D1457534

Also by Bonnie Traymore:

Killer Motives

Little Loose Ends

Contents

PROLOGUE..IX

ONE...1

TWO 10

THREE 17

FOUR...25

FIVE..34

SIX 43

SEVEN 48

EIGHT 60

NINE 70

TEN 82

ELEVEN..90

TWELVE 96

THIRTEEN 107

FOURTEEN 113

FIFTEEN 121

SIXTEEN 133

SEVENTEEN 140

EIGHTEEN 146

NINETEEN..152

TWENTY 156

TWENTY-ONE 164

TWENTY-TWO 170

TWENTY-THREE 183

TWENTY-FOUR 191

TWENTY-FIVE 198

TWENTY-SIX 204

TWENTY-SEVEN 213

TWENTY-EIGHT 223

TWENTY-NINE 235

THIRTY 240

THIRTY-ONE 246

THIRTY-TWO 257

THIRTY-THREE 263

EPILOGUE 269

ACKNOWLEDGEMENTS 275

ABOUT THE AUTHOR 277

PROLOGUE

Three months ago

She stands in silence, reading the weathered letter she holds in her trembling hands—over and over and over. A rage simmers deep inside her, about to erupt as she grasps the implications. Yet it all makes perfect sense for her now. The pieces of her life that never quite fit together suddenly snap into place as the truth reveals itself to her.

Her entire life, she now realizes, has been a lie. A fraud. A fractured fairy tale. How can anyone be expected to turn a blind eye to that kind of realization? How can anyone forgive that level of deception?

She's trying to hold it together, she really is, but the feeling bubbling up inside her is too powerful to suppress. It washes over her like a tidal wave, and suddenly she's willing to risk everything to get what she needs—and eliminate anyone who stands in her way.

ONE

I've never felt at home in this family because it's not really mine. But I try. Why? I don't really know. I could speak up. I could protest. I could leave. But I don't.

My husband is tenser than usual this morning. I can see it in his jawline when he walks into the kitchen.

"How's the approval coming?" I ask.

"Oh, you know, the usual hurdles. Nothing to worry about," he replies. He tries to hide it, but his discomfort breaks through. His voice is a little singsongy, always a sign that something's up.

He walks over to the coffee pot, pours himself a cup, and pops a slice of bread in the toaster. A dark blue tie hangs loose around his neck. He never wears one. Hardly anyone in Silicon Valley does, so it must be an important day. But for some reason, I don't think his unease has anything to do with work.

"Got a big meeting today?" I ask.

"The board wants an update," Peter replies.

"Aren't you just waiting for the FDA?"

"Yeah."

"So, isn't that the update?"

"Yeah." He smiles. "But you know how they are."

Then he shrugs, and I smile back. He butters his toast and pours some more coffee into a travel mug. I can tell that's all I'm going to get out of him. He's a calm man—most of the time. But he does have a temper, and even after twelve years, I still can't tell what might set it off. I can tell he's stressed, so I leave it alone.

I watch him walk over to the large beveled mirror that hangs in our dining room. He fastens his tie in one fluid motion. It looks sexy. Masculine. Commanding. The way he snaps it up and down at the same time to force it into compliance. He's older than me, but he still gets my heart racing with his salt-and-pepper hair and chiseled physique. His sleeves are rolled up a bit, exposing his muscular forearms.

He walks back to the kitchen and wolfs down his toast. Standing at the island countertop, I continue to make a veggie sandwich to pack for lunch. He places his dish in the sink behind me. We don't speak. It's a comfortable silence, but I can't shake the feeling that something is up.

I turn around to face him. "Well, I'm sure you'll dazzle them." I smile and rest my hand on Peter's bicep. I run my thumb across its taut surface.

"I don't know about that." He places his hand on my shoulder, leans over, and gives me a peck on the lips. "Have a good day." Then he grabs his coffee and heads out the side door to the garage.

I hear his car start and the garage door rise up. We have a two-car garage, but there's only space for one car because he's got all kinds of tools and sports equipment that take up the other half. It was like that when we started dating. Only one car in the garage. Twelve years later, my car still sits in the driveway.

I don't belong here. I'm still a visitor. Just like my car.

———

I'm searching through my clothes rack, second-guessing myself once again. I turn to look at myself in the full-length mirror that hangs on the opposite side of my closet. My navy skirt sits just above the knee, and I worry that people might think I'm playing up my sexy legs. But I'm not. It's just how my legs look. I don't want to wear pants. My blouse is modest, and I tell myself to stop being so insecure. I pull out a few different pairs of shoes from the cubbies and try them on. I land on strappy sandals with a medium heel. They're dark, almost the same color as my hair. I look professional but in a confident, sexy way. It's fine.

I have a big day today too. My career is really taking off. Finally. I was so young when I met Peter. Only twenty-seven. I'd just finished graduate school, a marketing MBA, and at first, there was too much going on in our lives to do much of anything with it. But I've made up for lost time. And I recently got a big promotion. Laura Sato Foster, Vice President of Monetization. Is that what's making him uncomfortable? The fact that I might not need him anymore? He's always been a big supporter of my career. It can't be that. But something is bothering him, that's for sure. He even rejected my advances last night, which he's never done before. He just turned fifty, and I hope it's not a sign of what's to come.

I make my way downstairs and out the front door to the driveway where my car sits. It's a silver Audi A6, so it's not an over-the-top choice, especially for this area, but it's certainly garage-worthy. I plop my satchel in the trunk, and then I notice something. A small stream of fluid is running out from under the car. We live in Los Altos Hills near the top of a long road—a very winding and steep one. Our driveway also slants down a bit; otherwise, I don't think I would have noticed the fluid. Thank goodness for gravity.

I'm a bit neurotic, the kind of person who runs back into the house to make sure the stove is off. I always pump my brakes before I back out of the driveway. Losing brakes on a hill like the one we live on could be fatal, and while that trickle of liquid could be anything, I have a sinking feeling in my stomach.

I open the car door and get behind the wheel. I press the start button and see the brake indicator light up. Then I step hard on the brake pedal. There's a slight resistance at first, but then my foot sinks to the floor. I realize then that it must be the brake fluid—one of my biggest fears. I feel a strange tingling in the back of my head.

I try not to catastrophize, but it's a pretty new car, although it's due to be serviced. Do brake lines start leaking for no reason? Probably not. Even before I call for help, I know this isn't good, and my stomach lurches as I consider the implications. It's quite possible that someone has tampered with my brake line.

Someone who's out to get me?

———

Peter's seated at the mahogany conference table at work, but his mind is a mile away. He's trying to forget about the email he found in his spam folder the other day, but it gnaws at him like a tick burrowing into his ankle flesh.

"*Peter?* Are you with us?" the chairman barks.

"Yes!" Peter snaps back into reality. He knows he has to get his head in the game, but he's missed the question completely, so there's no way he can fake it. He can get away with something like that once but not a second time, so he forces himself to focus.

"George asked if you have any concerns about what Sahil's team found when they tried to reproduce the results for the lung cancer experiments." It was the CEO, repeating the chairman's question.

"Sorry, I was looking over the FDA's last response. Yes, of course I have concerns."

"What do you plan to do about it?"

"We've already started on another round of experiments. I'm sure it was their mistake. We've performed those experiments numerous times for the study. They've only done it once, so I wouldn't worry just yet."

"We've already released that data in a preprint," the chairman says. "You better hope it was their mistake."

"Give me a week, okay?"

Everyone nods in agreement. Nobody wants this to be an issue, especially with a lucrative merger and FDA approval of their drug on the horizon. It will be fine. The data is good, he tells himself.

And even if it's not, it's the least of his worries right now.

———

"You look rattled. Is everything okay?" My assistant, Mina, looks up at me as I go rushing past her desk and into my office twenty minutes before my first important meeting as the new Vice President of Monetization—and two hours later than normal.

"Car trouble. I had to take an Uber," I call out to her and duck into my office. I wasn't about to tell anyone at work about the brake line. What if it was one of them?

Mina pokes her head in my door as I toss my half-opened satchel on my desk, spilling the contents onto the surface.

"Car trouble?" She's eyeing me with a curious look, hands on her hips, her dark hair cascading down the front of her tan sweater dress. She seems to sense that something's up, although it's hard to tell with her. She's got these mysterious coal eyes, the eyes of an old soul, with lashes so long they look fake, but she swears they're not. I'd kill for lashes like that.

"Car trouble!" I widen my eyes and shrug to let her know we're moving on. We've had a friendship of sorts over the years, although she's quite a bit younger than me.

But now that she's working directly for me, I've had to pull back a bit.

"Do you need anything for the meeting?" she asks.

I smile. "No, I'm good, thanks. Just a few minutes to collect my thoughts." She's a great assistant. I consider telling her about my car, but there's no time.

"I'll leave you to it then." She exits, and I decide I'll probably fill her in on the brake incident later. After I've had time to process it. If there's anyone I can trust around here, it's her.

The mechanic who came out to the house confirmed what I'd suspected. The rubber brake hose had been severed, but he couldn't say for sure that it had been tampered with. It's apparently hard to prove something like that. Sometimes road debris—a sharp rock, for example—could damage it enough to weaken it, and then it could simply rupture. And there's plenty of road debris where I live. I'm looking at a photo taken by the mechanic. There's a smoother-looking break on one side, and then it's ragged on the other like it tore apart. He also said that extreme heat could wear down the rubber more quickly, and we've certainly had our share of that this summer. But I'm not convinced by his road debris theory.

Instead of preparing for my meeting, I Google "brake line cut" and discover that there have been isolated pockets of this sort of vandalism in various communities across the country recently. Phoenix. Denver. The Seattle area. They've all been hit. I play a few videos of news broadcasts and listen to frantic residents recount their stories. Like me, at first, they thought that someone was out to get them until a pattern emerged. Who would want to cut the brake hoses of a bunch of strangers? No arrests have been made in any of the cases so far. Although it's a terrifying thought, that a random vandal is targeting my neighborhood, I suppose it's better than the idea that someone is out to get me specifically. I'll go to the police station and file a report. Right after my meeting.

"Laura?" It's my boss at my office door.

I finally have an office, and I thought it would be great. But it doesn't give me as much privacy as you might expect. Nobody closes their door around here. We're technically allowed to work from home if we want, but it's starting to feel like a bad career move if you actually do it.

"Hi, Bethany."

She's the CFO, and I report to her. It's my job to figure out how to start making money. We're venture-capital funded, like many startups in Silicon Valley, and the funding is drying up for this round. I'm supposed to have ideas about how to monetize our product. That's what they pay me for. I've got a few, and I'm sure they're terrible. But maybe that's how everyone feels. We're all just grasping at straws here.

"Are you ready for the meeting?"

"Sure."

"I'm counting on you, Laura. I went out on a limb for you." She holds up a finger, her eyebrows raised high above her translucent hazel eyes as they peer at me, boring into my skull. They look a little unsettling, framed by her wild red hair, which is especially unruly today. "Don't screw this up."

I nod, and she goes on her way. Nobody tells you this, but the gloves come off the closer to the top you get. All the polite formalities and HR-sponsored platitudes fall by the wayside. And what if I do screw up? Then it's game over. I'm out.

People would kill for an opportunity like this, Bethany said, when she told me I'd gotten the promotion.

But they wouldn't.

Would they?

TWO

A police officer sits across from me at our imposing dining room table. It's pretentious and formal—not my style—and I feel awkward sitting so far away from him. I would have rather sat in the living room, but this is where he sat. The officer is about forty, with a few extra pounds on his large frame. He seems less than enthused with the assignment. I decided to have the authorities meet me at home so the police could have a look at the car before it got towed in. I was too flustered earlier to make a decision about what to do. After the mechanic came and told me it was the brake line—or, more specifically, the right front brake hose—I told him to leave it there and hopped into an Uber to get to work for my meeting.

"So, what time did you go out to your car, again?"

"About eight thirty this morning," I repeat.

We've already been over this. Why is he asking me again? I can't tell if he's actually concerned about the possibility of a neighborhood vandal or if he's humoring me. He did inform me that the department has been on the lookout for this sort of thing based on warnings from other municipalities. But then he assured me that, as far as he knew, the Bay Area had so far been spared. I worry now that he'll think I'm paranoid if I ask him to dig further.

"And there's nothing on your security camera?"

"No. I have a pretty clear shot of the driveway from one of the cameras, and I didn't see anyone tampering with my car."

"The break is pretty jagged, at least on one side, based on these photos, so my best guess is that it probably got sliced by some road debris that got up into it like your mechanic suggested. Then it wore down and broke."

"Or someone could have cut it in another location," I say.

"True, but then they didn't do a very good job. That would mean they didn't know enough to cut it all the way."

"Maybe they got interrupted. Or wanted to make sure my brakes went while I was driving."

"Could be. But you'd probably have noticed it on your way home."

"The mechanic said it might take a few miles to notice if it was a small cut to begin with."

The officer nods. I can tell he thinks I'm being paranoid. I consider asking him to dust for prints, but since he doesn't bring it up, I assume it would be an inappropriate suggestion. The mechanic's prints are probably all over it anyway. And if someone was trying to kill me, wouldn't they be smart enough to wear gloves?

I hear a car pull up to the house and wonder who it could be. This doesn't seem like it would warrant another officer. The car stops in the driveway, and I hear a door slam. Then I hear someone running.

What the hell?

I stand up, and so does the officer.

A moment later, Peter comes bursting through the doorway. He runs up to me before I can react or say anything.

"What's happening?" Peter's face is pale, as if he's seen a ghost. I can see sweat beads forming, about to drip from his temples. I should have called to tell him about this, but I knew he had an important meeting. I didn't want to worry him until I knew more. But what is he doing home so early? It's only three in the afternoon.

After my meeting, which went swimmingly, I told Bethany about my car, and she encouraged me to go handle it. She's a hard-ass when it comes to work, but she's not a monster, and she seemed genuinely concerned. More than the officer standing next to me but much less so than my husband, who looks like he's about to have a stroke.

He takes my face in his hands. "Laura? Are you alright?"

"I'm fine, Peter."

"What's going on? Why didn't you call me?" My husband is frantic, and I don't get it. I'm obviously fine.

"Everything's okay, Mr. Foster," the officer informs him. "Please. Have a seat."

So we sit down and take Peter through the whole story from the beginning. I'm much more of a worrier than my husband is, so I expect him to brush it off. And he does, on the surface. But I can tell he's faking it. And I don't have a clue as to why.

"Well, Laura, if there's nothing on the security camera, I'd say it's pretty safe to assume that it was an accident," Peter says. But he's addressing the officer, avoiding eye contact with me. His lips are pressed together, and his jaw is tight. I feel like his words are at odds with his body language.

But then maybe his mood has nothing to do with the brake situation. Maybe it's the same issue that was bothering him this morning, and he came home early to talk to me about it. *But how would he know I was here?*

We wrap things up and see the officer to the door. He assures me they will "check into it," but I'm not holding my breath. I close the door behind him.

Then Peter lets out a deep sigh and almost collapses on the floor. He bends over and puts his hands on his knees, taking deep breaths, looking like he might pass out. *Maybe he's not feeling well, and that's why he came home early?*

"Laura, I thought..."

And then it hits me.

The last time a police officer was here, it was to give him some terrible news. He *has* seen a ghost today. The ghost of Cynthia Foster—his college sweetheart, the mother of his children, the woman whose home I inhabit.

I walk over, and he takes me in his arms, holding me close.

"I'm fine, Peter. I'm totally fine." I lean back and smile at him, my hands resting on his arms.

"I love you so much, Laura. If anything ever happened to you..."

"Peter. It's nothing. Really. I'm sure the hose just wore out like the officer said."

I rack my brain, trying to think if there is anything connected to his late wife that could have triggered his tense mood this morning. I watch for signs around the anniversary of her death, but that's months away. And it's gotten better over the years. He's genuinely concerned about me right now; that much is clear.

But then why wouldn't he press the officer to investigate further? He seemed eager to get rid of him. Maybe it's the bad memories. I can't imagine how hard it must be to live in those memories every day. And I still don't have an explanation as to why he's home in the middle of the afternoon.

"What are you doing home so early?"

"Oh, they're doing some minor renovations at the office and it was noisy, so I decided to come home to work."

"How did your meeting go?"

"It was fine. What about yours, hotshot VP? Did you knock 'em dead?" He brushes my cheek with his knuckle.

"Not quite, but they're worth more to me alive anyway." I smile at him.

He pulls me in for a kiss. Not a peck this time, but a deep, passionate one, and it's clear that whatever was bothering him last night has passed. He slips his hand under my skirt and slides it up my leg. Electricity courses through me. We haven't been very spontaneous lately, so this takes us both by surprise.

Then he takes me by the hand and starts to lead me upstairs. I'm not as excited as he is, though, because as we're walking up the stairs, I think about the look on his face when he walked through the door. All those terrible memories here. *Why won't he let go of this place and all it represents?* I love him, and I've tried to be patient, but I've been playing this game for too long. I decide that I have to put my foot down. I can't take a backseat to a ghost forever. We have to sell this place and move on. It's time.

———

Peter rolls over on his side and watches Laura as she gets out of bed and heads for the shower. Her petite, hourglass figure is a walking work of art. He loves her, and that terrifies him. If anything were to happen to her, well, he doesn't even want to think about that. He tries to keep his cool, but he has a hard time believing that the severed brake line was an accident. It's possible it was random. A neighborhood vandal. But he has a sinking feeling that maybe his past is catching up with him.

Then he tells himself he's being ridiculous. It's all a coincidence. He's letting his imagination get the best of him. It was vandalism. Or a piece of road debris. Regardless, maybe it's a sign that it's time to make a change. Laura's always hated this place. It's dark. And inconvenient, she says. The house isn't all that far from the Los Altos town center in terms of mileage, but it can take forever to wind up and down the hill, especially if you get behind a pack of cyclists, a slow-moving vehicle, or a garbage truck. And they're surrounded by woods. They live in California—one of the sunniest places on earth—yet it's always dark here. And then there's the fire danger, which has increased over the last few years. She never mentions the real reason she wants to move, and he loves her for that. Initially, he told himself he couldn't move because of the kids. But they're out of the house now. What's stopping him? Is it guilt? Maybe, but then he shouldn't punish Laura for his sins.

She comes back into the bedroom wrapped in a pale pink satin robe that sits halfway above her knee. Her dark hair is damp—wet and wild as it falls softly in front of her face—and she looks so sexy.

"What would you think about selling this place? Moving closer to civilization?"

"I thought you'd never ask." She throws off her robe and gets back into bed with him.

THREE

I know I should be thrilled that Peter has finally agreed to sell the house. And I am, for the most part. But I can't shake the feeling there's more to it, and I feel awful about that. There's a logical explanation at my disposal. He panicked when he thought something had happened to me. He realized how much he loves me. And then he decided to give me what I really wanted.

It's a nice explanation, so why doesn't it satisfy me? Is it my natural tendency to be a neurotic worrier, or is it my gut feeling that something is up with him?

Partly, it's because I've never doubted Peter's love for me. I've always felt that his wanting to keep the house had nothing to do with how he feels about me or that he somehow was still in love with his first wife. I've always gotten the feeling their marriage wasn't that great anyway, although he rarely talks about it.

At first, he said it was for the kids. He wanted to honor the memory of their mother. He didn't want to disrupt their lives. But they're pretty much grown now. His son is in his last year of college, and his daughter is in her mid-twenties with a life of her own. They're rarely here these days, although I expect when we tell them, they'll throw a fit. For some reason, they love this dark, desolate home, and they've never totally accepted me as the woman of the house. It's hard enough to come into a family after a divorce. But after a death, it's almost impossible to do anything right.

It's Saturday on a late summer morning that promises to be another scorching hot day, and I'm on my way to meet my triathlon team for a run. I'm late because a pack of amateur cyclists is hogging the road as I start up a rolling hill. I'm driving Peter's SUV, and it's not as nimble as my Audi, which is in the shop. They're riding three or four across, and they're struggling. They should know better. I'm a cyclist. I'd never do that. No wonder people hate us. I feel like honking at them, but I don't.

"Single file, people!" I call out my window to them in a pleasant voice to try to soften the blow. I say it with a smile but not a friendly one. More like a Chucky doll grimace. One woman almost loses her balance as she turns to me. They try to move into a more streamlined formation. I can tell they aren't very experienced. They're a danger to themselves as much as the rest of us.

I finally pass them and continue down the long, winding road, turning left onto Foothill Boulevard, which feels like the autobahn by comparison. Next, I turn off on Alpine, and then it's more winding roads through Woodside to my destination— the parking lot at Windy Hill Preserve. I get to the meeting point a bit late, but if I run fast, I might be able to catch the team. I park my car, grab my water bottle, and head out along the bone-dry trails of Portola Valley.

It's a hill run today, three miles to the top and then a winding five miles or so back down. Not overly long for us in terms of distance, but it's super steep, so it will be a challenging run—just what I need to get my mind off my problems. It's early August, and it's been hot as blazes the past few weeks, so I don't want to push myself too hard in the beginning or I'll run out of steam. We're training for the Santa Cruz Half Ironman in a few weeks, and we're starting to taper.

I'm running a bit faster than usual though, to try to catch the team, and I know it's going to mess up my pacing a bit. But it is nice to be alone with my thoughts, which I let float by. I notice the birds today because the air is still. Their pleasant whistling calls fill the air. *Sweet, sweet. Sweet, sweet.* It's fitting. If sugar had a sound, it would sound like that. I don't have any idea what kind of bird it is, but it's a nice distraction on my run.

I'm in a narrow passage now, and the bird calls have faded. I notice the sound of my own breathing getting heavier as I begin the incline. The gnarled trees form a tunnel over me as I run through it. A faint musty smell lingers in the air. There are patches of wet, mossy green here where the sun doesn't reach, and the Douglas firs and eucalyptus trees show off their verdant hues, but the leaves on the towering oaks look like kindling to me—whisper thin in variegated shades of brown, crumbling on their branches.

My quiet solitude is shattered when I hear someone coming up behind me rather quickly, like they're trying to catch me. It doesn't sound like the pace of a fellow runner. I don't dare to look back, but I suddenly feel very vulnerable all alone in the woods. I can hear their footfalls crunching along the trail. Normally, I wouldn't think twice about it, but today my senses are heightened, and I feel the hairs on the back of my neck stand up. The person is getting closer, and I start to feel panicky. Is someone chasing me?

But that's crazy, I tell myself. It's probably nothing. I think about turning around, but I don't dare. Instead, I run a little faster, trying to get to the open area up ahead. I hear them speed up to match my pace. What if someone did follow me here? Maybe the same person who cut my brake hose. My heart begins to race, so I have to slow down. I try to tell myself it will be okay.

"Laura?" a voice calls out to me. It's a male voice, but I can't quite place it. I turn around and look.

"It's me! Carl!" He's waving. Smiling.

Great. It's this odd guy who used to run with us years ago. He recently moved back to the area and rejoined the team. I'm a bit surprised he recognized me from so far away. And it's especially awkward because he tried to befriend me, but I was a bit reluctant to engage with him. Something about him made me uncomfortable. I have to wait for him, or it will be rude. He's almost caught up to me anyway.

"Hey, Carl!" I wave back as I jog in place.

He's a smaller guy. Very quiet. The kind you see people talking about on the news after he turns out to be a serial killer.

He seemed like such a nice guy. So quiet. So polite.

"Hi, Laura," he says as he jogs up next to me. We continue on the narrow path for a few paces, and soon we come out of the tree tunnel into a flat, open plateau. The Santa Cruz mountains pierce the blue sky, and it feels hotter already.

"Hi, Carl."

"You were really jamming there."

He's a good runner. He's just being polite. I'm out of breath, but he's fine.

"I'm trying to catch up with the others."

We make small talk for a bit as we continue our run, and it's slowing us down. I like running with a big group because you get the camaraderie, but there's no pressure to converse. With one person, it's different. There's this awkward obligation to chitchat. Along the way, he informs me that he's married and has a five-year-old son. I guess it's been a while.

After about a mile, I see a few people from my team stopped ahead of us. They're taking a water break. It's only seven thirty in the morning, and I'm already sweaty. I tell myself I need to get a grip. Carl's a nice guy. A family man. Not a serial killer. *What is wrong with me?*

———

Peter is sitting at the kitchen table in his workout clothes, drenched in sweat. He's just finished a massive cardio session on his Peloton. Laura is out with her triathlon team. Although they both like to keep fit, Peter's more of a gym guy, while she prefers the outdoors. The only time they exercise together is when they're on vacation. If it bothers her at all, she's never let on about it to him.

He pulls up the email again to try to figure out his next move. He hasn't been able to think about much since he read it. He'd discovered it when he was looking for something else in his spam folder the day before yesterday, but it had been sitting there over a week.

I know what you did. I won't tell anyone.

It could be a random spam email. It's pretty generic. He was planning to ignore it, but after what happened to Laura, he feels like he should maybe look into it. There was no call to action, so it probably wasn't a phishing scam. *Don't those usually have a link in them?* He needs to do some research. See if someone can find the IP address.

But how? Maybe he could hire a private detective. *Do they take on cases like this?* And how do you know which ones you can trust? Peter has a window of opportunity while Laura is out, so he starts to do a search. But then he thinks better of it. What if something comes of this, and the authorities take his computer? They'll see he was looking for a private detective. How would that look? He'll have to think of a better way to find one.

In the meantime, he calls the kids and asks them to come over for Sunday dinner. He has to tell them about his decision on the house before he takes any action, and he doesn't expect it to go well. But it's time. He's already told Laura he'd sell, although, in hindsight, he regrets not telling the kids first. Too late for that.

—

When I get home from my run, Peter informs me that the children are coming for dinner tomorrow.

"What should I make?"

"Whatever you want."

"Is Lydia still vegetarian?"

"I guess?" He shrugs.

"I'll text the kids and check in with them."

I'm the one who's kept up with all their changing tastes over the years. They were eleven and fourteen when I joined the family. It's hard to believe it when I look at Lydia, but I was around her age when I moved in with them and then married her father, only a year older than she is now. She seems so much younger than that to me. But then I had to mature into my role whether I was ready for it or not. It's the hand I was dealt, falling in love with a widower.

I'm happy that Peter is moving forward on the house sale, but we haven't talked at all about what this might mean. I'm not on the title. And I know the kids view it as their house, although they don't need the money. They have a trust from their mother's side of the family. Peter never had access to it. The bulk of her wealth went directly to the kids through her family's trust when she died, although Peter got the house and their other joint assets.

Lydia is twenty-six, so she's started getting her yearly allowance. Carson is still in college, so he doesn't get anything yet, although all of his college expenses are taken care of. We're very fortunate that way.

But what about the house? This is a community property state. And the house should be half mine anyway; I've done enough for this family. But then, he owned it before we got married. One thing for sure is we should talk about it before we tell the kids tomorrow, but I'm at a total loss as to how to bring it up to my husband.

I have only myself to blame for my predicament. I've let myself live so many years in limbo, and now I regret not speaking up sooner. Perhaps we could have moved earlier and saved me all these years of feeling uncomfortable and out of place. But then, it's not really my nature to assert myself. Time flew by, and here I am, in my late thirties, still living in someone else's home. I realize that I need to get over my reticence—at home and at work—and learn to assert myself. The more I live, the more I see that people will eat you alive if you let them. Maybe a cut brake line is exactly what I needed to push me out of my comfort zone.

FOUR

It's late Sunday afternoon, and Carson is here at the house with me. It's just the two of us. He attends a small liberal arts college in Santa Clara, only twenty minutes away, and he has his own apartment in Sunnyvale with some other students. He and I get along pretty well, although we're not particularly close. We were when he was younger, sort of. I used to host gaming parties for him and his buddies, and they all thought I was cool because I played video games with them. I pretended to like the games, but I didn't. I was doing it to make sure that they weren't overly violent. I cared, and I did what needed to be done. I tried to pick up the pieces of a broken family.

I got him to eat his vegetables. "You better eat your carrots, or your nose will fall off," I'd say. And he'd smile. "Okay, but when you're walking around with no nose, don't come crying to me." My dorky banter worked on an eleven-year-old boy, but as he got older, I found it harder to relate to him.

Looking back, I was probably more like a cool nanny than a mom. I never got on his case when his grades dropped or grounded him when he stayed out too late. I didn't do any of that "mom" stuff. I'm not his mother, but I'm all he has. And he seems to get that.

"How's senior year?" Probably a stupid question since it only started a few days ago, but I can't think of anything else to say. Maybe I should have said something like *How does it feel to be a senior?* No. That's too touchy-feely.

"It's not that bad so far. It kinda just started." He shrugs and looks back down at his phone. He's been texting someone. I wonder if he's in a relationship. Carson rarely talks to either of us about things like that, although I did know about his high school sweetheart, from whom he's since parted. I think Peter knows less than I do. That's Carson's nature, to play it close to the vest.

"Are you...um, when do you start looking for jobs?"

He looks up, his dark bangs covering his eyes. He needs a haircut. He looks like a wiry version of Peter, and I wonder if he'll grow into his body.

"I don't know. Second semester, I guess. That company I interned with last summer already made me an offer, but everyone says I should pass."

I want to say *Who's everyone?* but I don't.

"Well, it's an employee's market. If you need any help..."

"I'm good. But thanks, Laura." He smiles at me in a mildly condescending way, but he doesn't mean anything by it. He can't help it that he's grown up with connections and privilege and gotten everything handed to him.

Not that I grew up poor or neglected. I always knew I was loved, but my Jewish American mother and my

Japanese American father had extremely high standards, and they pushed my brother and me hard in school. Both are college professors and even though I make more than the two of them put together ever did, I know they're disappointed that I only have a master's degree. But my parents are still alive and well and always there for me when I need them, and that's something I can't say about Carson and Lydia. Their maternal grandmother showered them with affection and money in an attempt to ease their pain. Peter didn't seem to have much say in any of it. He was just along for the ride. It's hard to have a say when your children have a higher net worth than you do.

Their grandfather died of a heart attack two years before Cynthia's accident, and Peter thought that might have contributed to his wife's emotional troubles, which had flared up occasionally over the years. According to Peter, she was a total daddy's girl and had a difficult relationship with her mother, who seemed to compensate for that by doting on Lydia, her granddaughter. He thought something may have snapped in Cynthia after her father's death.

I head into the kitchen to put the finishing touches on dinner, knowing that the worst is yet to come. I didn't bring up the house or the money issue last night with Peter. *So much for asserting myself.* And I have absolutely no idea where his head is at or how he's going to break it to the kids.

Dinner is going well so far. Lydia informed me that she's now pescatarian, so we had shrimp cocktail, then salad, and now we're finishing up my homemade eggplant parmesan.

Lydia's in a particularly good mood. She and I are actually doing better now than years ago, but that's not saying much. She hated my guts in the beginning, but we've settled into something a bit better than mutual toleration. Mutual respect, maybe? She's in social media marketing at a startup company that's developing a new dating app, so we have something in common, sort of. *Does she ever think about the fact that she's almost as old as I was when we first met?*

She's a regal beauty—the perfect corporate-woman look—smart and savvy with a serious countenance. Her long, dark hair falls perfectly as she turns her head to talk to Peter. I'm sure she'll go far. She adores her father, and the feeling is mutual. I knew right away not to make it a competition. I've never said a bad word about her, even when she treated me like garbage.

"So," Peter says, clearing his throat, and we all look over at him. He has a commanding presence when he chooses to play it that way. "We've got something to tell the two of you."

My husband is sitting at the head of the dining table, and we're seated too far from each other to have a comfortable conversation. The table is bigger than it needs to be for the size of our family and too formal. I feel like it adds to the distance between us. Plus, the style is hideous to me: a thick slab of rosewood sitting on large, ornate pedestal legs that get in the way if we have too many guests. *When we move, we're not taking it with us.* His children are on opposite sides of him. Peter turns his head from one to the other, stopping to look them each in the eye. They both stop eating, and Carson looks over at Lydia; he often takes his cues from her.

"What is it?" she says. "Is everything okay?"

"Yes, of course. Nothing to worry about." Peter pauses.

He's stalling, and it occurs to me that maybe he hasn't thought this through. He's a shoot-from-the-hip kind of guy.

"Well?" Lydia says, her blue eyes—the one feature she inherited from her mother—wide with anticipation.

"Laura and I have decided to sell the house and move closer to town."

"Oh! I thought you were going to say something else." Lydia doesn't look very upset. In fact, I notice that the corners of her mouth lift up a bit as if she's trying to suppress a smile.

Then she looks at me. "I thought you were going to say you were pregnant."

We all have a laugh, but it's a tense one. I can imagine Lydia being quite upset about a baby, especially if it was a girl. She barely tolerates sharing her father with Carson and me. I can't imagine how she'd feel about additional female competition for his attention.

"Oh. No, it's for sure not that." I smile back. I've never wanted children of my own, being a stepmom is enough for me, and I think that's one thing she's grateful for.

We finish up our meal, and Lydia excuses herself and goes up to her room. Even though they don't live here anymore, their rooms are still theirs, just like when I moved in. They feel more at home here than I do. It won't be like that in the new place, and that makes me smile inside.

I look over at Carson. He's only a senior in college, so he might be taking this a bit differently. I'm sure living with a bunch of guys is fun for now, but what if he was planning to come home after graduation? He's so quiet. Lydia tends to suck up all the air in the room, and his needs often go overlooked.

"Carson, are you okay?" I ask.

"Yeah. I'm fine."

"There'll be a place for you at the new house, so you don't need to worry about that."

"It's fine," he says. "I don't care."

Peter jumps in, and they start to discuss the logistics. I leave them to it and clear the dishes. I'm getting dessert ready in the kitchen when I hear Lydia coming down the stairs. It's all going pretty well so far, but I can't help feeling it's going a little too well. I expected this to be more of a big deal, but she hardly batted an eye. *Maybe I need to think positively, stop looking for problems before they even start.*

I'm serving pound cake with vanilla ice cream and chocolate shavings on top. I've sliced individual servings, so I can only take in two at a time. I walk in and place their dishes in front of Carson and Lydia. She's smiling now. I go back for the other two, convinced that she's saving something up. *Did she go call her attorney?* I expect she'll hit us with whatever it is as soon as I sit down. So much for positive thinking.

I set a piece of cake down in front of Peter and then go to my seat opposite him, at the far end of the table, and prepare myself for what's to come.

And then she starts.

"So, I talked to Gran."

We all know this means her maternal grandmother because Peter's mother has passed.

"And guess what?"

She waits, and an uncomfortable silence hangs in the air. Carson has his head propped up on his elbow which is resting on the table. Peter is sitting up straight. He swallows and looks over at me, then back to Lydia.

"What, sweetie?"

"Gran's agreed to release the money from my trust so I can buy the house from you. Isn't that great? Carson and I can live here together. As soon as we agree on a price, we can move forward." She's wearing a smug smile, and I feel like I'm going to be sick.

"Well, um, that's...I mean, it's..." He's obviously as shocked as I am. "It's an interesting solution. Don't you think, Laura?"

I should have seen this coming, but I didn't. The money, who gets the proceeds, it's not even an issue for the kids. They have so much it's probably not even on their radar. At any rate, I try to remain optimistic. We can move. Peter and I will own our new house together. Then I can finally start to feel at home.

"Yes, very interesting," I say.

"It's perfect! Eventually, I can live here with my own family. And we can all have holidays here like we always do." Lydia's beaming.

Carson doesn't seem to register the fact that Lydia's assuming it will be her house. But then, if her part of the trust is buying it, maybe that's okay? I can also see that I'll never be free of their past, but at least I won't have to live in it every day.

"What do you think, Carson?" I ask.

"Whatever. I don't even know where I'm getting a job yet."

By the time we finish dessert, it's all settled. Peter will get an appraisal, and we'll agree on a price. *We can start house hunting!* It's convenient, but it has to be a bit humiliating for Peter, his kids buying his house from him. Whatever he might be able to give them as part of their inheritance after decades of hard work won't make any difference to them. But then, I guess it's pretty good news for me.

But Peter knew the deal going into it, marrying into a big-money family. It's always awkward. I wonder how it was between them, with his wife holding the purse strings. He makes good money by most people's standards, although not in relation to the cost of living here. And like me, he's self-made. Did it bother him? He's never let on if it did, and I never pry. But I do wonder.

After a bit, Peter sees the kids out the door, and I clear the table. I'm thinking about Cynthia as I'm rinsing the dishes and placing them in the dishwasher. I don't know why. I rarely do. Maybe it's because of what happened yesterday on my run when I heard someone coming up behind me. I think about his wife, falling to her death off that cliff out there, all alone. Did anyone hear her scream?

FIVE

I'm in a decent mood for a Monday. Work is going well. I pitched my idea this morning, and it seems like maybe my solution to our money-raising challenge isn't so terrible after all. Everyone at the meeting seemed pleased. For the entire morning, I didn't think about dinner last night or Cynthia or my brake line being cut. But as my stomach starts to grumble, indicating to me that it's past noon, domestic thoughts start to creep back in. I'm meeting a friend for a late lunch, and I normally eat earlier. I pop a few almonds in my mouth to tide me over.

"I'm going to lunch," Mina says. "You want to come?"

"No, I'm meeting my friend soon. But thanks."

Mina goes on her way and leaves me with my thoughts.

I told Mina and my boss about the brake hose. I didn't tell them I think my car could have been tampered with at work. If someone here is out to get me, I don't want them to know I'm suspicious. And something is bothering me about the way Peter reacted, but I can't put my finger on it. I want to hash it out with my best friend over lunch before I bring anyone else into this.

When I met Peter twelve years ago, he'd been a single dad for six years. From what his friends told me, he hardly dated before he met me. Or if he did, he didn't let on about it to anyone. He had help with the kids—from his mother before she passed, their maternal grandmother, and a nanny who had been with them even before his wife died. He was very protective of the children when it came to relationships with women, so being the first to meet them, I'm the one who had to blaze the trail. I think I've done a decent job, and we've all come a long way from those early days.

He rarely talks about what happened to Cynthia or how it affected the children. I'm sure it was horrible. They were so young. From what I can piece together from the bits Peter's told me, she liked to live on the edge—literally. Rock climbing, skydiving, extreme skiing. And I believe that's what attracted him to her in the beginning, sort of like with me with my races. But when the kids were born, he wanted her to stop, and it was a point of conflict in their marriage that, although she took things down a notch, she still dabbled. The day it happened, she was out for a hike, not a climb. Alone. There was a brief investigation, and her death was ruled an accident. But I've always wondered: *How could they know for sure?*

"Laura?" It's my boss, Bethany, at my door. "Can I come in?"

"Sure." It's not like I have a choice.

Bethany closes the door and seats herself in the dark swivel chair across from my desk. The closed office door is odd. Something is up. She's wearing a tweed Chanel

V-neck dress that flatters her tall, slim figure. She's from New York, and her wardrobe is impressive, but it's overkill for here. She reaches back and shimmies off the scrunchy from her hair. Her red mane springs back to life as she fluffs it with both hands. She leans back and crosses her legs, a nervous energy emanating from her as she moves the chair ever so slightly from side to side. I've never seen this look on her face before. It's not a happy look, but I don't get the feeling that I'm in any sort of trouble. It's more like the look a doctor gets when they're giving you bad news: a look of concern.

"So, what's going on with your car?"

My eyebrows raise. That wasn't what I was expecting, and I guess she senses that.

"Oh, and nice job this morning," she adds.

"Thanks."

I pause. The car is the last thing I want to talk about, although I suppose I should be pleased that she remembered. But then, it is a bit of a juicy story. Why would she forget about it?

"What did the police say?" she asks.

"They didn't seem too concerned. They said it was probably just a piece of road debris that got in there and sliced the rubber tubing. Then it wore down and broke in half."

"Oh, that's great news. I didn't tell anyone here about what happened."

What an odd statement.

"Um, thanks?"

"Sure." She gets up to leave, but I stop her.

"Bethany, *why* didn't you tell anyone about what happened? Is there something I need to know?"

"No. I mean, not anything in particular." She settles back into her chair, and an awkward silence fills the air.

"What does that mean?"

She's my boss, but right now, I don't care. Right now, she's simply a person holding something back, something that might be important for my safety.

"Nothing! I mean, you remember I told you your promotion would ruffle some feathers around here. You know how competitive people are."

"Competitive enough to cut my brake line?"

"No! I'm being ridiculous. I've been watching too many thriller movies."

"Any competitive people in particular that I should be looking out for?"

"No! Ignore me. Forget it, Laura. I'm happy it was nothing. I shouldn't have said anything. Of course nobody around here would do something like that."

I nod, but I'm not sure I'm convinced. Why would it cross her mind? And why would she say it if it wasn't a valid concern? Exactly how upset are people about this?

She starts out the door but then turns back to me. "Now, if your car happens to get keyed…"

She flashes a sly smile. It turns out she has a nice set of teeth. And a sense of humor. Five years, and it's the first I've seen of either of them. I smile back.

"Don't worry. I've got your back, Laura."

"Thanks, Bethany." And she goes on her way.

So, people around here are only car-keying pissed at me, not brake-line-cutting pissed at me? Good to know.

—

Peter knows he needs to do something. He's going to hire a private investigator. And he'll have them look into the issue with Laura's car along with the email he received. The police already know about the car, and it wouldn't be out of line to hire someone to look into that if he needed an explanation. They certainly don't seem to be doing much about it, which doesn't surprise him. He's narrowed his choices down to two, both referrals from an attorney friend he's retained, just in case, and he's trying to decide which way to go. There's a large, well-known firm in San Jose and a smaller one closer by. The larger company has more positive reviews, but they have a team of investigators, and he wants to keep this quiet. More people, more chances that someone will find out. He chooses the boutique firm that lists "digital investigations" as one of its specialties.

He's thinking about how much to disclose. He decides he'll give them the basics and then turn them loose. See what they can find out. Laura called earlier and told him she heard back this morning from the officer who was at the house last week. They don't think it's a vandalism spree. There haven't been other cases reported in the neighborhood, as there were in other areas of the country. The officer thinks it's either a freak accident or someone targeted her specifically, but he's leaning towards accident. Peter's not so sure.

Since they know the car wasn't tampered with at their house based on the security footage, Peter asked Laura to email him a list of all the places she went earlier that day. He hasn't told her about the PI. He can't tell her about the email he received, and if he tells her about hiring an investigator, she'll probably want to meet with him too. That's the trouble with secrets. They breed more lies, and then things spiral out of control. So far, he's never had to outright lie to her, mostly because she doesn't ask a lot of questions. He doesn't like that he's keeping things from her. But right now, it's the only choice he has.

He picks up the phone and punches in the number of Shackler Investigative Services.

———

My friend Sophie comes bursting through the door of Chef Chu's exactly ten minutes late. At least she's consistent— meaning she's consistently ten minutes late. It's been like that ever since I've known her, which is since grad school. The pungent smells of garlic and ginger, the bright reds and greens of the sizzling hot dishes rushing by got the best of me. I got here early and ordered pot stickers to munch on, so it's fine. I was enjoying the alone time, but I'm glad she's here now. She's my closest friend, and I really need to talk to someone today.

"Sorry, Laura." She offers me a sheepish smile as she slides into her chair, wearing a cute red dress and overly high heels that compensate for her shorter stature. She plops her giant handbag down on the floor, and it lands with a thud. *What is she packing in there?*

I nod, my mouth full of pot sticker, and then hold up a finger and swallow. "No problem."

"Are you in a hurry? I'll order fast." She's a natural blonde with short wavy hair, a compact, curvy figure, and just enough imperfections to make her alluring but approachable. In sum, a total guy magnet. Although she's married now with two kids, she was a great wing woman when we were single.

"No. I'm just hungry."

"I'm starved!"

The waiter spots her and comes rushing over. Sophie is a regular, and they treat her like a celebrity. This is an iconic Silicon Valley spot, frequented by the movers and shakers of the tech and VC worlds. They do get their fair share of famous clientele, but they value their regulars even more. "Sophie!" He smiles, and they engage in a quick chat.

She orders her usual, and I follow her lead. Sophie is what you'd call a force of nature. She's in PR, and she's great at it. She's got the perfect mix of drive, style, and irreverence to render her irresistible. She tells it like it is, and clients pay her handsomely for it. She doesn't mince words, especially when it comes to the people she cares about.

She takes one good look at me and starts right in. "Something's up. What is it? What's wrong?" She pinches a pot sticker with her chopsticks. It slides off, but she recovers her grip and takes a bite.

"I thought we'd ease into it."

"Oh my God, just spit it out." She's chewing as she's talking, so her words are a bit muddled.

I mull over how to start, and I decide to get straight to the point. "I think someone might be trying to kill me."

Her eyes pop open as she gasps, almost choking on her food. She holds up her hand as she tries to regain her composure. Then she swallows and takes a sip of her ice water.

"What the hell, Laura!"

"You told me to spit it out!" I flash her a smug smile, and it's almost worth an attempt on my life to get this kind of rise out of my normally unflappable friend. She's usually the one with the dramatic stories. I'm the boring one.

"Okay. Start from the beginning. Tell me everything."

She's riveted as I take her through it all. How I saw the fluid on the driveway, the mechanic's conclusions, the police officer's take on it, what Bethany said about my promotion bothering people in the office, Peter's reaction when he came home to find the police officer at our house.

"Hmm." She has a faraway look in her eye.

"Hmm? That's all you've got?"

"I'm thinking, Laura!"

Our meals arrive, and we stop talking about my crisis for a bit to fill our plates with a crispy sesame chicken dish and some spicy Szechuan veggies. I haven't even gotten to the part about Peter finally agreeing to sell the house. Sophie's uncharacteristically quiet, and it's freaking me out, so I start filling the silence. I tell her about the house, Peter's abrupt decision to sell it, and Lydia's plan to buy it from us.

I see her brow furrow as she finishes chewing and takes a sip of her water.

"So, why would Peter suddenly make this decision now? After all this time? You've been living there for over a decade. Married for what? Seven years?"

I nod, and she continues.

"And he's known all this time you've wanted to move. I mean, why now? There must be a connection to what happened."

"I don't know. I thought it was because he was frightened that day when he thought something had happened to me and wanted to make me happy. Give me what I want."

I can tell by the skeptical look on her face that she's not convinced. I'm not either, but I was hoping that was just me, letting my imagination get the best of me.

"Why? What's your take on it?"

She hesitates, which makes me even more nervous. We nibble on our food, and she's not making eye contact. Then she stops and looks up at me.

"It seems like something a person would do out of guilt, maybe?"

"Guilt?"

"Yeah."

"You think he feels guilty about something?"

"That's what my gut is telling me."

"Guilty about what?"

"I have no idea. But if I were you, I'd want to find out."

SIX

It's Tuesday afternoon, and Peter is in the lobby, if that's what you'd call it, of Shackler Investigative Services. It's more like a hallway with a few dated office chairs—metal ones with olive green vinyl cushions that seems to be doubling as a storage area. The brittle cushion crunches as he sits. There are boxes stacked up in one corner, and the door to the office is closed. An issue of *People* from five years ago sits on the lone wooden side table. *Maybe I should have gone with the well-known firm.* Too late for that now.

After a few minutes, the door opens, and a man and a woman come out. The man is tall with light brown hair, about fifty, and stuffed into a pair of ill-fitting gray slacks that pinch at the waist. His tucked-in white button-down shirt spills over the sides of his belt. He's not particularly overweight, but the cut of his slacks gives that impression. The woman is patting her eyes with a tissue, and the man has his arm around her. She's maybe in her early forties, wearing a stylish fitted red dress and designer shoes, carrying what looks like a Birkin bag. Even if it's a knockoff, he still takes it as a good sign that the client appears well put together. The man walks her to the door, and she turns around to look at him.

"Thank you, Shep," she says, looking into his eyes.

He places a hand on her shoulder.

"Anything you need, Melody, you call me. Okay? Anytime." He sees her out and then turns to Peter, who stands up to greet him.

"Shep Shackler." He holds out his hand.

Peter shakes it. "Peter Foster. Nice to meet you." Shackler's grip is firm, dry, and confident.

"We're in the middle of a remodel, so please excuse the clutter."

Shackler escorts him into his office, which is about the size of Peter's walk-in closet. He's got more boxes piled up near his metal office desk, which is covered with stacks of paper. It looks like an organized mess if he had to guess. The saving grace is a large window with a nice view of the tree-lined street outside.

"So, what can I do for you, Peter?"

Peter thought about it on the way over and decided he'd start with Laura and the car and then go from there. He takes the investigator through the story, and Shackler furiously jots it all down on his small notepad. *He's a good listener.* When Peter finishes, Shackler throws up his hands.

"Peter! This must be making you frantic. Does she have any enemies that you know of?"

"No. She recently got a promotion at work. Her boss said there were some jealousies, but cutting her brake line seems a bit much."

"It's not unheard-of, but it would be unusual. It's a rash move, though. If it was someone in her office, she'd probably have an inkling about who it was. Has she said anything about anyone in particular?"

"No. But I'll ask her."

"How long have you two been together?"

Peter takes him through the broad strokes of their twelve-year relationship. His first wife's death. His time alone as a single dad with two young children. How he and Laura met at the bar at Los Altos Grill. Their whirlwind courtship. Their stable, happy marriage.

"Any disgruntled exes in her past?"

"None that I know of."

"What about her present?"

Peter narrows his eyes at Shackler. "What the hell is that supposed to mean?"

For a moment, Peter feels like storming out. He hasn't given anything away yet, so he could. But then he realizes it's a natural question to ask, so he takes a deep breath and settles back in.

Shackler walks it back a bit. "Sorry, Peter. I mean no disrespect. I'm only trying to cover all the bases here. Could she have had, perhaps, a dalliance that turned sour?"

"No. I mean, I can't imagine it. No way. Not Laura."

"What about an admirer? Someone who got the wrong idea?"

He hadn't considered that, but maybe he should. She's an attractive woman. It's possible. Someone from her triathlon team?

"She hasn't said anything, but I can ask her. She's not the flirty type, so I doubt it." Then his mind flashes back to his first wife. All that drama. And he appreciates Laura even more.

"What about *your* present?"

"Look, Shep, I'm sorry to disappoint you, but we're happily married. There's no story there. There's nobody in our present except each other. You can move on."

Peter's eyes are trained on the investigator, who seems to get the message. Shackler offers Peter a firm nod of his head.

"Okay, then. Nothing in your present." The PI pauses as he spins his pen between two fingers, his head tilted to the side. "What about your past?"

Peter's stomach sinks, and he avoids Shackler's gaze. Peter needs to tell him about the email, but he only wants to disclose the bare minimum. An awkward silence fills the air, and Peter feels the familiar tingling in the back of his head that occurs when his buried past resurfaces.

"There might be something. What I tell you is completely confidential, correct?"

Peter did some research and found out about the *Kovel* rule, stemming from a federal case in the early sixties that extended attorney-client privilege to other professionals working for clients through their attorneys, which is why he went through his attorney friend to arrange the meeting with the private investigator. It's not ironclad protection, but it's better than nothing. He's sure Shackler knows about this but wants to hear it from him anyway.

"Absolutely. We're covered," Shackler confirms. "I work for you."

"Laura might want to meet with you once I tell her I've hired you to look into the car incident, and she can't know about this. I need to protect her. Understand? I'm not even sure it's connected. Do I have your word on that?"

"As I said, Peter, I work for you." He puts down the pad and pen and leans back in his chair, his arms folded across his chest. "This is completely off the record."

Peter mulls over exactly how much to disclose. As little as possible, he decides. He's still not sure he can trust this guy, but then he doesn't have many options.

"I received an email the other day."

"Go on," Shackler says.

And Peter does.

SEVEN

The week is flying by. It's Wednesday already, and Peter and I have barely spoken, aside from some perfunctory small talk. That's mostly on me. I can make more time for him if I choose to, but I've been distancing myself a bit. We've both been very busy, so I don't think he's noticed.

But what Sophie said has been nagging at me. Why has he decided to sell the house after all this time? Does he feel guilty about something? And why can't I get him to open up more about his past and what happened to Cynthia? I need to broach the subject with him, but I want to do some research first. It's late afternoon, and the office is quiet, so I start to dig.

It's not the first time I've looked into Cynthia's accident. I have to admit that morbid curiosity got the better of me after I found out what happened, and it took a while before he started to open up about it to me. Even then, I only got bits and pieces.

Our courtship was a whirlwind one. After our first date, I knew he was smitten. He texted me right after he got home that night, and I was impressed by the fact that he was confident enough to tell me how he felt about me. No games. Not like the young guys I'd been dating.

We'd been seeing each other for a month or so when the conversation about his late wife finally happened. We'd seen each other almost every day, but I had yet to meet his children. I was fine with that—things had been moving fast enough for me—but apparently, it had been weighing on him.

"Laura," he began, as we held hands and gazed into each other's eyes across a candlelit table tucked in the back of his favorite Italian spot. We were finishing up for the night, and for a few long moments I was afraid he might pop the question. I wasn't ready for that. "I know I've been a bit closed off about my children."

"Your children?" I tilted my head to one side. That wasn't what I was expecting.

"I haven't introduced you to them."

"That's okay, Peter. I understand." I wasn't ready to meet them anyway, not that he was asking me if I was.

"No, it's not okay."

"Peter, really, it's—"

"No. Wait. Please." He held his hand up to silence me. "Let me finish."

"Okay."

"Look, Laura, you know I'm not one to beat around the bush. I see a future with you. I *want* a future with you. I love you more than you know. I never thought I could feel this way again. I'm just not sure you feel the same way, and I don't want to involve them until I'm sure you do."

That made my head spin. I was twenty-seven with my whole life ahead of me. Was I ready for this? I was crazy about him, that much I knew. The sex was great. I couldn't get enough of him in bed. But what did I know about love? I thought I was in love before, twice, in fact, and looking back, it was laughable. It would never have worked with either of them. And taking on his two children? After they'd lost their mother? I felt like a horrible person for having those thoughts, and I didn't share any of them with him. I just stuffed them down and replied.

"Of course I feel the same way, Peter. I love you too."

And that was that.

After I'd sealed my fate, we talked about the kids and how they'd been handling their mother's death. And then I just had to ask.

"So, I'm not sure if it's okay to ask, but that day? The day it happened? It must have been horrible for all of you. You can talk to me about it if you want. I'm here for you."

Peter rested his forehead on his fingertips.

"I'm sorry, I—"

"No, it's okay." He took a deep breath and looked up at me. "I need to talk about it." He stared down at the table-cloth, fiddling with the few bread crumbs dotting its crisp white surface.

"Take your time."

I already knew some of what he told me that night from my research, but I let him continue. He'd concluded that Cynthia was an adrenaline junkie, that she was wired that way, to need the rush that her escapades provided. But they'd been having issues, mostly because he was on her case about toning it down. Oddly, she'd given up most of her adventure sports after the kids were born, but then she started climbing again out of the blue about two years before she died.

He also told me she'd suffered from mood swings over the years, and he thought maybe the buzz of the adventure sports somehow mitigated her pain. He wanted her to get help, and she had done so periodically, but most of the time she resisted and tried to tough it out. He said she'd been diagnosed with borderline personality disorder in her teenage years, a controversial diagnosis that he wasn't sure fit her symptoms. It was a difficult syndrome to treat, requiring intensive therapy and not tending to respond well to medications.

"She was spending too much time on her hobby. Those climbs, they take all day. I had a career that was taking off. And we had two small kids."

"Did she go with other people?"

"I guess. I didn't really keep track."

That seemed odd to me at the time, but then he never asks about my social life, either. Still, this was the mother of his children. Wouldn't he want to know who she was with?

Peter continued. "We'd been having issues for a few years. She'd turned cold all of a sudden. Distant. She didn't really speak to me very much. I tried to get her to go to counseling, but she wasn't interested. Then, a few weeks before the accident, she did a one-eighty. Said I was right. That she was being selfish. That she wanted to change. Wanted to make the marriage work."

I nodded, not wanting to interrupt, although a slew of sordid thoughts bounced around my head. Was she having an affair? Could her lover have...

Peter broke my train of thought.

"We even talked about having a recommitment ceremony, at her suggestion, if you can believe that. I have no idea what changed her mind. And I guess I never will."

Peter went on to explain that on the day she died, she went out for a hike, not a climb, supposedly by herself. Instead of his wife, the police showed up at his door that afternoon around the time she was due to return, informing him of her fatal fall and shattering their family into as many pieces as her broken body.

I'd known the broad strokes for some time, but when he opened up a bit more about it, the whole incident started to sound a bit fishy to me. She's an experienced climber, out on a hike, not a climb, and she falls to her death? I was surprised there wasn't more of an investigation.

What if she was seeing someone and she broke it off? Maybe that's why she had a change of heart—the guilt of an affair would do it. What if there was an angry lover out there somewhere, a climbing buddy perhaps? Or was it a suicide? Is that where all of Peter's guilt was coming from? I got the impression that Cynthia's mother wanted to sweep it all under the rug and move on; a suicide would certainly explain that. It would be too much of an embarrassment for the family and too much to process for the kids. But I'm not the type to ask a lot of questions, so I kept all those thoughts to myself.

Of course, any outsider would probably be thinking something even more sinister. His first wife dies in a freak accident, and then his second wife gets her brake line cut? I know how it looks, and I'm sure there's an explanation for all of it, so I'm not going there.

Am I?

—

My twenty minutes of sleuthing at work earlier today turned up no useful information of any value, but it did up my guilt, so I abandoned my little mission and got back to work for a bit but not before calling Peter and asking him to make time for a romantic dinner at home.

Now Peter and I are enjoying a quiet midweek dinner at our kitchen table—takeout from a Greek place we both like in downtown Los Altos. He sounded happy for the distraction when I called him at work this afternoon. Relieved, even. Maybe my aloofness this week hasn't been lost on him. After all he's been through, he's likely on the lookout for signs of trouble in our marriage. I should be more trusting. This is crazy. *Why am I snooping on my own husband?* I need to stop.

We're finishing up a chat about my promotion when he abruptly changes the subject.

"So, I met with that private investigator."

"You did what?"

"To look into the brake line thing. I told you about it. Remember?"

"Oh, yeah. Right." *Did he?*

It doesn't help that my mind is still back in the past, with Cynthia out there on that cliff. I'd almost forgotten that someone might be trying to kill me.

"Did you forget about it?" Peter gives me a curious look, his head tilted to the side.

"I, well, no, not about my car. Of course not. I sort of forgot about the investigator. Sorry. I remember now. You asked me to tell you where my car was that day. But I thought we'd leave that for a bit. See what the police turn up first."

"They won't do much of anything. Can't you tell? They've moved on already, so I went ahead and met with him."

"I guess you're right. So, tell me. What's he like? This PI you found."

"He's right out of central casting, I swear. A real character. But he seems to know his stuff."

"How did you find him?"

"A referral from my attorney."

"Your attorney? Why would you call an attorney?"

Sophie's voice rings in my ear. *It's something he might do out of guilt.*

Guilty people call lawyers.

"I didn't 'call an attorney.' I called my friend Tom for a referral, and he happens to be an attorney."

I guess that makes sense. But still.

"And what does he think? This investigator fellow. What's his name?"

"Shep Shackler."

"Shep Shackler? You've got to be kidding me."

"Nope. That's his name." Peter smiles, engaging his crow's feet, which give his eyes a twinkly look that I find attractive and endearing.

"With a name like that, what other choice does he have?"

Peter takes a hearty bite of his falafel and shrugs. "Used car salesman?" Tzatziki sauce squirts out the side of his mouth as he talks. "Sorry." He wipes it away with his napkin.

"Can't take you anywhere."

"You should talk. Look at your blouse."

I look down and see a white blob clinging to my front, which I promptly remove. We both have a laugh, and it feels nice. Comfortable. Normal.

He continues to give me the rundown, gesturing as he speaks. He says we'll both meet with Shackler soon, after he's had a chance to look into the information we've given him thus far.

"So, do you think he can help?"

"I'm not sure, but he probably can't hurt."

"True."

"He's checking camera footage on all the places your car was that day, and then he'll get back to us."

We continue with our meal—a Greek salad, some shrimp kabobs, and rice—and he fills me in on the FDA situation at work. Peter is an executive vice president at a biotech company. He's leading a research team that's hoping to get approval on a promising drug for ovarian cancer, and all eyes are on him. So far, so good on that, he says. But he's not smiling. His lips are pursed and his jaw looks tight to me. He's worried about something, I can tell.

"So it went well? The meeting?"

"Yes…" His brow furrows.

"I sense a 'but' in there."

"Well, remember I told you that we got some early indications that the drug might work for lung cancer too?"

"Yes, but I thought that was in the preliminary stages. And isn't that a good thing?"

"It is, but we put out a preprint on it. And that made the stock go up. A lot."

"And that's a problem?"

"The team from the company we're merging with hasn't been able to reproduce the results from our lung cancer experiments."

"That does sound like a problem."

"Maybe, maybe not. But if someone on my team screwed up, it's ultimately on me."

"I see."

I wonder how much this means for us, financially speaking. *How much has the stock gone up?* He told me once that we stand to gain a nice profit if they get the approval, but I haven't really looked into it in any detail. I'm superstitious, and I don't like to count my chickens. But I suppose I have a good explanation for his tense mood as of late. I can tell he doesn't want to talk about it, and I'm not surprised when he changes the subject.

"Anyway, I've got a real estate agent lined up, so we can start looking for a new house anytime. Want to go online tonight and see if we can narrow it down?" Peter's eyes light up, and I can see he wants me to return his excitement.

I don't say anything for a bit. Then I recover, not wanting to disappoint him. "Sure! Yes, that would be...great."

"Laura? Isn't this what you want?" He looks puzzled and a little hurt at my lack of enthusiasm.

"Yes. Of course."

"Then what's wrong? You don't seem very excited."

I decide I might as well confront him and get it out in the open. "I am excited. It's just, I mean, why now? After all this time?"

"Huh?"

"It seems rather abrupt. The decision to sell."

"Isn't it obvious?"

"Not to me."

"Well, when I saw the police, it all came rushing back at me. That day, you know...the trauma of it all."

I nod. That makes perfect sense. *Why didn't I think of that?*

Peter continues. "I always knew you weren't crazy about this place—you said so in the beginning—but then you never made an issue of it, so I guess it dropped off my radar. But then—"

"I get it, Peter. I do."

"And the thought of something happening to you. Maybe this place is just, I don't know, bad luck?"

He hangs his head, and I place my hand on top of his. I love his hands. They're powerful and smooth, and I think I'd like to feel them on me tonight.

"That sounds so stupid. I know."

"It's not stupid, Peter. It makes perfect sense."

Of course. All of those horrible memories here. It's not about me. It's about him and his past. He's ready to move on, and I feel horrible for doubting him. He's a kind, sexy, devoted hunk of a man, and I vow to dig no further. I don't think he senses anything about my bizarre suspicions, but I still plan to make it up to him later tonight.

—

Peter is lying in bed, waiting for Laura. She's in the bathroom engaging in her nightly ritual, and he's waiting for her to come join him before he turns out the light. Normally, he'd be reading. Instead, he's reflecting on his talk with Shep Shackler.

Provided the email wasn't a phishing scam—which Shackler agreed was unlikely with no call to action—it could be linked to one of two things, and Peter had told the detective only about the one that won't land him in prison. The statute of limitations has run out on that particular transgression. He didn't give away anything more than was absolutely necessary, so Shackler is checking into the car incident and the email. Peter has to trust someone, and the PI is his only option right now.

He's initially more shocked than delighted when Laura strides in wearing a black lace teddy he didn't even know she owned. That's one more thing he loves about her— she's full of surprises.

"What's the occasion?"

"We're the occasion." She smiles, her head tilted down, a sly look on her face.

"I'll drink to that."

"To us." Laura feigns a toast with a raised hand, and Peter returns her gesture. Then she climbs into bed.

Soon she's all over him, and thoughts of the email, the data, and all the other bullshit in his life simply evaporate. It's only the two of them, and he couldn't care less if the world ended outside their door. His hands caress her tight, hot body, the smoothness of her skin a stimulating contrast with the scratchy lace of her garment. He tries to go slow, make her wait, but it's not that kind of night. He rips the snaps open, tearing her teddy a bit.

"Sorry," he says.

"Don't worry." She kisses him as she talks. "I hate this freaking thing." And then she sits up and rips it off, and they melt into one.

EIGHT

It's Saturday, and lunch with my mother is going as well as can be expected. I knew what her reaction would be about Peter's daughter buying the house from him. I got an earful, but I'm thankful she doesn't harp on it for too long. My parents love me; they really do. But my mom's got a certain outlook on life that can rub people the wrong way—a stuck-in-the-sixties mentality—although she's too young to remember much from that decade. My parents met at the University of Hawai'i in graduate school in the eighties, and I was born in the islands—just like Obama, they often reminded me when I was younger, as if he'd somehow upped the ante. My brother and I were destined to disappoint.

"So you're looking for a new place?" Mom munches on her vegan stew as we chat at a sidewalk café down the street from their house. I'm picking at my salad; I don't like the dressing. Bonkers, their small golden-haired rescue, sits at her feet, staring up occasionally in hopeful anticipation. He came by that name honestly—he was a handful in his early days—but at ten, he's rather outgrown it, although he still has that same mischievous look in his eyes. They live in San Francisco's Outer Richmond district, and I came into the city to meet her. Their neighborhood is decidedly bourgeois; my mom has mellowed on her militancy over the years. They moved to the city from the South Bay after my brother and I graduated from college.

Their neighborhood, a bit far from the city center, was populated later than the more central sections of the city near Union Square and the Financial District after the 1906 earthquake and fire destroyed much of the city and people pushed out to this area to regroup. Bordered by Ocean Beach and Golden Gate Park with access to walking trails and paths where Dad can run and Mom can walk Bonkers, the area offers dramatic vistas and a touch of nature but with quick and easy access to the city. It suits them in this later phase of their lives.

I drove the Pacific Coast Highway on the way up from the Peninsula, and seeing the rolling whitecaps break along the shore made me miss the islands. We moved to the Bay Area when I was in middle school, but I spent my early childhood years digging in the alabaster sand and bodysurfing the warm, frothy waves of Kailua Beach on the windward side of O'ahu. I hate the fact that I need to wear a wet suit to get in the water here. I'll never get used to it.

"Yeah. We've got some appointments for later today." I haven't told my mother anything about the brake line incident. I know it will make her frantic, so I'm weighing the pros and cons of disclosing it.

"I know you've been wanting this move for a while. So why aren't you more excited?" My mother knows me too well.

"I *am* excited." I try to put some zip into the statement, but it falls flat.

"Laura?" My mother eyes me, her fingers tapping the table. "What's up? What are you not telling me?"

I sigh and then bring her up to speed about my car incident. It's a bit of a relief. Underneath her bohemian façade, she's a mom—my mom—and although I don't want to worry her, I sort of need my mommy right now.

"Oh my God, Laura! Do you think someone at work is out to get you?" Her eyebrows lift, and I see myself in her right now, which I rarely do. I have her straight, classic Greek nose, but otherwise, I look more like my dad.

"No! I mean, I don't think so."

"You know how cutthroat the corporate world can be." She goes on to explain why I should perhaps consider working for a nonprofit or some other more socially conscious vocation.

I quickly change the subject. I'm not in the mood for her propaganda.

"Peter's hired a private investigator to look into it."

"How very Dashiell Hammett of him." She smirks. My mother's a retired English professor and often speaks in literary code. I'm fairly well-read, and this one I get, but often she stumps me. "Has he uncovered anything of interest?"

"Not yet." I recount what Peter told me, and I remind her of the officer's road debris theory, trying to convince her that I'm buying it myself.

"That makes sense, Laura. Maybe it was an accident like the officer suggested." Mom offers me a shrug, and I decide we should leave it at that. She's pushing seventy and doesn't need the added stress. If she wants to tell herself it's nothing, I'll play along.

"I think so too, but he's going to check all the places my car was to make sure."

"Well, you let me know, sweetie." My mom smiles, and I feel grateful that I have such caring parents. Peter had a rough upbringing, although he rarely opens up about it, and I know I'm fortunate.

We enjoy the rest of our meal as she fills me in on my older brother, an M.D. who lives in New Jersey with his wife and tween son, and I remind myself that I should call him or go visit. We used to be close, but we've both been so busy lately. I've often wondered why my parents don't move closer to their only grandchild, but then they hate the cold as much as I do. My father is there now, combining his visit with a conference he's speaking at in New York City. He's an economics professor and pretty well-known nationally. I don't know if he'll ever retire.

We wrap up and say our goodbyes, and as I look back at my mom walking away with her little sidekick bouncing alongside her, I notice that she's getting older. It's not the way she looks; it's how she carries herself—as if she could easily break apart with one wrong move.

I feel nostalgic for my childhood on the beach as I drive home, gazing at the familiar coastal view to my right, headed back to the South Bay to meet Peter and the real estate agent. And now, finally, I start to feel excited about our new beginning.

———

We've looked at six houses already, and I can already tell this isn't going to be easy. It's dinnertime, and I'm hungry, so that might be affecting my mood. We decide to call it a day. Supposedly, the market has softened a bit, but it doesn't seem like it to me. Although our place is a drive from the Los Altos town center and not very convenient, we have a very large lot and a great deal of privacy. If we want to be closer to town, we'll have to settle for a smaller yard, and Peter's not crazy about that idea, although it doesn't bother me. I'm more concerned about aesthetics, and none of the homes are acceptable to me. The agent's trying to get us to consider townhomes, but that's not going to happen. Although I'd prefer to stay in Los Altos, I'd look in a different town before giving up on a single-family home.

We stroll around town, and I take it all in. I have grown to love it here over the years, although, in the beginning, it was a bit much for me, given how I grew up. There are wealthy people in my home state, of course, but it's hard to pick them out of a crowd. The beach is the great equalizer there; nobody owns it, and the ocean doesn't care how much money you make. At first glance, Los Altos looks like any quaint California small town: picturesque sidewalk cafés and boutiques, nail shops and salons, banks, and insurance companies. But then we pass the ASKA shop, a storefront where consumers can get a glimpse of a flying car that is under development—and preorder one for just under a million dollars. The fact that they've chosen this town for a retail outlet says a great deal about the demographics, although most people here are surprisingly down-to-earth. Still, it can all be a bit overwhelming, the thought of how much wealth resides in this region of the country. I wonder how it feels to be a longtime resident, with so much change happening over the last few decades, and how most people manage to even survive.

Speaking of money, we still haven't talked about the house, but I plan on bringing it up. Neither of us should be making assumptions, and something Peter said to our real estate agent earlier nags at me: *I'll have the proceeds from the house to put down.*

If we're in this together, shouldn't it be "we"?

"So, what do you think?" Peter asks as we walk towards our car.

"About?" My mind was a mile away. I realize he's been talking, but I have no idea what he just said.

"The houses. The agent."

"Well, we agreed we don't like any of them, right?"

"Does that include the agent?" Peter flashes me a smirk.

She's very attractive. Does he think I'm jealous? No, he knows me better than that.

"She's fine. Easier on the eyes than the houses she showed us."

Peter smiles and takes my hand as we stroll along.

"Maybe we should sleep on it. There's no rush. Right?"

"Right," I reply, reminding myself that there is indeed a rush, at least on my end. I don't want to drag this out for too long. Strike while the iron is hot. Even if I have to settle, I'm getting out of that house. Soon. Before he changes his mind.

"Wanna grab a bite to eat? I know it's a little early, but—"

"I'm starved." I raise up my hand. "Say no more."

We're too hungry to be picky, so we land on a sandwich spot around the corner, sit down, and order, but the money issue is still top of mind for me. I fill him in about my visit with my mother, waiting until we've gotten some food in us to bring up the house sale. I'm about to start in on it when his cell gets an incoming call.

"It's Shackler. The PI." My husband seems to be asking my permission to answer the phone.

My eyes widen. "Answer it!" But he's not reacting. *Why is he hesitating?*

Finally, Peter answers his phone and then gets up and walks to the hallway near the bathrooms, away from people. I would have rather listened in, but I suppose he's being polite to the other diners.

After a few long minutes, he comes back with a puzzled look on his face.

"Well?"

"He found something. Take a look at this. Tell me what you see."

He hands me his phone. A video is cued up, ready to play. It's a view of the parking lot at work, taken from somewhere across the street. It's grainy, but I spot my car in the frame. The front part of the car, where the wheels sit, is hidden from the camera, tucked behind the building's façade.

"And?"

"Just play it."

I press the button, and the video starts up. Soon I see something come into view above the hood before it disappears again a few moments later.

I feel my heart start to race a bit. "Is that someone's head?"

The head—if it is a head—appears to belong to someone with darker hair, although it's hard to tell on the video. It was taken around five thirty in the afternoon, and it was still light out, but the building cast a shadow over the area.

"Could be," Peter says.

"I'll be damned."

"You can say that again."

"So what do we do now?"

We sit in silence as I take in the fact that someone was apparently crouched down by my car the day before I came out of my house to find brake fluid on my driveway. I'm flabbergasted. *Could someone actually be that upset about a promotion?* I tell myself that it's very unlikely, but my hands are trembling a bit as I hold the phone in my palm, staring at the image. One thing for sure is we need to check into this. Soon.

Peter covers my hands with his to steady me, and we decide to call Bethany and let her know what's going on. I have to trust someone, and I'm sure she's on my side.

Shep is sitting in his office reflecting on his brief phone conversation with Peter Foster. The case has him intrigued. It's not your run-of-the-mill cheating spouse or stalker situation, which have come to be his bread and butter. Foster's playing his cards close to the vest, which makes Shep think there's more to this than he's letting on. Although it was hard to tell over the phone, Foster seemed initially more relieved than disturbed by the video, although he caught himself towards the end of the call and voiced the requisite indignation.

Shep looks again at the email Foster forwarded to him. **I know what you did. I won't tell anyone.**

The email came from a burner address that is no longer in existence. Shep traced the sender's location to a street in Sunnyvale near a public library. It was a fairly unsophisticated move, but in its simplicity, it left few clues as to who the sender was or, more importantly, why they sent it to his client and what it means.

Peter Foster has a skeleton in his closet. A potential SEC violation from decades ago. Out of desperation, he leaked a fake story to the press to manipulate the stock price at a company he was with—a "pump and dump." He was being blackmailed, he claims, and he had no other way to obtain the funds.

Blackmailed for what, he wasn't saying. And now that the finger is pointing towards someone at his wife's workplace for the car incident, his client has instructed him to back off the email investigation. Foster claims he's convinced it was a random prank. Maybe a teenager, he posited—the twenty-first-century version of a phony phone call; nothing to worry about.

But Shep isn't worried; he's curious, and Foster's eagerness to close the lid on the email investigation entices him to dig further.

NINE

It's Sunday morning, and we're at my office, poring over security camera footage. Peter and I talked about it and decided not to go to the police until we investigated further. Bethany, Peter, and I are with the security chief, who's not too thrilled about being called in off-hours. We're about to review the footage from a camera that gives us a different vantage point from the one across the street.

We haven't told anyone else about this, and my boss is visibly shaken by the notion that someone from work could have tampered with my car. *Does she really care that much about me, or is she afraid that she'll be next if this is payback for my promotion?* I still can't believe that anyone cares enough about this to try to kill me. It's all very surreal.

But soon we are all breathing a collective sigh of relief. We see Emily—our college intern with shoulder-length dark hair—walking along the sidewalk near my car. We can't see her face, but it's obvious from her mannerisms and clothes that's who it is. She steps off the curb and stumbles, falling between the two cars. Her handbag flies up in the air, and then she falls down and disappears from the frame. We see the top of her head bob around before she stands back up, brushes herself off, and limps away.

Nobody is trying to kill me. It was an accident, and I'm glad we didn't go to the police with the video that Shackler found.

"Oh my God, I'm so relieved!" Bethany says.

"Me too," I say.

"Who is that?" Peter asks, squinting at the screen. Bethany and I are smiling, almost ready to leave, but Peter is still focused on the screen.

"Emily Swanson," Bethany says. "Our summer intern."

"Oh." He shrugs. "Well, I guess that settles that."

We apologize to the security manager for making him come in on a Sunday, and we say our goodbyes.

Driving home, Peter is pretty quiet.

"What's up?"

"Nothing," he says.

"You don't seem relieved."

"I am. But let's not get complacent. This was a false alarm, but we still don't know for sure that it was an accident."

I'm a bit surprised that he's being so cautious.

"True, but what do you suggest I do? Hire a body-guard?" I smile.

"Just don't let your guard down for a while, Laura. Let's see what else Shackler comes up with."

"Right."

My husband's being overly cautious, I tell myself. He lost one wife, and he doesn't want to lose another.

"Listen, I have to go into work for a bit. I'll drop you at home, okay?" he says.

"Sure."

I've already missed the morning cycling ride with my team, but I need to squeeze in some kind of a workout before I meet Sophie for our mall crawl. I'm behind in my training because of all that's happened, and I thought about dropping out of the race next weekend in Santa Cruz, but I've decided to go through with it. I have a bit of an ego about my times, but I tell myself that's silly. It's something I enjoy, and even if it's not going to be my best showing, it will be good for me to race. It'll get me out of my own head and away from all of this nonsense. I don't need to be so competitive. I've got nothing to prove.

———

Sophie and I are strolling around Stanford Shopping Center, one of the only malls I frequent. I'm more of a boutique shopper if I shop in person at all. Online suits me fine most of the time. But this is an outdoor mall, appointed with brick pavers and lovely planters with colorful flowers that almost make me feel like I'm in an English garden. That is until Sophie grabs me and whisks me into the next shop—mostly handbags and other accessories—where she engages in an intense conversation about stitching with a wide-eyed salesperson, the dollar signs flashing before her eyes. We've been at this for over an hour, in and out of shops, and Sophie's wearing me out. After this, I'll ask her to take a breather. She's a power shopper, and although I tire of waiting around for her, I enjoy seeing her having so much fun.

"I think I'll pass," Sophie says after a bit and hands the bag back to the disappointed salesperson. She can be a bit of a tease.

We walk out the door into a perfect late summer day. The weather is a bit cooler, and there's a faint smell of coffee in the air. I haven't told her anything about what happened at work earlier today. I suggest we grab a Starbucks and sit for a bit, and she agrees. After we get our coffees, we sit at an outdoor table under the awning, where we watch the world go by. I fill her in on all of my happenings.

"I don't think it was someone at work. I mean, would someone really try to kill you over a promotion? There are other ways to ruin someone's career that won't land you in prison. It doesn't make any sense."

"You're right. I'm leaning towards this being a freak accident."

Sophie looks past me, her lips pursed. When she turns her gaze back to me, she says, "Did you ever press Peter about why he's decided to sell all of a sudden?"

I'm not sure how much to tell Sophie. We're best friends, but she can be a bit of a provocateur, and I've always had the feeling that she doesn't really like Peter. She thought I was making a mistake years ago, taking on all of his baggage, and she warned me it would hamper my career, which it did. But I've made up for lost time, and I'm doing fine now. *We're* doing just fine.

"He said the incident stirred up bad memories for him, seeing the police at the house. He panicked when he thought something had happened to me. And he decided we need to move on."

She tilts her head to the side, biting her lip as she speaks. "I guess that makes sense."

But the look on her face tells me she's not buying it. I should probably drop it, but I don't. Because it's not a look of salacious delight—the kind of look she gets when she's knee-deep in the latest piece of gossip—it's a look of genuine concern.

"Sophie? What is it?"

"It's nothing. I have a vivid imagination, that's all."

"What?"

"It's nothing!"

"It's not nothing."

"Well, okay. It's probably nothing. But, I mean, his first wife dies in a freak accident, and then you have a freak accident? I'm just saying." She throws up her hands. "What are the odds?"

My mind flashes to that documentary I watched last year about a husband who was charged with the murder of his second wife, whom he claimed accidentally fell down the stairs, just like his first one. No. That's ridiculous. What motive would Peter even have? He loves me. I know that. It's not that. I'm sure of it. But I also know how it looks, and I know where people's minds go when things like this happen. The husband is always a suspect. I decide we need to shut this all down immediately. A hint of suspicion can ruin a person these days.

"Sophie! Stop it!" I glare at her. "That's just ridiculous."

I think about telling her my suicide theory, that maybe that's where Peter's guilt is coming from, but I decide to hold back. It feels like too much of a betrayal to my family.

"I'm sorry, Laura. I am. I'm not trying to be alarmist. It's where my mind went, and you're my best friend. I care about you."

My mind flashes back to Peter. The look on his face when he came home to find a police car at his house. He was terrified—white as a ghost—and that is nearly impossible to fake. He'd have to be some kind of major psychopath, and even then, it would be hard, if not impossible, to manifest the physiological signs.

"I know it's not that."

I take a deep breath and search inside myself, trying to figure out what it is I'm feeling. I don't think Peter's trying to kill me, but if I'm being honest, I do feel like he's keeping something from me. Something important.

"I sense a 'but' in there," Sophie says.

"Can we drop it for now? Please?" I give her a stern look, and she seems to get it.

I feel very conflicted about this. It's hard for me to keep anything from Sophie. We met when we were still single. Back then, we told each other everything, especially about guys. We dissected every text message, scrutinized every argument. Looked up their exes on social media. Did our background checks and analyzed their Linkedin profiles, looking for signs of anything amiss before we gave them our bodies or our hearts. But at some point in a relationship, especially a marriage, the loyalty starts to shift, and it feels like a violation of trust to give up too many intimate details about your relationship, even to a best friend; we'd long since passed that point. It's the right move, most of the time. Unless, of course, you're married to a sociopath.

"Sure. Sorry. Let's change the subject."

We take a pause and sip our coffees.

"Now, did I tell you about my new client? The one with the sordid affair I have to spin?"

Sophie goes on to entertain me with the latest Silicon Valley gossip, although I sense it's a bit forced. She's still worried about me, I can tell, and I love her for it.

———

I'm home from my shopping excursion, upstairs in our bedroom, putting away the workout clothes I bought at the mall. It was a fun day, and I needed it. But I have more to do. I want to go look at some open houses later. Peter said he would be a while at work, so I'm planning to go on a little reconnaissance mission by myself. It's only three thirty, so I've still got time. I'm determined to find a new home and get out of here.

Walking down the stairs, I think I hear someone. It's not Peter because I've just gotten off the phone with him. Plus, I didn't hear a car drive up. I have a sinking feeling in my stomach when I realize the alarm isn't on. I rarely use it during the day. I'm pretty sure I locked the deadbolt before I went upstairs. It's a habit. I can't imagine forget-ting to do it.

The house is pretty isolated, as homes go around here, nestled in the bosom of a cluster of towering oak and eucalyptus trees that cast a perpetual darkness over the home, even in the daytime. To the back, there are nearly two acres of woods, which give the property a much higher value than the home itself would normally fetch. Although the privacy is nice, I've always felt somewhat vulnerable here. The house is set back from the street, far away from the neighbors, and we have no gate or other method of keeping out intruders. If I forget to put on the alarm, we don't have much of a barrier to keep anyone at bay. I felt better when we had our German shepherd, but he died a year or so ago, and with the kids out of the house, we didn't want the responsibility of a new puppy. Of course, we get our share of animal interlopers, and it's possible it could be a deer, a coyote, or even a mountain lion, which is rare but not unheard-of. And I realize now that I can't wait to move out of this place and live closer to town.

I go back into the bedroom, looking for something to use as a weapon, just in case. All I can find is a giant-size umbrella sporting the logo of a now-defunct company Peter worked for. I use it to shade myself when I cheer on my friends at the finish line.

This is ridiculous. What if the person has a gun? Then I remind myself: There's no person. It's my imagination. Still, the umbrella makes me feel better, so I head down the stairs, clutching my pathetic weapon in my right hand, my phone poised to dial 9-1-1 in my left.

"Hello?" I call out. Nobody answers. I think about calling the police, but then I realize the noise could have been anything. They already think I'm paranoid. There's no further sound. I breathe deeply, in and out, to slow my racing heart, and will myself to calm down.

I take a spin around the living area and the dining room and make my way into the kitchen. The lights are out, and the trees shade the house so much it's hard to see at first. But when I flick the lights on, it's all clear. With a sigh of relief, I turn around to go back upstairs to finish what I was doing. Then I hear something rattling around in the garage, off the kitchen. Maybe it's a squirrel or a raccoon. I turn around and head into the kitchen.

The side door to the garage starts to open. My stomach lurches, and I grip the umbrella tight and lift it in the air, poised to strike.

"Get back!" I call out. "I'm calling the police."

The door swings open, and my hand goes to my heart. Then I do a one-eighty as my brain struggles to catch up to the image in front of me. It's Lydia, wide-eyed, looking at me and my raised umbrella like I'm some kind of crazy person.

"Laura? What the hell are you doing?"

"What are *you* doing, Lydia? Jesus, you scared the crap out of me!" I take a deep breath and let myself absorb the fact that I'm not in any danger.

But after the relief passes, I start to feel upset. I try to suppress it. I don't want a conflict. She has a key to our home, although she's never let herself in like this before, at least that I know of. I'm trying to calm myself, but my fear is turning to anger.

"I texted you that I was coming over. Didn't you see it? I need to get some measurements. I was looking for a tape measure in the garage."

"I must've missed your text. But still, you shouldn't just let yourself in." Texting in advance doesn't justify letting herself into our home. But then it dawns on me. To Lydia, it's her home now, and I realize we need to move fast to find another place before this all explodes and destroys our family.

"Sorry, Laura, you're right. I'm excited, that's all."

"Well, please call next time. And wait for confirmation before you come over."

"I will. Sorry. Dad told me about your car. I know you must be on edge."

So now it's my fault because I'm on edge?

I don't have the energy to counter that my being on edge is not the point, and I feel uncomfortable letting her stay in the house when I'm planning to leave, but I can't very well kick her out. It's been awkward enough already.

"I'm fine, Lydia."

"I'm sure it was a freak accident," she says.

"Right."

I check my phone and see that she did text me. And she drives a Tesla, so I wouldn't have heard the car drive up. She didn't mean anything by letting herself in, so I let it go like I always do.

"Okay, well, I have to run out. Do you want to stay for dinner?"

"No thanks. Christopher's taking me out." She offers me a girlish grin, and although it's not much, I take it as a nice moment; she's letting me in on the fact that she's smitten.

"Sounds like it's getting serious."

"I really like him. And he's great. He treats me like a princess."

He'd have to, wouldn't he?

I smile and play the devoted stepmom.

"I'm happy for you, Lydia." And I am, because if she finds her Prince Charming, maybe she can finally move on and let me have a normal life with her dad.

When Peter and I first got together, Lydia was accustomed to being the woman of the house, and she wasn't about to give up the role without a fight. She'd take the front seat when we all drove together. I'd ride in the back with Carson. Lydia sat at the foot of the table; I was sidelined. I remember the first time she beat me to the front seat of the car. We were headed out to dinner. Peter was about to protest, but I held up my hand to stop him. I didn't want to rock the boat. She was young. Fragile. But that moment wasn't lost on Lydia. She flashed me a smug victory smile from the car window, letting me know that this was a contest—and that she'd won.

Her actions weren't always so overt, but they were pretty consistent, at least in the beginning, especially if her father wasn't around. If looks could kill, I'd be a dead woman. When we were all together, it was more subtle. She'd bring up memories from their past before I was in their life to let me know that I was an outsider.

Remember when we all went to Costa Rica, Dad? And I got so sunburned?

For Christmas, she'd give her dad photos of the three of them from before I was in the picture. Over time, the acting out started to fade, like the memory of her mother, I imagine. Which is sad, so I try not to judge her too harshly.

But I am looking forward to a new life for us. Lydia can have this house with all of its bittersweet memories, and Peter and I can finally move on. I pull up the list of open houses, determined that one of them will become our new home, and we can finally begin to move on from this somber, haunted abode.

TEN

Two weeks have gone by since Shackler found the video of my car in the office parking lot, and there have been no further developments. The brake incident is starting to recede from our lives. We found a house that's acceptable to both of us, and they accepted our offer. The lot is a bit smaller than Peter wanted, but mature trees lining the property offer some privacy. The courtyard-style backyard has a Zen-like ambiance, lined with uniform Italian cypress trees and accented by a large Australian weeping willow and a flowering dogwood whose white blooms look spectacular at this time of year. It sits on a quiet street, within walking distance to the town center—super convenient, which I love. It's not very large, but it is tasteful—a three bedroom, two bath, just over two thousand square feet. The interior is clean, modern, and functional, and I'm excited to finally be able to decorate in my own taste. It's hard to fathom that a house this small is a deal with the staggering price tag. But then, this is the Bay Area, and we live in one of the most expensive zip codes in the country. It's a cash sale, so thankfully, we'll be able to move soon.

We'd never be able to afford a home like this on our salaries alone, without the proceeds from the family home. Even with that, things will be tight as we've put in all the cash we had on hand, but I'm not complaining. It's ours—mine and Peter's—and I'll finally be rid of the ghost.

My race is tomorrow—a half Ironman. I'm looking forward to getting back into the swing, even if it might not be my best time. With all of our house hunting and brake line sleuthing, I haven't been training with my team as much as I'd like. But in a way, it's good that I've mellowed a bit over the years. It used to be a bit of an obsession, my training. Even if I was injured, I still worked out, pushing myself to an unhealthy degree. It went hand in hand with an eating disorder that surfaced when I was a teenager and stayed with me through my midtwenties. I had therapy over the years, but becoming a stepmom is what really snapped me out of it. I had to take care of the kids and be a role model, especially for Lydia. That voice is always there in the back of my head, though. The one that points out all my flaws, the one that sees flab that isn't there, the one that tells me to keep running on a twisted ankle. But now, I can ignore it most of the time.

Peter comes into the kitchen as I'm getting ready to go out for a short bike ride to test out my time trial bike, the one I use to race, which is different from my road bike, the one I use to train.

"Hey there." He takes my face in his hands and gives me a gentle kiss. We had a nice evening—dinner at home followed by an especially romantic lovemaking session—and the memory is still fresh in my mind.

"Don't try to distract me." I smile, and he looks me up and down. I'm in my biking gear.

"You're going for a ride? Today?"

Peter still worries about me, and he'll throw out an occasional comment if he thinks I'm getting too obsessive.

"Just a quick ride around the neighborhood. To get the kinks out of the bike before the race." I head out the side door to the garage to get my racing bike, and I blow Peter a kiss on my way out.

———

Peter hears the garage door go up as he sips his morning coffee and thinks about what he wants to eat. He doesn't have much of an appetite, but he feels like he should force himself to put something in his stomach. He's on the verge of finally leaving the past behind, but for some reason it's haunting him now more than ever. Maybe that's to be expected. Part of the process of moving on. Or maybe it's the phantom email combined with the car incident that's bringing the past up for him again. He tries to convince himself that it's all meaningless. Random. That it has no connection to his past. But it's not working.

The last day of Cynthia's life is playing over and over in his mind. It was a terrible day, even before she left the house to go hiking. They'd had a rough two years but had been making headway towards some sort of reconciliation. And then it all turned sour.

"Where are you going?" Peter asked as Cynthia headed out the door in her workout gear. "Lydia has her soccer game today."

"Is that all you care about?"

"You didn't answer my question."

Peter felt thrown off-balance. A few days before, his wife had seemed eager to patch things up. She'd even suggested they have a recommitment ceremony. But that day, the coldness had returned, and he had a gut feeling that he knew why.

"Peter, can you stop trying to control me?"

"Cynthia? What's going on?"

Her icy blue eyes peered into him, chilling him to the bone. She was a striking woman, small but formidable, and she had a look that could disarm a terrorist. It's the kind of look that comes from knowing that, at the end of the day, you're holding all the cards. Always.

"Stop the bullshit, Peter. I know."

Those two words were a death sentence for their relationship.

She knows.

It didn't matter that she was the one who'd started it all. Her two-year affair with her climbing buddy Clint, another silver spoon trust-funder, who Peter thought was perfect for her. During those years, he'd sometimes hoped that Cynthia would divorce him and move on. But when he thought about the children, he kept at it. Tried to make it work. The woman had no maternal instincts to speak of. She seemed to have been born like that, missing some essential biological ingredient. Her mother made up for it, doting on the kids. Peter knew that his mother-in-law understood her daughter had issues, although they'd never spoken about it. Cynthia's teenage years were full of rebellion, and she'd embarrassed the family on more than one occasion.

"It's over, Cynthia."

"It certainly is over. Especially for you."

Cynthia was referring to the prenup, which clearly stated that Peter got next to nothing in the event of a divorce involving infidelity. From the time she was old enough to date, she was obsessed with the notion of someone using her, marrying her for her money. It had taken years for him to build trust, yet she was the one who went and broke their vows. Since he had nothing further to lose, he decided to let out years of pent-up frustration.

"You're such a freaking hypocrite! For years, I worked. Raised our kids while you were out messing around with Clint."

"Why didn't you try to stop me?"

"What are you talking about?"

"If you loved me so much, why didn't you say anything?"

"So that was a test?"

Cynthia stood a few feet away, looking at the ground with watery eyes, and Peter couldn't help but feel a pang of sympathy for his twisted wife. He knew there was something wrong with her. Was she actually that confused, or was this simply a way to throw it all back on him? Had she ever loved him at all? Was she even capable of love?

"We have two children, Cynthia."

"You should have thought about that before you started banging Jeanine."

"I told you. It's over with her."

Or so he hoped. His brief affair with his longtime work colleague had filled a void in him, a need to be needed, but he'd gone from one extreme to the other. At first, Jeanine's fawning was a welcome change from his wife's chilly demeanor. He thought he was in love, and he could kick himself for voicing that to her. But it quickly morphed into something troubling, even obsessive, especially when he broke it off after Cynthia came to her senses and decided to give the marriage another try. Peter had made it clear to Jeanine from the start that he wasn't going to leave his wife, but she still blew a gasket when he ended it.

"You'll say anything now, with all that's at stake."

"You're the one who cheated first, Cynthia. I have proof. And if you try to mess with me and take our children, I'll use it to get custody. I'm not losing my kids."

"Your children? Is that all you care about?"

"What are you talking about? They're *our* children, Cynthia."

"Take your precious children, Peter. You can have them. I'm done with all of you." She headed out the door, off to go on her hike, the hike that would result in her death.

But that wasn't even the worst part of the day. The worst part was when he turned around and saw his seven-year-old daughter standing at the bottom of the stairs, staring at him.

"Lydia. How long have you been there?" Peter's stomach sank as he watched Lydia's eyes well up.

He started to walk towards her, but she turned from him and ran back up the stairs. Peter heard her bedroom door slam, and he stood in helpless silence as the sound reverberated through the house.

———

Shep is pleased with himself. He likes it when his gut delivers. It helps that Peter Foster has a tell. When his client was asked about his present relationship, Shep was sure he was telling the truth. He doesn't suspect that either of the Fosters is having an affair. But when he asked about the man's past, his client hesitated, his blink rate increased, and his body leaned towards the door—both signs of discomfort and, quite often, deception. Foster later told him about the SEC violation, but Shep suspects that's an incomplete explanation for his behavior. Maybe that's part of it, but he's sure there's something more.

As a PI for hire, he doesn't normally go snooping around behind his client's back. But this is a special case. Foster's first wife died in a freak accident. According to the records, there wasn't much of an investigation. When Foster was questioned, he had an alibi, but it was shaky. Then the death was ruled an accident, and the family seemed eager to move on.

Still, it seems a bit suspicious that now his second wife has also had a freak accident, and if his client is some kind of serial spouse killer, he has to take action. He's uncovered the fact that Peter Foster was having an affair back then, and so was his wife. He wonders if his client will get around to telling him about it.

In the meantime, Shep continues investigating the whereabouts of his client's former mistress, but, curiously, Jeanine Randall seems to have vanished into thin air.

ELEVEN

The morning of the race is clear and cool in Los Altos, but there will likely be some fog at the coast. It's still pitch-dark outside. The house is quiet as I check off all the gear in my mind, savoring the silence and sipping my coffee. I triple-checked it all last night, and the gear is already in my car, but I still go through the list in my head. I find it calms me down.

It's quite a production, getting ready for a race, and I sometimes wonder why I keep at it. I'm always worried that I've left out something critical—one bike shoe, perhaps—but I never have. But I know once I'm out on the course, pumping away trying to catch the person in front of me, it'll all be worth it. There's nothing like it for me. That total commitment to being in the moment, my entire body a well-oiled machine with a singular goal—passing the person in front of me. It's the only time I feel completely free and totally at peace. I even look forward to the aches and pains the next day. There's something cathartic about it for me.

Peter is still sleeping. When we first started dating, he came to a few races. I don't blame him for quickly losing interest. It's long and very boring for spectators. Sometimes he comes to meet me at the finish line but not often. Today, he's planning on it. He's trying so hard to make me happy, and I appreciate it. We also cleared up my concern about the new house and my stake in it when we wrote up the offer.

"How would you like to hold title?" the agent asked.

"In the entirety," Peter replied. I knew what that meant: the marriage owns the property. It's mine and his together.

Why was I even worried? I need to stop being so suspicious. I'm getting everything I ever wanted. Although I'd be lying if I said I didn't still harbor some concerns about the brake incident, I chalk it up to my natural tendency to catastrophize and force myself to move on. Even when things are perfect, I'm always waiting for the other shoe to drop. It's my nature.

Nobody is out to get me. It's going to be a great day.

———

Peter is lying in bed, wide awake. Laura's as quiet as possible when she leaves for her races, but it still wakes him when she leaves their bedroom. He thinks about what his life would have been like if he'd met Laura, or someone like Laura, earlier. She's so…*normal.*

It's not like he went looking for high-strung women in the past. Neither Cynthia nor Jeanine had set off any alarm bells in the beginning, but looking back, he probably should have known. Laura was different. He knew that right away. She was confident in the right ways—pragmatic and mature beyond her years. But she also had a touch of humility and a healthy sense of humor, something the other two lacked. On the other hand, Laura's never wanted children, so what kind of a life would that have been?

He can't help but think that might have something to do with the way his children treated her—Lydia, in particular. His daughter was so young when she found out the sordid truth about her parents' sham of a marriage—only seven—and then she lost her mother that very same day. Peter should have stuck up for Laura more when she acted out, but he couldn't bring himself to reprimand Lydia. They seemed to be getting along better these days, so perhaps it's all fine. He did the best he could in a difficult situation.

He tells himself to put it all behind him. He and Laura will have their own home. The kids are moving on with their lives. If the past is going to catch up with him someday, there's not much he can do to stop it, so he decides to try to live in the moment—and this moment is pretty good. He gives his tired body a stretch, rolls over, and tries to get a few more hours of sleep.

———

I emerge from the freezing cold water of Santa Cruz Bay and step onto the cool, muddy sand of the wide, flat beach. A beam of sunlight peers through the fog and into my already irritated eyes, causing them to water. The nasal, braying caws of the sooty shearwater birds as they glide across the water grate on my nerves, pushing me to hurry up. I scramble to the transition station, hoping I don't step on something sharp and cut my foot. I hate this part, and I'm glad to get it over with early on.

I peel off my wet suit, fumbling as my hand slips off the zipper that appears to have a coating on it that wasn't there earlier, and I wonder what the hell I've immersed myself in. I'll never get used to this water. After growing up in Kailua, I'm a total beach snob. I wrestle off the sleeves, and then I pull one foot out, tugging against the suction, balancing on my other leg, and then pull out the other leg and put the suit aside. I'm very happy to get the wet suit off, but then I realize I'm dawdling a bit.

Hurry up, Laura.

My time was great on the swim, and I don't want to screw it up by taking forever on the transition, so I push myself on. Soon I'm at the bike station, where I mount my bike and snap in my shoes. I'm shivering a bit, but I'll warm up soon. I push off, head out, and join the flow.

This is the critical part of the race, the longest leg, and it's not my best sport. I'm a fast runner and swimmer, but it's the biking that really makes the difference. The deal I made with myself earlier—to simply enjoy the race and not worry about my time—is now off. Who was I kidding? I want to place. I want to win.

I start out hard and vow to keep pushing until I cross the finish line.

—

Peter is in his SUV headed to Santa Cruz. He stopped and bought some flowers for Laura. He hasn't been to one of her races in a long time, and he wants to make that up to her. He admires her dedication, and it's kind of a turn-on that she has her own thing that she feels so passionate about. Unlike his first wife, she toned it down when he and the kids needed her, and he's never properly thanked her for that. Had it not been for Cynthia and his baggage from their issues, he'd probably have been more supportive about her races.

He told Laura he'd meet her at the finish line, but he's now aiming to see her after the bike ride and before the run. She's always so nervous about her bike time, and he'd like to be there to support her. It's the least he can do after all she's done for him.

—

I've passed the halfway marker on the bike course, so the uphill is done. My time is good but not great. Now I've started sailing away on the dangerous downhill section.

I see a few cyclists ahead of me, and I'm gaining on them. I'll need to be careful when I try to pass them. I'm in the aero position, tucked, my hands on the upper bars. I lean left to swerve and pass, but something is terribly wrong. It takes me a few seconds to process what's happening.

The handlebars are loose!

I'm thrown forward as the aero bars collapse on me, catapulting me headfirst towards the ground. I tuck and close my eyes as the ground races up to meet me.

Everything goes black.

TWELVE

"It could have been a lot worse," I hear someone saying. *Where am I?* I open my eyes and look around. I see a white cloth partition to my right. I'm inside a medical tent, I think. The pain hits me right away. Is it my arm? My shoulder?

"She's waking up," someone says.

"Laura?"

I turn my head to the left.

"Aggh," I moan. That made it worse.

"Try not to move, honey. I'll come around the front. You broke your left collarbone."

It's Peter standing in front of me. With flowers. *What's going on?*

"Where am I?"

"In the ER."

"What happened?"

"You wiped out on your bike."

"I did?"

"You don't remember?"

I'm trying to think back. *Do I remember?* My brain is foggy. I look over and notice an IV in my arm. I must be on pain meds.

"I...um, yeah. I was on the bike, and then it's all kind of a blur."

"It's fine, Mrs. Foster. Your memory, it might come and go," someone says. I think she's my nurse.

"What day is it?"

"It's Sunday still. It's only been a few hours."

"Have I been unconscious the whole time?"

"No," she continues. "You blacked out for a bit, according to the other riders, but you were awake when the ambulance came. They gave you some pain meds, and you went back to sleep."

I don't remember any of it, and I wonder if that's normal.

"Do you need more pain meds?" Peter asks.

I think about this. More meds mean more fog. And there's something I'm struggling to remember. It's right on the edge of my memory, and I'm trying to pull it in.

"Um, let's wait a bit. Maybe later."

"How do you feel, honey?" Peter asks.

"Like I'm floating. But not in a good way."

"You tell me if you need more," the nurse says. "Do you need anything else before I go?"

"No," I say.

I hate the side effects of pain meds. I'm not even big on drinking alcohol. I like to be grounded, in control. This haziness feels terrible to me, but I realize that with a broken collarbone, I need the meds. I start to take inventory.

My left hip hurts, and I feel like I've got some scrapes on the left side of my arms and legs. My face, thankfully, seems okay.

But is it? I flash on a memory of the ground racing up to me, and I feel my stomach lurch.

"Peter!" I call out. "My face. Is it okay?"

"Yes, yes. It's fine. It seems like you tucked into a ball when you fell. Your left arm, shoulder, and hip took the brunt of the impact. Your helmet hit the pavement, but it was a secondary hit."

"Oh." I guess that's good? I'm not thinking straight, and I can't tell if it's the pain meds or the blow to the head.

I'm very confused about something. I don't remember making a mistake on my bike. *How did this happen?* But I'm too tired to think anymore, so I let the dreamy haze envelop me.

———

I wake up to the sound of people talking. The first thing I notice is my dry mouth. Then I smell something. I think it's eggs, and I realize I'm a bit hungry. Is it the next day?

"Good morning, Mrs. Foster." An orderly is standing in front of me with a tray. "Would you like some breakfast?"

"Okay. Can I get some water first? I'm really thirsty." I look around, and I don't see Peter or anyone else I recognize. It's a weird feeling. Being so alone.

"I've got some ice water right here. How are you feeling?"

"A little hungry, I think. And I want to sit up. Please." The orderly takes the remote and helps lift the head of my bed, although in hindsight, I could have done it myself.

"Is that good?"

"Yes, thanks." I reposition a pillow behind me with my right hand.

He hands me a cup of ice water, and I drink it down. It feels like heaven. He puts the tray of food in front of me. Then I see someone come rushing in the door.

"Laura! Sweetheart, you're awake."

It's my mother entering the room with a cup of coffee in her hand. My dad is right behind her. She comes up to me and takes my right hand. "How are you feeling?"

I think about this. I'm better than the last time I woke up, that's for sure. I feel clearer, more awake. Hunger is surely a good sign. "Better, I think."

My dad comes over, puts his hand on my head, and kisses my forehead. "My little Laura Loo. I've missed you, sweetie."

He's been calling me that since I can remember. He's such a kind, wonderful man. He's a fitness nut, like me, and he looks great for his age. Slim and neat. His jet-black hair has mostly faded to gray, but it looks good on him. Very distinguished.

"Do you know what day it is?" Mom asks.

I feel my stomach clench a bit. Is this when they tell me I've been in a coma for ten years and my husband has long since moved on?

No, I tell myself. My parents still look the same. I'm definitely slow on the uptake today. Damn these pain meds.

"I'm guessing Monday."

"Monday. Yes." Mom smiles.

Then my mind flashes to work. "Did somebody call my office?"

"Yes, of course. Peter did. Yesterday. Bethany sent flowers. Don't worry about that."

But I *am* worried about that. This is exactly why I've never told them about my racing. It's a distraction from my job. Now that they know, I may never be taken seriously again. I may even get demoted. Or fired.

"Let's get some food in your stomach," Dad says.

I stab the eggs with my fork and start to bring them to my mouth. Then something hits me. It's about the race. There's something I'm trying to remember, and I know it's important. I was starting the downhill. Leaning on the aero bars. I wanted to pass someone. And that's all I've got. I don't remember any kind of collision.

"Eat, dear," Mom says.

I realize that I've stopped with my fork in midair, scrambled eggs balanced on the tines, threatening to fall to my tray. I quickly bring the fork to my mouth and clean it off. I take a few more bites of my eggs, and my mind feels like it's starting to clear a bit.

Then it hits me. I remember a wobbling feeling under my forearms. *Oh my God. I didn't wipe out. My handlebars. They collapsed on me!*

"My bike. Where is it?" I ask.

"I don't know, honey," Mom says. "I'm assuming Peter took it home."

"Where is he?"

"He went home to change. He stayed all night. We relieved him," Dad replies.

"When's he coming back?"

I don't want to tell my parents my suspicions regarding the bike: if my handlebars collapsed, it could have been intentional. It will only cause them to stress out, and more stress is not what I need right now. *I wonder why nobody mentioned anything about the bars.* But as I think about it, they probably thought they broke because of the fall. But they didn't. They were loose before I fell.

"He'll be back in a few hours," Dad says.

I'm on pain meds, so I don't freak out as it dawns on me that someone might have sabotaged my bike and that a broken collarbone might be the least of my problems. I'm starting to see why people get addicted to opioids. Someone might be trying to kill me, and I feel absolutely no stress about this as my mind drifts aimlessly from random thought to random thought.

"I want to go home," I proclaim.

"I know, honey. They wanted to keep you overnight because you hit your head. They have to examine you today, and then they'll probably let you go."

Mom is talking more than Dad, as usual. My father is a man of few words, especially around my mother, who can be a bit of a chatterbox. They complement each other, although when it's only Dad and me, we converse much more. I miss that. Father-daughter time. I need to have more of it, but with Mom retired and Dad still working, there's rarely a time when we can be alone together.

"When's Peter coming back?" I want to tell my husband about the handlebars.

Then I realize I asked that question only a few minutes ago, but I'm too foggy to walk it back.

"A few hours," my mom says, offering me a sympathetic head tilt.

"Where's the nurse? I want to dial back the pain meds. I can't think straight on this stuff."

"I'll buzz for her."

My mom hits the call button, although I could have done that myself too. I hate feeling this helpless.

"In the meantime, eat your breakfast. It will help."

She's right, so I take another bite of my scrambled eggs and then go for the toast. I know the drill with hospitals. I'll have to wait around for hours to see the doctor and get the approval to leave. I want to get out of bed and walk around. I'll eat my food and then ask to get up. I'm going home today, getting off these drugs, and getting on with my life.

My father takes my mother's hand as they sit side by side, filling me in on my brother and his family, and I can't help but feel very fortunate that I have parents like them. I love the way they fit together, the way they finish each other's sentences. They're still in love; we're still the same. We're still a family, and they're both here for me. It's a comfort right now, so I sit back and take it all in, pushing the negative thoughts about bikes and sabotage and danger aside as I fill my growling stomach.

———

Peter's finally back at the hospital. He had to stop by work because there was a time-sensitive inquiry from the FDA, so he popped into the lab to give his team some direction. The rest of the work he can do from anywhere, so he brought his laptop with him. He thinks Laura will get out today, but he knows the discharge might take a while.

"Hey," Peter says, and he notices Laura is sitting up, looking much perkier.

"Hi there."

"Feeling better?"

"A bit, yes. They decreased my meds a bit."

"Is it okay? The pain level?"

"It hurts a little more, but it's a fair trade-off. They'll taper me off this stuff and then get me on over-the-counter meds. It's nothing I can't handle."

"Did your parents leave?"

"Yes. You just missed them. Peter. Where's my bike?"

"I took it home. It's pretty mangled."

"I remembered something important."

"What?"

"The handlebars, Peter. They were loose. Right before I fell."

"What do you mean?"

"I remembered earlier today. I had my arms resting on the aero bars, the upper handlebars. Then they started to wobble. I didn't lose my balance and fall. The bars collapsed on me."

"What? How?"

"I'd just started the downhill, and I was going pretty fast. I leaned to my left to pass. Then I felt them wobble. And then they failed, and I went crashing down to the ground."

"That's terrifying. Did you notice anything before it happened?" A wave of panic hits him as he considers that this could have been intentional. But maybe he's getting ahead of himself.

"No. It was pretty sudden."

"Does that happen? Normally, I mean?"

"It's rare, but it happens. There could have been a loose bolt."

"A loose bolt."

"Or someone could have loosened it."

Peter's stomach sinks. "You think someone may have sabotaged your bike?"

"It's possible. Especially after what happened to my car."

"Who would want to do something like that? And who would be able to pull it off?"

"I guess that's what we need to figure out. So, get me off these meds, and let's get out of here and find out."

———

It took all day, but a bit after four in the afternoon, I finally got sprung from the hospital. We stopped on the way home and filed a police report about the bike at the Santa Cruz station. It's in a different jurisdiction than the car incident, and I don't think they took it very seriously. I can't even say for sure that it wasn't an accident. It happens sometimes; the bolts could have loosened on their own. Still, we briefed Shackler, and he's going to try to gather footage from the race and see what else he can find. We'll meet with him once he has something to report.

We're home now, and it's dinnertime. Peter is setting out some Italian takeout we picked up on the way. It smells good. Getting the IV out felt wonderful, but now that I don't have a steady dose of meds dripping into my veins, I realize I'm pretty banged up, but at least I have an appetite. In addition to my shoulder, my hip is bruised, and I've got a bunch of scrapes and contusions that will take some time to heal. Thankfully, I'm proactive and organized, so I've already packed up most of my essentials for our move. The movers can do the rest. Peter suggested we postpone it, but that's the last thing I want. Even if I have to keep the stuff in boxes for weeks and eat off paper plates, I'm moving out of this place—pronto.

"Laura? Do you want to eat at the table?"

I'm sprawled out on the sofa.

"Sure. Yes." Anything to feel normal.

I stand up and hobble to the dining room. I'm pleased to note that walking feels fine. My hip is sore, but it doesn't seem to be affecting my mobility much. I won't be able to run for a while, but I'll probably be fine using the exercise bike and walking to maintain some level of fitness during my recovery. It could have been worse.

Peter has set the table, and we're kitty-corner, like he wants me next to him, just in case. It's sweet.

"How're you feeling?" He places his hand on mine, looking over at me as if I might break.

"I'm hungry. It smells good." I smile at him. He's filled my plate with penne marinara and some sautéed spinach, and I start to eat. It hits the spot.

"How's the pain? The meds should be wearing off. Do you need more?"

"No. Not now. I'll get some food in my stomach and then take some Advil and Tylenol. I don't want anything stronger. The nurse said if I mix them together, it will probably do the trick. Two different mechanisms." They gave me a prescription for oxy, but I don't want to take it. Still, I had Peter fill it just in case, not knowing what I was in for in terms of pain level. Better to have it handy.

"Don't be a hero, Laura. If you need something stronger, take it."

"I don't like being in a fog."

"I know."

I resign myself to the fact that I'll have to work from home for the rest of the week. This is a disaster, with all that's going on there. But I know I'm too groggy to go in. I need a day or two before I try to drive. Plus, the scrapes need to be cleaned out a few times a day, at least for the first week, so they don't get infected. I'm planning to attend the key meetings remotely, and that will have to do for now. In the meantime, I'll distract myself by ordering new furniture and assorted goodies for the new house, trying to stay positive, and making the most of the downtime.

THIRTEEN

A lot can happen in a week. I'm back at work now, and the vultures are circling. They can smell weakness. And here I sit, with my left arm in a sling, the wounded wildebeest. Bethany and I are in my office, trying to do some damage control. At least I've figured out a way to drive. And I can type—sort of.

"So," says Bethany, "where do we go from here?"

While I was recovering from my biking accident, the shit hit the fan, and Brent, my nemesis, was trying to pin it all on me. He was the other candidate for the VP of Monetization position. Although he's gracious to my face, I know inside he's seething. He's been here longer than me. He even has a personal connection to the CEO—college buddies—but the bro card wasn't enough for him this time. I'm sure he views my promotion as reverse discrimination, a byproduct of all the media buzz about the lack of women in the tech and VC worlds. It was Bethany who pushed for me, and as she sits here glaring at me, I know I have to think of something to salvage my career—and hers.

"We need to spin it a different way," I say.

"So spin," she says, her arms crossed and her hair pulled back tightly, taking her face with it.

"We reach out to CBOs. Let them have it for free. Tell them that it's a way to level the playing field for low-income students."

Our launch product, ApplAI, uses AI to help students fill in parts of their college applications by prepopulating information based on their selected majors and other inputs. It provides suggestions for questions like *Why this school?* or *Why this major?* to speed up the research and writing process, and also provides grammar suggestions and essay ideas that are a cut above the standard bearers out there. It's proven quite effective and popular in beta testing, but now that more awareness has been generated, there's been some pushback. That's not on me, of course. If they'd vetted it with the general public earlier, as I suggested, we wouldn't be in this position. But I'm not in marketing or PR, and that wasn't my call. I'm only supposed to figure out how to make a profit.

Like most startups, we were venture-capital funded in the beginning, so the users had free access. But that phase is ending. Rather than putting the costs totally on the students and families, I suggested having the colleges cover some of the costs by having an opt-in advertising program to court students. We can provide some very granular data for the colleges, which would help target their marketing and reduce wasteful mailings and unwanted email blasts. Students would pay a nominal fee, but much less than the cost of a private college counselor. The colleges would foot the bill and get something in return.

Of course, the private college counselors who help students with essays are up in arms about it, but the bigger concerns are about data sharing, although that's already happening with other platforms anyway. If people only knew the half of it. And if we can offer it free to community-based organizations that help low-income students, we can come out looking like the good guys. This was actually something my mother suggested to me earlier, and it may just save the day.

"That's not a bad idea." Bethany looks genuinely surprised that I'm not more rattled, that I have a comeback. And I decide then and there that my best defense is a good offense.

"Why is this our problem, anyway? This privacy issue, it's something that should have been vetted earlier, as I suggested. The public would have found out eventually. So what if my idea sped up the timeline? Isn't it better we get it out in the open now? And why are we doing Mark's job for him?"

I'm referring to the VP of Marketing, and my tone is unusually forceful. Brent works for him. Maybe it's the fact that someone may be trying to kill me, but something in me has shifted, and I'm not putting up with this crap anymore. I've had it.

"You're right, Laura. I'll call a meeting with Chad," my boss says, referring to our CEO. "And keep that fire going. They need to see you like this so they stop screwing with you."

I smile and give her a nod, and she starts out the door. As she leaves, I call out to her. "Bethany?"

She turns to me. "Yes?"

"Thanks. For everything. Really."

I realize that I owe her a lot, and I promise myself I won't let her down.

"I told you, Laura. I've got your back."

Bethany exits my office, leaving me to my thoughts, which are growing increasingly dark. I didn't tell anyone at work that my bike was likely sabotaged. But I'm less inclined to think it was someone here. I don't let on much about my racing here at work. I feel people might think I spend too much time on it; they want total devotion. I didn't even tell Bethany I was racing. But everyone knows now, so there's no walking it back.

My assistant, Mina, knew about the race, and Emily the intern, because she heard Mina and me talking about it. But they don't have anything against me, and Brent's too smart to pull something so juvenile and risky. Plus, it seems he's figured out another way of sabotaging me. He still has the CEO's ear, and I'm sure Chad's heard "I told you so" more than once over the last week.

So, I'm back to two possibilities. Either I'm so unbelievably unlucky I have had two freak accidents in the space of a few weeks, or someone in my personal life is out to get me. Initially, my mind flashed to Lydia, rustling around in the garage where my bike was the day before the race. But why would she do something like that now when she's getting me out of her house? And we're getting along so much better now. It doesn't make sense.

But I still feel like Peter's not telling me everything. I insisted we meet with the private investigator after work today. As with my professional life, I need to start going on the offensive. If someone's out to get me, I want to see it coming.

———

It's midmorning, and Shep's client is sitting in front of him. He also has an appointment later today with the man and his wife, so he finds it odd that Peter Foster is here now.

"How can I help?" Shep asks.

"I need you to find someone for me. This may or may not be connected to what happened to Laura, but I have to find out."

"Okay. Who do you want me to find?"

Foster takes a deep breath and hangs his head, and Shep has an inkling about where this might be going.

"It's related to my first marriage." Foster hesitates for a moment and looks down to his right, then back up.

Shep nods. "Please continue. I'm not here to judge, Peter."

"I was having an affair. We both were, actually. Cynthia, my wife, started it. Not that I'm using that as an excuse for what I did. Then mine, it just sort of happened." Foster shrugs.

"I understand."

"Cynthia and I, for about two years, it was…well, let's just say we'd grown apart. There wasn't much there.

Jeanine and I worked together. It started on a business trip. You get the picture."

"Right."

"But then Cynthia had a change of heart. Rather suddenly. Said she broke it off with the guy. She wanted to try again. She said she was all in. So, of course, I wanted to. We had little kids. Seven and four. I had to give it another chance. So I broke it off with Jeanine."

"And how did Jeanine take the news?"

"Not well. Not well at all."

FOURTEEN

I'm sitting in the lobby, if that's what you'd call it, of Shackler Investigative Services. It's more like a foyer. *Is this the best we can do?* It's not like Peter to cheap out on something this important. Why didn't he go with a more formidable firm? And Peter isn't here yet, which is odd. He's very punctual. We're about five minutes into our three o'clock appointment time, and Shackler's door is still closed.

Another minute passes, and I'm feeling annoyed. I notice my foot is tapping against the floor. Then the door opens—finally—and I'm not too thrilled at what I see, because Peter's already here. They both walk over to greet me. I stand up, unable to mask my surprise. *Why did he get here before me?* I didn't see his car in the parking lot. I arrived a few minutes early. He must have planned it like that, which is doing nothing to quell the feeling of distrust percolating in my gut.

Peter jumps in. "I got here a little early. Sorry. I was filling Shep in on some of the details."

Shackler holds out his hand. "Shep Shackler. Nice to meet you."

I shake his hand and try to keep my cool, but I shoot Peter a look, and he gets the message. We get settled in the cramped little space that Shackler calls his office. As we sit down, my knee touches Peter's leg to my right; our chairs are very close together. I quickly pull my legs to the left. It's not lost on the investigator, and I don't want to give him the wrong idea about us, so I take a deep breath and try to smile, but I still don't want to touch my husband.

Shackler starts in. "Peter was telling me about your bike incident. I'm so sorry for what you're going through. How are you feeling?" His head leans to one side, a sympathy tilt. *Great. This isn't what I need.*

"I'm fine. Shep, can you run me through what you've uncovered so far with your investigating?" So far, I'm not very impressed with the guy.

"Sure, Laura. Regarding camera footage of your car, all I've found is the video you've seen of the parking lot at your workplace. But you said your car was parked in downtown Los Altos for an hour or so the day before, and there's no good footage of the car there. It could have been tampered with then. I'm still working on the race day footage. Can you walk me through what happens on race day with the bikes?"

"The bikes are in the transition area during the swim, waiting to be picked up by the racers after they finish." I run him through the process, going through all the details, unsure of how much he already knows about triathlons, but I assume he wants me to be thorough, so I am. "So any of the volunteers working the race would have had access to the bike. Loosening the handlebars would only take a few seconds," I say.

"How would they do it?"

I take him through the mechanics of my time trial bike and show him a photo on my phone. "There are two sets of handlebars," I explain. "The lower ones on the sides have the brakes, and the higher ones, called aero bars, are up top, where racers rest their forearms when they're jamming along. My arms were on the top handles when they failed. It looks like one of the bolts came loose on the underside of the handlebars, tipping me to the left. Anyone with a pocket tool could have loosened it a bit. Then over time, with stress, the bars will fail and collapse."

"Did you notice anything before it happened?"

"Not really, but the first half is uphill, so I wasn't putting much weight on them. On the downhill, all my weight's on the upper bars. I'd just started downhill when it happened."

Shackler is nodding, jotting it all down. He asks me the make, model, and year, and I give them to him.

"And Peter tells me it could be an accident. What do you think?"

"It's not unheard-of. But I've used the same bike mechanic for years. It's unlikely he would have made a mistake like this, but it's not impossible. But then it's also hard to believe I could be this unlucky twice in the space of a few weeks."

"You don't think it's an accident, then," Shackler says, twirling his pen between his thumb and forefinger.

Peter is leaning back in his chair, arms crossed over his chest, letting the investigator do his thing.

"No," I reply.

"But then maybe we're looking for a connection that isn't there."

"I'm not sure what you mean."

"The two incidents could be unrelated. One could be deliberate and the other, an accident."

"True," I say. "The brake tampering is potentially more deadly. It's hard to kill someone in a biking accident."

"Even the brake incident wasn't likely to be deadly. Most people would notice the brakes before they started driving. Let's say for the sake of argument that nobody is trying to kill you. We've already established that you can't think of anyone who would want you dead. But what about someone who would want to mess with you or lay you up for a while? Or scare you? Does anyone come to mind?"

"Someone from work, maybe?" Peter asks. "I mean, you said yourself that Bethany—" He turns to the PI. "That's her boss." Then he turns back to me. "You said that Bethany told you some people in the office were upset about your promotion."

My mind flashes to Brent, going in for the kill during my absence. I suppose it is possible. He's chatty with everyone. He could have found out about my race. But it seems so risky and amateur. I feel like he could find a better way to get at me. Still, maybe that's part of the strategy. Try to mess with me but make it look like it's too brazen to be him.

Wow, I'm getting very paranoid.

"There might be someone. I suppose it's worth looking into." I update them about the latest happenings at work and the impending coup by Brent, and Shackler takes down his name, along with the names of his supporters.

"Did anyone at work know about the race?"

"Only my assistant." Shackler asks for her name so he can check her out as well, and I feel terrible going behind Mina's back. But that's the way it has to be.

"Now, let's run through everyone who could have had access to your bike." He leans back, his arms crossed. "Take me through all of it. One more time. Before the race too."

I finally have an opening to disclose what's been nagging at me, but should I? I've already walked them through the process on race day. I remind Shackler that there are myriad people with hands on the bike during the day, but I also point out that rarely would someone be alone with the bike, away from other people. I explain that it would have to be someone on the inside, a volunteer, and there are tons of them.

"I can get a list," he says, "and we can comb through it. See if you recognize any names."

"It wouldn't be that hard for someone to insert themselves into the process. Someone not officially signed up," I say, thinking out loud.

"Well, we have to start somewhere. You've both given me a lot to go on, so I'll get on this and circle back."

Peter leans forward, about to stand up. "Thank you, Sh—"

"Wait." I hold up my hand, and they both turn to me. Peter settles back into his chair. "There's something else. About the bike."

"What?" Peter asks.

"It could be nothing," I say.

"Any of this could be nothing, or it could be something," Shackler says. "Please continue."

"There's someone else who had access to my bike. At the house the day before."

Now they're both riveted, but I know this is a delicate situation. Once I say it, I can't take it back, so I'm stalling.

"Who?" Peter asks, his eyes wide.

I take a deep breath and look away.

"Laura? Who was it?" My husband looks terrified, and I realize he may think I mean him, so I finally spit it out.

"Lydia," I say to Peter.

"Lydia?" Shackler asks.

I turn to the investigator. "My stepdaughter. Peter's daughter." Then I turn back to Peter. "Lydia was in our garage that day. Where my bike was stored."

I take them through the story. How she let herself into the house. How I thought there was an intruder. Me and my silly umbrella.

"And how is your relationship with your stepdaughter?" Shackler asks.

I look over at Peter, and his eyes narrow at me. This has been weighing on my mind, Lydia in the garage, so I had to get it out there. But this isn't a marriage counseling session, and I don't want to give up too much about our personal struggles to Shackler or have him get the wrong idea.

"It's fine now. It was very strained in the beginning when Peter and I got together years ago. She lost her mom at an early age, and she had to became the woman of the house. Then when I came into the picture years later, she was a bit territorial. It was totally understandable. But things have gotten better over time."

"I see." Shackler's wheels are turning, I can tell.

Peter's lips are pressed together, and his jaw is tight. I don't want to air our family issues in front of the investigator, so I walk it back a bit.

"I'm only trying to give you the complete rundown on where the bike was, since you asked me. And I thought it was very strange that she let herself into the house. But it was probably nothing."

"Has she ever done that before? Let herself into the house?"

"Not that I know of."

"Well, she's buying the house from us, Laura!" Then Peter turns to the investigator. "We decided to sell the family home, and Lydia's decided to purchase it. She has a sizable trust from her mother's side of the family."

"Yes, and there's something I should have told you earlier related to that," I say, trying to soften the blow. "She did text me before she came over, but I somehow missed the message. She needed to get some measurements. She was in the garage looking for a tape measure."

"Well, see, there's your explanation," Peter says.

"Of course. I shouldn't have even mentioned it." But I catch Shackler's eye, and a moment passes between us. If he's any good at this, he'll see that I want him to look into it further. We say our goodbyes and head out. There's always been an edge to Lydia, and if there's even a remote chance she's behind all of this, I need to know.

When we get outside, Peter turns to me, a death glare on his face.

"What the hell was that, Laura? *Lydia?* Are you kidding me?"

He storms away towards his car, which is over in the far corner of the parking lot. I'm at a loss for words, so I don't try to stop him; I need some time to collect my thoughts. This conversation has been a long time coming, and it's going to be a hell of a night.

FIFTEEN

Peter's steaming as he drives home from the PI's office. But as the tangled threads in his mind start to unwind, he realizes that although some of his anger is directed towards Laura for blindsiding him, there's much more wrapped up in his feelings than what happened today—disappointment in himself for the failure of his first marriage; allowing himself to be seduced by Jeanine and her fawning instead of fixing what was broken at home; and most of all, the guilt about the pain he caused his daughter.

Sure, Cynthia started it by cheating on him first, but he knew going in that it wasn't going to be a marriage based on equality. He'd thought long and hard about marrying into a family with that level of wealth. Now that he has a basis for comparison, he knows he's much happier married to his self-made equal. But the truth is, he fell in love with Cynthia. Or at least that's what it felt like at the time. She was so alive, so exciting and vivacious. Life was a perpetual adventure with her. He'd never met anyone quite like her. He'd grown up with a mildly abusive father plagued with financial problems, which he took out on the family and a complicit doormat-of-a-mother who drank to ease her pain. As a consequence, he took his studies seriously. Very seriously. Success was his way out.

Cynthia was the opposite. Born with no incentive to accomplish much of anything, she had the luxury to tempt fate, and opposites attract—at least in the beginning. But there was a darker side to his wife that came out after Lydia was born. She was given to dramatic highs and lows, which were made worse by the birth of Carson and the death of her father. She seemed so confident at the beginning of their relationship, but he soon began to see that it was all an act. Inside, she was painfully insecure, and that manifested itself in jealousy and mistrust. He thought back to their argument the day she died and the comment about her affair.

Why didn't you try to stop me?

It was a test, and he'd failed. She had the affair, he assumed, to get him to fight for her, to prove his love. And he'd turned to another woman instead.

Lydia, unlike Carson, was old enough to be aware of what was going on at the time of her mother's death but too young to understand it all. After her mother's death, she acted out at first, playing mean tricks on her brother as if she viewed him as competition for her father's attention. After some counseling, she shifted gears and took on the woman-of-the-house role. At the time, it was a big improvement. Seeing herself in this light, she mothered Carson, took him under her wing. A popular girl in middle school, she sent some tween thugs to warn Carson's elementary school bully that Lydia Foster's little brother was off-limits. Peter had been called to school for that incident, and although he played the outraged parent for the sake of the principal, inside, he was proud of her for defending Carson.

When he finally introduced Laura to his kids, it took some getting used to on Lydia's part. She directed her pain and anger towards his new love—whom she viewed as a competitor—and the therapist said her jealousy was completely normal. Laura never gave him any indication that she was concerned about it, although, in hindsight, they probably should have gone to family counseling or at least talked about it more. But that was all water under the bridge, and despite how it looks, he's certain that Lydia had nothing to do with Laura's bike.

But who was it, then? Could both incidents have actually been accidents? What are the chances of that? He's seriously thinking about trying to calculate it mathematically. That's the kind of mind he has. But he thinks better of it because he doesn't believe in coincidences, and Peter thinks it's starting to look like someone at her workplace. An hour or so ago, he thought differently, but that was before Laura disclosed the latest work drama and before Shackler informed him that his number one suspect was now off the list.

The woman formerly known as Jeanine Randall couldn't be behind it—she's been incapacitated with a traumatic brain injury for the last three months.

———

I'm pulling into our driveway. I stopped at the store on the way home to pick up some fresh salmon and arugula for dinner, allowing Peter to beat me here. I planned it this way to give him a chance to cool off a bit before we try to talk this out. Over time, I've realized this usually works out better, giving him time to see things from my perspective, even though this goes against my nature. I like to deal with our marital issues right away and not let them fester; I get that from my mother. But this is marriage, and you either learn to adjust, or it ends.

I know he's home because I see his keys in the porcelain dish that sits on our walnut foyer table, but I don't see him. I'm pretty sure he's in the basement, his unofficial man cave. The kids hung out down there with their friends when they lived here, and now it serves as his office. It also has a big-screen TV he watches sports on when one of his buddies comes over, which isn't often. He's not very social.

I go about my business, unloading the groceries, and getting started on the dinner prep. After a bit, while I'm searing the salmon, Peter comes into the kitchen, still in his work clothes. Our eyes meet, and it's not at all what I expect. His eyes are glassy and full, like the dam is about to burst. I've never seen him cry, and he's doing everything in his power to keep it that way. *What happened to the anger?*

"Thanks for picking up dinner," he says.

"Sure," I reply.

Then there's this awkward silence. I've learned not to push him to talk when he's angry. But I've hardly ever seen him like this. He looks so sad.

Two empty water glasses sit on our island countertop, along with a pair of plates and salad bowls from our vegan bone china set—white with a geometric pattern—a gift from my mother.

"Is one of these for me?" He's pointing to the glasses.

Who else would they be for?

"Yes," I say.

My eyes land on my husband, searching his face for clues, but he avoids my stare. Then he fills a glass with ice and water, chugs it down, and fills it up again.

"I'll set the table," he says and starts rifling through the cutlery drawer.

"Thanks."

I let the salmon cook on low and cut up some tomatoes and add them to the arugula. I think about adding some avocado, but I'm not in the mood to go to all that trouble. I'm not even particularly hungry, but I feel like we should eat.

We both go about our tasks in silence. I dress the salad and bring the bowls to the table, but Peter has left the dining room. The slightly smoky smell of garlic and charred fish starts to stimulate my appetite. Back in the kitchen, I transfer the fish from the pan to the dinner plates and leave the pan to soak in the sink. I hear him walking back, and I bring the fish in. He's changed into a t-shirt and shorts. We sit at the table in an uncomfortable silence.

Peter breaks the standoff, seeming eager to move on.

"Looks good." He takes his fork, wiggles off a piece of fish with the side of it, pops it in his mouth, and starts chewing. Then he does it again. The glassy-eyed look is gone, and I'm at a total loss for how to deal with him.

I'm still a bit put out that he got to Shackler's office before me, but my Lydia comment was worse, so it should probably be me who offers the olive branch. I should have talked to him about it first, but I was concerned he might shoot down the idea. Then, if I brought it up to the investigator, it would have been even worse. Easier to beg forgiveness, as they say.

"Sorry I blindsided you." I'm eyeing him, but he's fixated on his plate, eating methodically. A forkful of salad, a bite of fish. I rest my hand on his, and he finally looks over at me, meeting my gaze.

"Do you really think Lydia could do something like that?" He doesn't say it in an angry way. It's like he's actually asking for my opinion.

I realize now that I probably overreacted. All those years of putting up with her insults, her acting out and taking out her anger on me. The worst of it, Peter never saw; she was smart enough to keep that from him. Maybe I should talk to someone about it. A professional. A therapist. Before the resentment eats me alive. But I don't want to tell Peter about it right now. What would be the point? It would only make him feel worse about everything.

"No, I don't. But she frightened me that day, Peter. She shouldn't let herself into the house like that. I thought we had an intruder."

"Agreed, but why didn't you tell me about it sooner? Why do it in front of him?"

"It slipped my mind."

That's a total lie, of course, and I wonder if he suspects. Peter's more trusting than I am, so probably not. I knew he'd be blind to the idea of her doing anything to hurt me, so I said it in front of the PI, who has the capacity to be objective.

"Let's put it behind us, okay?" He takes a forkful of salad, and I can't understand why he doesn't want to discuss this further.

I need to get to the bottom of whatever is going on, so I press him further. "So, I have a question. Why did you get there earlier than me?"

"Huh?"

"When I arrived, you were in Shackler's office with the door closed. Why? What couldn't you say in front of me?" I put my fork down and cross my arms. My eyes narrow on him, and he hesitates.

"Nothing. I was early, that's all, so we got started."

"Sure. Okay."

"You know, I really do think it might be someone from your work based on what you told us today. What's your take?"

"Someone from work who wants to kill me? Or mess with me?"

"Maybe they only wanted to mess with you. Even the brake thing. It wasn't likely to kill you, like Shackler said. Most people would step on the brake and realize something was wrong before they started driving."

"Wouldn't slashing the tires be easier than cutting the brake hose?"

127

"Maybe not. But then, I'm not an expert on those things. Maybe the car and bike were meant to slow you down, divert your attention so you'd slip up at work. Make you worry and lose focus."

"Maybe."

"Let's see what Shackler comes up with," he says.

But it seems weird to me. Someone at work would have to know a lot about me and my whereabouts at all times to have done both of those deeds. It seems unlikely. I'm also not sure why he's so eager to put all the eggs in the work basket, but I let it go for the moment.

We eat in silence for a while longer. I don't believe that he got there early for no good reason at all. I'm trying to keep calm, but I'm getting more upset about his lack of an explanation for his behavior as the moments pass. But I decide it's futile to pry any further, so I change the subject. I know he's hiding something from me, but maybe it's better to play my cards close to the vest. He's less likely to hide something if he thinks nobody's looking for it, so I'm trying to play it cool, although I'm heating up inside.

"So, how're things with the FDA approval?"

Peter goes on to tell me that it looks hopeful that their drug will be approved for ovarian cancer soon, and I know we stand to gain financially if it does, but he hasn't elaborated on that too much. He seems pleased with these developments, and he also seems to be enjoying his dinner now, which I find bizarre. Me, I just pick at the food on my plate.

I make a halfhearted attempt to tell him about my talk with Bethany and about how we decided to go on the offensive, trying to keep up the ruse that things are back to normal. But I'm getting more and more upset because I know he's keeping something from me. I can feel it.

"Good for you. Don't take any crap from Brent or any of them. You've got this, Laura. They made the right call."

"Thanks."

But I don't feel thankful, I feel upset, and Peter finally picks up on it.

"What's wrong?" he asks, finally giving his fork a rest. "You're hardly touching your food. Don't you feel well?"

I stand up. I've had it.

"I need some space. I'm going for a drive."

I start to leave the table, hoping he'll try to stop me. That he'll finally come clean. But he doesn't. He picks up his fork and keeps eating.

I turn from him, walk over to grab my purse and my keys, and then I head out the door, still hoping in vain for a protest from my husband.

———

It can't go on like this, Peter decides, as he watches his wife walk out the door. He knows he should stop her, but he needs time to think. He's got to level with Laura. Tell her about the affair with Jeanine, at least. She's picking up on it anyway—the dishonesty—and it's eroding their trust.

And if it's someone at Laura's company who's after her, they need to work together to figure out who it is. He runs through it all again in his mind. The chain of events. First, he got the strange email. Then her brake hose was severed.

Then her handlebars collapsed. Could they be unrelated? Could both of those incidents have been accidents, or only one, as Shackler suggested, and the other intentional? There's no connection that he can see between the email he received and Laura's incidents. But then, what was the meaning of that email if it had nothing to do with Laura? He's so far not gotten another one, so maybe he was over-reacting, and it was simply a random spam email. That's a nice thought, so he decides to hold on to it for a bit longer. Right now, he needs to figure out a way to fix things with Laura, and the only way to do that is to level with her to the degree that he can.

Sophie and I are at a little dive bar we used to frequent in Palo Alto, hashing it all out over beers and a bowl of fries. The smell of stale beer hangs in the air. I thought she'd be eager to bash Peter, but now she's trying to calm me down. She knows I really love him, and she's a good friend.

"Peter loves you, Laura. I'm sure of that. Even if he has a hard time expressing it. You need to be the one to open him up. He's always been a closed book."

"What happened to your serial spouse killer theory?" I grab a french fry, dip it in ketchup, and pop it in my mouth. I'm only having one beer, but I don't want to drink on an empty stomach. I hardly touched my dinner.

She offers me an apologetic smile. "Sorry about that. You know how I can get. But it is strange that he seemed so sad about Lydia. There's something there, I'm sure of

it. And in my expert opinion, sadness is not typical serial killer behavior. So, he's off the hook as far as I'm
concerned."

"What if he's a psychopath who's trying to lull me into
a false sense of security?" I flash her a smirk.

"Then sleep with one eye open, dear."

"Awesome advice, Soph."

"Seriously. Describe it again for me. The dinner conversation. What did he say again? About Lydia?" Sophie takes
a bite of her french fry, then she dips it again in the blood-
red ketchup, the same shade as her upturned pinky nail,
and finishes it off, eager to play detective with me.

"He asked me if I really thought she could do something like that," I repeat, "but like he was actually asking for my opinion. Like he has some doubts about her
himself."

"Well, that's where you need to look, then. Find out
why he has doubts. But I thought things have been better
with her lately."

Sophie's well aware of all the drama I've been through.
She kept me sane during those turbulent first few years of
marriage when I thought about leaving, giving up on all
of them.

"They have been. I'm sure it's not her. I mean, do you
think she could do something like this?"

"Who knows? She could have pushed her own mother
off that cliff for all we know."

"You're impossible."

"Sorry. I couldn't resist." She offers me a cheeky grin.
"No, I don't think it's Lydia, but there is something he's not

telling you, and you need to find out what it is. Stop beating around the bush and ask him. Don't be such a wimp."

She's right. I am a wimp. But I can change.

"I will. But what do you think about the work theory?" I've already walked her through the meeting with Shackler and shared his theories with her.

"I didn't think so before. But now? Maybe."

"Why? What's changed?"

"Just a hunch. Bethany. Her concerns. Maybe she knows more than she's letting on. Let me do some investigating, okay? I have a good ear to the ground. I'll fish around for dirt on Brent. See if he's got any kind of history we should know about. And that assistant of yours too. I'll check her out."

"My assistant? Mina? Why?"

"She knows everything about you and where you go."

"What would she have to gain?"

"Money, maybe. Or she could be sleeping with Brent. Or someone else who wanted your job."

"Maybe you should be a PI."

"PR. PI. What's the difference?" She shrugs. "Basically, the same job."

"So, what's new with you?" I ask. I need to get out of my own head, so we leave my problems behind for a while as Sophie entertains me with her latest adventures. But I realize I can't stay long and decide I'll wrap it up shortly. I need to go back and confront Peter. Wherever it leads, it leads. I can't live like this anymore.

SIXTEEN

I walk back into the house about two hours after I left. The living room lights are on, and Peter's waiting downstairs for me, sitting on the sofa drinking a beer. *Has he been there the whole time?* I don't say anything, but I give a nod in his direction. I can see from my vantage point that the dinner table is clean; the kitchen isn't visible from where I'm standing. *God help him if he didn't do the dishes.*

I know we should talk, but I can't bring myself to initiate it, so I start to walk upstairs.

"So. Where'd you go?" Peter asks.

I turn around to face him. "I went to meet Sophie."

He rolls his eyes. He's not her biggest fan.

I think he's picked up on the fact that she's had reservations about him in the past. I never told him the worst of it—about her trying to talk me out of the marriage all those years ago—and I'm sure he'd be shocked to know that she somewhat stuck up for him tonight.

I turn back to head up the stairs.

"Wait," he says. "We need to talk. I have something to tell you."

I turn towards him. My hand is on my hip, and I realize it's an overly assertive posture, so I try to relax my arm, but now my right arm dangles aimlessly, while the left one sits in its sling. It's very hard to find a snarky posture with a broken collarbone.

"Come. Sit with me." He waves me over, patting the space next to him, trying to soften the mood a bit.

I sigh. I'm happy that he's finally seen the light, but I'm still pretty pissed off at him. I walk towards him slowly and sit down next to him. His head hangs for a long moment like he's trying to process some terrible news. Then he looks over his shoulder at me.

"There is something. You're right. I should have told you earlier. It's about my first marriage, but I was afraid you'd judge me."

"Whatever it is, it's probably not as bad as what I'm thinking, so just tell me."

"Okay. I was having an affair."

I feel my eyes widen, not because I'm upset but because it makes perfect sense. An affair. *Of course.* Why didn't I think of that earlier? That would explain so much. The guilt. The cagey behavior.

"Oh." It's all I can muster.

"'Oh'? That's all you've got?" He smiles.

"Do you want to tell me about it?"

"Do you want to hear about it?"

"Just give me the broad strokes. Spare me the sordid details." The corners of my mouth lift a bit, relieved that my husband is only a cheater and not a serial spouse killer.

"Well, I already told you part of it. Cynthia. For about two years, she was—"

"Yes, I know. She was having an affair. And you said she broke it off. Wanted to reconcile."

"Right. Well, about a year or so after she started, uh... withdrawing? I started seeing someone too." He purses his lips. "I'm not proud of it."

"Who?"

"A woman at work. It wasn't very serious. And I broke it off after Cynthia came to me and said she wanted to try again."

"Did Cynthia know about her?"

"She found out. Towards the end."

"How?"

"I don't know. She didn't tell me. And I never had the chance to find out."

Peter recounts that, on the day his wife died, she confronted him about his affair, and he told her he'd already ended it. Cynthia was still furious, they fought, and she left to go on a hike. Then he repeated the last words she said as she walked out the door.

Take your precious children, Peter. I'm done with all of you.

My mind is swirling as Peter pauses to collect his thoughts. Does this mean that he thinks she might have—

Peter continues, interrupting my train of thought.

"But that wasn't the worst part," he says.

He proceeds to tell me that Lydia, barely seven years old at the time, overheard their argument. All of the ugly details. The fact that they were both having affairs. That she was "done with all of them," including her own children. How horrible that must have been for a little girl to be confronted with all of that sordid information. And then her mother's death the same day. No wonder Lydia has issues.

"My God, Peter. I had no idea. Why didn't you tell me this sooner?"

"I don't know. I was embarrassed, I guess. I should have been stronger. I lost it that day on Cynthia. Years of pent-up frustration. It all came out. I called her a freaking hypocrite." He lets out a sigh. "And Lydia. My poor little girl. She heard it all."

Now I'm almost certain he thinks it was suicide. It certainly seems that way to me. And he blames himself. But I don't want to bring that up. What would be the point? So I focus on the situation with Lydia, which seems to account for the bulk of the guilt that's eating at him.

"Peter, you're a great dad. Lydia adores you. Don't beat yourself up."

"I know she's had issues in the past, Laura, but she went to therapy. They assured me that she was fine. I should have talked to you more about it. I'm sorry for the way she treated you. She took so much of it out on you."

He doesn't know the half of it. But now I see why he got so upset when I brought it up. And I'm his wife. I need to try to ease his pain.

"Peter, Lydia's fine. We're doing fine. We're better now. I'm sorry I even brought it up." I do wish he had leveled with me years ago, but I don't want to lay that on him now. *But would I have even stayed?* Then another thought occurs to me.

"Peter?"

"Yes?"

"Who's the woman? And where is she now?"

"The woman?" His head tilts to the side, and his brow furrows. *Is he this clueless, or is he simply stalling for time?*

I throw up my hands. "The woman you had an affair with, Peter."

"Oh, right. Of course. Her name is Jeanine Randall. We lost touch. I don't know where she is now."

"How did she take it? When you broke it off?"

"You know, she was upset at first. But it was understood from the beginning it wasn't serious. I was married. She was seeing someone else too. She knew it wasn't going anywhere. It was a mutual understanding."

"But how did it all wrap up? And what do you mean, you don't know where she is now?" I'm very skeptical about this "mutual understanding" that it wasn't going anywhere. I've never been with a married man, but I can't imagine any woman would waste her time with a man if she didn't think it had the potential to go somewhere.

"She decided to leave the job. Move away. She thought people at work knew about us, although I didn't think so. I'm not really sure what happened to her."

This is all sounding very suspicious to me. He doesn't know what happened to her? How hard is it to keep track of someone these days? And if it wasn't that serious, why would she leave her job? But then, if it was serious, why wouldn't she have tried to reinsert herself into the family after Cynthia was out of the picture? *There has to be more to this story.* But in the name of marital harmony, I think it's best to keep all my doubts to myself—for now.

"Well, thanks for sharing this with me."

Peter nods and puts his hand on my knee. I place mine on top of his, but that's as far as things are going tonight. I decide I've had enough and tell him I'm headed up to bed.

When I get upstairs, I fire off a text to Sophie.

Me: Put Jeanine Randall on your PI list.

Sophie: Who's that?

Me: The woman Peter was having an affair with. Before his wife died.

Sophie: Holy shit.

—

Peter feels much better, getting some of the story off his chest. He's been living with secrets since the day Cynthia died, waiting for something to surface. It's probably taken years off his life, all the stress and worry. He decides that he's been living like this long enough. Laura now knows most of what happened, and he's pretty sure they're okay. And they're moving on. Leaving this sad place and its melancholy memories behind.

Plus, the news he got from Shackler proves that Laura's incidents aren't related to his transgressions. He knows what Jeanine is capable of, and he was starting to think that she could be behind it all. But then, that never made sense to him. Why now? After all this time? Why wouldn't she have come after Laura earlier, when he married her, if she was still keeping tabs on him? It's not Jeanine, so he can let go of that fear and all the guilt surrounding it.

He's not tired enough to go up to bed, so he sits, sipping his beer, thinking about all of it. If he'd never gotten involved with Jeanine, would he and Cynthia still be together? That thought sends a chill up his spine. It was so long ago he can't even remember his own emotions, but he knows now that what he felt for his first wife wasn't love, especially compared to what he has with Laura. It wasn't happiness. It was some twisted, bizarre form of codependent obligation.

Still, he remembers feeling relieved when Cynthia came to her senses and wanted to reconcile. But that was out of a sense of duty to his family and his children, he surmises. Looking back, being married to Cynthia was a kind of prison, although he couldn't see that at the time. It's understandable that he sought comfort in another woman's arms, and it's time to forgive himself. He has everything he's ever wanted. So, from this point forward, he decides he'll leave the past behind. They're moving to their new house next week. No more living in the past. A fresh, clean start for both of them. Finally.

SEVENTEEN

It's our second weekend in nirvana. We've been in the new house for over a week, and I'm still looking at boxes stacked all over as far as the eye can see. My injury is slowing me down a bit. It feels better, but I still have to keep it in a sling much of the time. Being one-handed is a major drawback, but it's healing faster than expected, so I don't want to overdo it and have a setback. Plus, we're still waiting on some of our new furniture, so I can't unpack everything until it gets here.

I love it here, though, and I love my new life, so I'm not complaining. It's spartan because we left much of the furniture at the old house, but that suits me. I hate clutter. Most of the furnishings in the old place were Peter's from before I moved in, although we did change the living room a few years back, replacing the sofa and recliner with a stunning sectional in a pearl fabric, complemented by a pair of wingback chairs that looked out of place in the old house but fit in perfectly here—just like me.

We brought our bed; I insisted on replacing that when I moved in with him, but we left behind the bedroom furniture and replaced that with a teak set I've had my eye on for years. We ordered a new dining table, breakfront, and some other pieces and accessories, which we're still waiting for, so we've been eating at the kitchen counter or in front of the television. It feels fun, like we're camping out.

Since we moved here, we've been like newlyweds. Peter even picked me up and carried me over the threshold the first day. It's been so nice, in fact, that I've been ignoring Sophie's messages to call her. She apparently has some news, but I'm regreting getting her involved. It's starting to feel like a betrayal of my marriage, having her dig around in my husband's past. Things have been fine at work. No further incidents or attempts on my life, and the police have turned up nothing of concern. I don't want to fill my mind with negative thoughts, so I'm trying to think positively as I putter around the house.

Bam!

I startle as I hear a car door slam, snapping me out of my musings. My stomach lurches. It's not a delivery person. I'm not expecting anything. It's not Peter. He said he'd be a few hours when he left.

Then there's an insistent, angry pounding on the front door that reverberates through the house. I suddenly feel very defenseless, with my still-broken collarbone and my half-healed contusions.

"One minute," I call out.

Could it be Sophie? Upset that I haven't gotten back to her?

I peek out the window and see Lydia's Tesla. *What on earth is she doing here? Did I inadvertently take something of hers?* She keeps hammering away.

"Hold on, Lydia." I'm stalling.

What if she really is behind all this and is having some kind of breakdown? What if she's coming to do me in, once and for all? No, that's ridiculous.

But is it?

Peter said she went to therapy before we met.

I can't very well leave her standing out there. She knows I'm home. I've got to open the door and face her.

I open it, and she's got her fist up, ready to pound the door again. Her eyes are wide and wild, and she's breathing out of her nose. Her look is somewhere between anger and fear, and I'm totally perplexed.

Her hand relaxes when she sees me. Her palm opens, and her hands go to her head. I'm trying to process all of this while she stands there, holding her head like she's trying to keep it from exploding.

"I have to tell you something. And it's terrible," she says.

Then my stomach lurches.

"What happened?" I ask. "Is it your dad?"

She shakes her head no. Then she opens her mouth to speak, but nothing comes out. I see her start to shake, and she collapses, curling into herself. Sobs rack her body. *What is going on?* Maybe her boyfriend broke up with her. But why would she come to me about that?

She's crouched on the stoop, trembling. I reach down and pat her on the back. "Lydia. Come. Let's go inside."

I stand her up, ferry her through the door, guide her over to the sofa, and set her down. She seems so fragile. I've never seen her like this before. I go to get some tissues and let her cry it out for a bit. The sobs have slowed to a trickle when I return, and she seems to have calmed down to the point where she can explain herself.

"I'm sorry to barge in like this. I had nowhere else to go." She takes a tissue and pats her eyes.

"It's fine, Lydia. Do you want to tell me what's going on? Is it Christopher?" I'm pleased with myself for remembering his name.

She shakes her head no.

"Then what?"

"You know that dating app I'm working on?"

"Yes." This is work related? Could she actually be this upset about something that has to do with her work?

"It uses DNA. Did I tell you that?"

"What do you mean, it uses DNA?"

"It matches people based on personality type from a questionnaire and preferences you set." She blows her nose with the tissue and seems to be getting a grip on her emotions. "But there's also a feature that allows you to use your DNA. To see if people are compatible. Based on genetics. Like, to flag any future problems. And to eliminate any potential relatives."

"Huh?" I'm still wondering why she's coming to me about it. "How does it work?"

"We have a data-sharing arrangement with the big players in the field, and you can opt to upload their DNA analysis if you've had it done."

"Oh. Like, so you don't end up dating your own long-lost brother or something?"

"Exactly."

Is Christopher related to her somehow? That would be troubling, but I don't see her showing up here and sobbing to me about it.

"I still don't understand."

"We're beta testing that feature, so a lot of us offered to give it a try. I put in my genetic data. And his too, to see what it said. And I found out something awful."

"What is it?"

"I think I have a half sister, Laura."

"What?" My hand goes to my mouth. That's not at all what I was expecting. "How do you know?"

"The app flags relatives if you opt in to that feature. And I matched. With an anonymous female. She's a fifty percent match to my DNA, Laura. She has to be my sister."

I'm totally shocked. Could it be a mistake?

"How old is she? Can you tell?"

"She'd be about nineteen or twenty. It only has the birth year. They don't give names or contact information."

My mind is reeling. If it's true, it must be on Peter's side. Cynthia couldn't hide a pregnancy. Besides, she was dead by the time this child was born. Is this why his lover disappeared? Was she pregnant with his child? Does Peter know about this? I can't take any more secrets. But then I tell myself I'm getting carried away. It could be a mistake. *Couldn't it?*

As if reading my mind, she continues. "I don't think it's a mistake, Laura. My parents… I'm not sure if you know this, but they both had affairs. I could have a bunch of half-siblings out there for all I know."

"I, uh, yes. I do know. Your father told me. Recently." I place my free hand on her shoulder. "I'm so sorry, Lydia.

And especially for the way you found out. He told me about that too. How you overheard them."

"I never told Carson. I wanted to protect him."

I see her in a totally different light now, as a protector of what was left of her shattered family. The "other woman," Jeanine, took away her mother and broke up her family. And I'm convinced now that Cynthia took her own life; it must have been her reaction to finding out about Peter's infidelity, and Lydia blames this other woman. No wonder she was so reluctant to let me in. All that pain.

"You're a good big sister, Lydia."

"I'm sorry I was so hard on you, Laura. You really hung in there with us. And you're all I've got now."

She reaches over and hugs me. Although it hurts my collar bone, I don't complain. I'm too much in shock, trying to process all of this, and I don't want to ruin this tender moment. It's nice that we're finally on the same side.

"It's fine, Lydia. It's all okay. We're good now."

But where is this all going?

I need to find Peter and find out what he knows. I called him right before Lydia started pounding on our front door, but it went to voice mail. On a Saturday. That's never happened before. But I don't want to get suspicious. He leveled with me about the affair. We're happy. We're moving in a new direction. I want to be on the same side as my husband. I'll give him a chance to explain.

But what does this mean for us? For our family?

EIGHTEEN

Peter's trying to play it cool, but he's spinning too many plates. It's all going to come crashing down around him. He's not a very good liar, and although he hasn't been outright lying to Shackler, he's been selectively revealing different parts of his story to different people, and it's hard to keep up with what he said to whom, especially when he gets nervous.

It's Saturday, and he's at Shackler's office to talk about another threatening email he received, from a different address. It came the other day, and he's even more concerned than before.

I won't tell if you don't.

Before he can get to that, Shackler has some information about Jeanine Randall's daughter, Ella—the nineteen-year-old he'd identified after he'd located Jeanine outside Las Vegas in a long-term care home. The young woman who may be his daughter.

"Her daughter. She's had some issues in the past. Her file is sealed. Juvie case. But the scuttlebutt is, she was a bit..." Shackler's scrunching up his nose, searching for the right word. "Unhinged," he says eventually, with a firm nod.

Peter's eyebrows raise as he thinks about the emails, trying to make sense of it all. *Unhinged? What does that mean?* But then, it shouldn't really surprise him, based on his knowledge of her mother.

"Unhinged. How so?"

"It's hard to say with what I can gain access to. But she's had some psychiatric issues and a few minor run-ins with the law. Reading between the lines, I'd guess shoplifting. Petty theft, maybe. That sort of thing. She got expelled from one school in ninth grade. But she turned herself around. Graduated with honors from a decent prep school. Good student, it seems. Smart. Got into college. A state school in Nevada, where they live."

"That sounds like a dangerous combination. Smart and unhinged."

"You said Jeanine was seeing someone else at the time of your affair."

"She was. It was sort of a cover, she said. So people in the office wouldn't get suspicious about us. She brought him to company parties and that sort of thing. I'm not sure how serious it was. She wouldn't have told me the truth anyway."

"So this child. She could be yours. Or she could be his."

"Yes. I suppose. Let me see that photo again."

Shackler shows him the photo he pulled off her social media feed. She's got light hair, like her mother and the other guy.

"Her hair color. It's more like his than mine." Peter scrutinizes the photo a bit more. "But there's a slight resemblance to my daughter, Lydia, although it's hard to tell from one photo."

"Do you have some photos of your children?"

Peter pulls up some photos of Lydia and Carson and shows them to Shackler. The detective's eyes dart back and forth between the phone and the computer screen. After a bit, they agree that it's inconclusive. It's obvious that Lydia and Carson are brother and sister, but with Ella, it could go either way.

"And what did this other fellow think about all this when she up and disappeared?"

Peter's already told Shackler that he engineered a pump and dump, a move to inflate the stock price at the company where they were working so Jeanine could cash out her stock and start a new life. It was right after Cynthia died, and all of his assets were frozen during the early stages of the investigation. Jeanine—raw and vengeful—was blackmailing him, and it was the only way he could think of to get her the money. This was after Peter made it clear that he had no intention of getting back together with her, even with Cynthia out of the picture. Jeanine, hurt and angry, threatened to go to the police about their affair. He knew how that would look; he hadn't yet been cleared of wrongdoing. So he did what she wanted, trying desperately to save himself and his family.

"I have no idea. I didn't really know the guy."

"And you didn't know about the daughter until I told you?"

"No. I told you already. I never looked back. We lost contact."

"Right."

Peter's starting to get annoyed with all of this back and forth, and he's wondering if he's maybe given up too much to the investigator.

"Listen, Shep. You work for me, no?"

"Yes, of course, Peter."

"This is starting to feel like an interrogation."

"Sorry. I'm going somewhere with it."

"Get there faster."

"Maybe this daughter has something to do with what's happening to Laura."

"What? Why now? After all this time?"

"Maybe it has something to do with what happened to her mother. When she had the accident. It would make sense that she would come looking for you. She's got no father figure or anyone else in her life that I can find. She's all alone now. And we know she's a bit off-balance."

"She'd have to know about me."

"True. If there's anything you can think of about Jeanine, what kind of backstory she may have told everyone when she changed her name and started over. It might help me figure out what's going on."

"I have no idea what she told everyone. And I thought you said Ella's out of the country on some kind of service trip to Mexico."

"She is, supposedly."

"So it can't be her." Peter doesn't want to think about this possibility. What a disaster that would be. It can't be that. There has to be some other explanation.

"Maybe she faked the trip," Shackler says.

"I doubt that. She's only nineteen. How would she pull it off? And what about the emails? If they're connected, what could they mean?"

Shep looks again at the second one his client received. **I won't tell if you don't.**

Shackler presents his theories. Either the emails are from the daughter and it's her way of trying to reach out, which he doubts, or they have nothing to do with her, and they're related to work and the stock manipulation, which he feels is more likely. If that's true, he expects a blackmail demand or some sort of other request soon.

They talk a bit more about Laura and her work. Shackler has some information to present to both of them, but the long and short of it is he found nothing to implicate either the assistant or Laura's nemesis at work. Since Peter didn't tell Laura about the emails, they'll have to call a separate meeting and pretend this one never happened. He hates keeping it from her, but if he lets her in on it, she'll start asking more questions, and he can't answer them without putting her in jeopardy.

They wrap things up, and Peter goes on his way, weighing his options about the mystery daughter and this new revelation about her emotional issues. He has a hard time believing Jeanine would have kept something like this from him, so he tells himself it's more likely that she's the other guy's kid. He decides there's no point in telling

Laura about this new development. Not until he has more information.

———

Shep's more convinced than ever that there's more to this story. Why would Jeanine Randall take a payoff to skip town and get a new identity simply because she felt humiliated and heartbroken? It doesn't make any sense. Especially if she was carrying a child. She could have stayed and asked for child support from either one of them, depending on whose it was. Why start over? Alone? And why hasn't she married after all this time? It's been nineteen years.

He no longer thinks that Peter Foster is dangerous or that he had anything to do with his late wife's death. But he is hiding something; Shep knows that for sure. And the only thing that makes any sense is that Jeanine Randall *did* have something to do with Cynthia Foster's death, and his client is hiding it for some reason.

He always thought it sounded strange. That Cynthia Foster simply fell off a cliff. He decides he'll go get the old case file from one of his police contacts. Look into it and see what he can find. He realizes he's getting a bit obsessed with this case, but it's making him feel alive and engaged for the first time in a long while, so he indulges himself.

NINETEEN

When Peter pulls into the driveway, Laura is waiting at the door for him. He can tell from her body language that she's not happy. On his way out of Shackler's office, he noticed that she tried to reach him, but he decided to head home and talk to her in person. Now he feels like that was probably a bad move. He doesn't like talking on the phone, but he knows it annoys her when she can't reach him. It's a sticking point with them and an easy one to fix. He could kick himself for making an issue of it again.

But as he gets closer, he notices the strained look on her face, and it's clear there's more to this than a missed call. He doesn't bother opening the garage door. Instead, he parks the car in the driveway, jumps out, and steps up his pace to the screen door, concerned that something terrible may have happened.

"What's wrong?" Peter asks as she opens the door to let him in, obviously frazzled and eager to see him.

"Where the hell have you been, Peter? I've been trying to reach you."

"Sorry. You know how I am. I went to work. I ran some errands. I lost track of time. Are you okay? Is everything okay?"

"I'm okay. Yeah. But Lydia's not."

She steps aside, and Peter walks through the door and into the living room ahead of her.

"What? Lydia? Is she hurt?"

"No. Nothing like that. She found out something that upset her. And it upset me too, Peter. We're both upset."

"About?"

"You. And your past."

"Me?" Peter feels like they should sit down, but Laura is still standing by the door. He tosses his keys on the foyer table. "Do we want to have a seat, maybe?"

His stomach sinks as the possibilities swirl around in his mind. He steps over to the sofa and waits to see what she will do, completely confused about where this is going. Laura follows him but seats herself across from him in a chair, keeping her distance, which isn't a good sign. But he respects her choice and sits on the sofa.

"Lydia found out she has a half sister. Through the dating app they're working on. It uses DNA data as part of its matching service, and it flags relatives."

"A half sister?"

"You didn't know?"

His mind flashes to his talk with Shackler. Jeanine's daughter. She must be his, but he can't let on to Laura that he knew about this, even though it's only been a few days since he found out. Technically, he tells himself, he didn't really know because, until this moment, he wasn't sure whose child she was. *This isn't a lie. I didn't know for sure.*

"No. I didn't know."

"I find that hard to believe." Laura's sitting back with her arms crossed. Her eyes are trained on him, and it feels like she can read his mind. Maybe he should come clean and tell her, but it seems pointless. What good would it do?

"I mean, it happens. It's actually happening a lot more these days. And sometimes guys don't know, Laura. Women don't always tell them. You and Cynthia aren't the only women I've slept with. Does she know her name? Or where she is?"

"All Lydia knows is that she's around nineteen or twenty. The app doesn't reveal identities."

Peter looks down towards the floor and then back up at Laura. It's good to have this information, so he can tie it all together for them and move on.

"Based on the timeline, it has to be Jeanine's child. She's the only woman I was involved with at that time."

"So you and this woman, Jeanine, had an affair. Your wife died. She was pregnant with your child, and then she simply up and left town without telling you about it?"

This part will be harder for Peter to fake. He knows it makes no sense. It doesn't make sense to him, absent the part he can't tell her about. But he has to try to sell it to her.

"I wasn't the only person she was seeing, Laura. Maybe she didn't know whose baby it was. And she felt humiliated. And hurt. She thought some people at work knew about us, although I doubt it. I'd broken it off with her before Cynthia's death. But after the accident, she got her hopes up. When I made it clear that things were over, even with Cynthia gone, she decided to leave town. Start over. Get away from me and the situation. She told me she was going to change her name, and I assume she did. And she probably found out about the pregnancy after it all happened. After she'd left town."

"So she was in love with you?"

"I suppose maybe she was. And I feel terrible about that. I never meant to hurt anyone. It just happened. And if she'd told me about the child, I would have done right by her."

Peter's not about to tell Laura what he knows about the young woman's past; it will only worry her more. But it's weighing heavily on his mind. Could Shackler be right? Could she be targeting Laura? He needs to get ahead of this if there's any chance the PI's theory is correct and take care of it before he has a disaster on his hands.

"I need some space," Laura says, then stands up and makes her way upstairs, leaving Peter alone with his thoughts.

He has to admit he feels quite conflicted. He knows he needs to protect his wife. But this child. She's his flesh and blood, and if there's any chance she's behind the attempts on Laura's life, he wants to find her before the authorities do. Try to reason with her. Tell her it doesn't have to be like this. Assure her there's space for her at the family table. With her mother in the condition she's in, Ella has nobody. He realizes it's probably a crazy fantasy, that there could be some kind of happy ending to all of this insanity, but it's all he has right now to keep him going.

TWENTY

Peter seemed just as shocked as me when I told him about his surprise daughter after he finally returned home yesterday afternoon. He had no explanation as to where he'd been all day, but I didn't press him because, naturally, we were distracted by this bombshell revelation. I could tell his hair was shorter, so I presumed he got a haircut while he was out. But that doesn't take hours. And I would have felt better if he'd offered me an explanation without my having to ask for one.

Lydia was long gone by the time he got back. I wanted her to wait for Peter to come home, but she was too upset to face him. She said she needed a day to process all the news and invited us to her house this afternoon. *Just what I need.* I wanted to be rid of that place, but less than two weeks in our new home, here we are, in Peter's SUV, winding up that dreaded hill, headed back over there. I feel carsick already, and we're only halfway up.

My husband insists that he knew nothing about this daughter. That Jeanine never told him. I wince every time I hear her name, even in my own head, and I can't help but think there's something else he's not telling me. Peter said he called Shackler, and the detective's looking into it. To see if he can track them both down. What good is this guy if he couldn't find this on his own? How will he ever find out who's out to get me if we're the ones who have to tell him about the daughter? He hasn't even gotten back to us about my work investigation. *Some private investigator.*

I did some sleuthing myself. But all traces of Jeanine Randall seems to end abruptly in 2004, a few months after Cynthia died. That's even weirder to me. It's too soon for her to have gotten married. Where did she go? And why did she leave her old life behind?

Peter says she was embarrassed about the affair and decided to leave town. Change her name. Start a new life. She thought people knew about the two of them, or at least suspected. And when Peter told her there was no future for their relationship, she decided to make a clean break. Start over fresh. I have to admit, it must have been a bit humiliating. Even with Cynthia out of the picture, Peter still didn't want her. I guess it's possible she might have wanted a do-over, given the circumstances. But still. It's weird, especially given that she was pregnant. But then, she was seeing two men, according to Peter. Maybe she didn't know whose child it was, or maybe she didn't find out she was pregnant until she'd already left, as Peter suggested. But it doesn't make sense to me, not in the bigger picture. I'm convinced there's more to this story.

I finally called Sophie back yesterday, after Lydia left and before Peter came home. She assured me that Mina and Brent aren't having an affair. Mina's not into guys, and

Brent is indeed a player, but he's apparently smart enough to keep it out of the office. I feel terrible for entertaining her idea about Mina being in on this somehow, but I suppose it's wise to cover all the bases. I'm not so sure about Brent, though. I don't trust him.

We've been driving in silence. So much for our new home nirvana. The honeymoon's over already. I'm dreading this meeting. I don't think Carson knows anything about any of this yet unless Lydia told him. Poor kid. He was only four when all of this started. And even though he looks fully grown, he's still pretty young and vulnerable. With Lydia, we always know what she's thinking, whether we want to or not. Carson's different. He holds it all in, like his father. Although that makes it easier on us, I worry that he'll be more upset than he lets on.

Peter parks the SUV and looks over at me. "I'm sorry. I'm so very, very sorry, Laura. For all of it."

I take a deep breath and let out a long sigh. "I just wish you had told me everything sooner," I say.

"I know."

"I don't like having secrets between us."

"I only kept it from you to protect us. To protect what we have. I didn't want you to judge me. To start getting jealous and suspicious. I had enough of that with Cynthia. It destroyed us. It destroyed our family."

"I know, Peter. I'm not the jealous type. Don't worry about that. I know you love me, and I wish you'd trust me enough to tell me the truth."

He reaches over and takes my face in his hands, looking deep into my eyes. "There's only one thing you need to know, Laura. You're the love of my life, and I'd do anything to protect what we have."

What does he mean by that? *Protect what we have.* Is he worried that this daughter will make a claim on our assets or something? That hadn't even occurred to me. But I guess she could try. And Peter said if the FDA approval goes through, we're likely to get a windfall profit through his stock options.

He still hasn't said what I'm longing to hear, though: that he's told me everything. That there are no more secrets. But the way he's looking at me tells me one thing for sure. What he's saying is true. He'd do anything for us. He loves me. And that's going to have to be enough. For now.

———

Lydia and Carson greet us at the door, and we get seated at the dining room table. We took our living room sofa and chairs, so there's nothing else to sit on; my stepdaughter's still waiting for the furniture she ordered. It feels very formal, sitting around the large, clunky table with no food on it, like I'm at a tense board meeting waiting for some terrible news like the company's going under or we're all being sued. There's a pitcher of water on the table and some glasses.

"Would you like some water?" she asks.

Peter is silent. His eyes are wandering around the room, landing anywhere but on his children.

"That would be nice," I say.

Lydia eyes her father as she fills the glasses, placing one in front of each of us. Carson has one elbow on the table, and he's resting his head on his fist. There's a faraway look in his eye. I'm sure from the look on his face that his sister told him the news.

"I had no idea about this child," Peter says. "I'm sorry you had to find out this way."

"You had no idea?" Lydia asks, her tone sharper than I've ever heard her use with her father. "How could you have no idea?"

"The woman never told me."

"Mom knew, didn't she? About your affair, I mean?" Carson's sitting up now, his eyes like daggers narrowed sharply on Peter. It's a look I've never seen on him before.

"Yes."

"She found out that day?" Carson asks.

"Yes. Well, she confronted me about it that day. I'm not sure when she found out. Or how. But I'd already broken it off. I told her that."

Lydia starts in. "So, let's get it all out in the open. How long was Mom having an affair?"

Peter clears his throat. "For about two years, as far as I could tell. But she broke it off. A few weeks before she died. She said she wanted to try again."

"And you?"

"Mine started later. About a year before your mom's accident. But I broke it off too. When your mom did. We both wanted to try again."

"She didn't want to try again!" Lydia says. "That's not what she said that day, Dad. I heard her. You know I heard her."

For a moment, I feel like I've traveled back in time. Her demeanor and her voice are childish, impetuous, like when she was in her early teens, and it's clear this is bringing up some unresolved issues from her past.

"Well, yes. I know. She was upset because she'd recently found out about my affair. I figured she'd cool down. She didn't mean what she said, Lydia. She loved you both very much. She just had some…issues."

Peter goes on to tell them a bit more about their late mother's mood swings, and he tries to assure them that none of this was their fault. To convince them that she loved them both very much. But they don't seem to be buying it, and I have to say, I can't blame them.

"And you really had no idea about this love child of yours?" Lydia asks.

"I…uh, no. I had no idea until recently. The woman moved away right after your mom died. We didn't keep in touch."

Carson rolls his eyes, and I have to fight not to follow suit. As they're talking, the hole in his story begins to widen. Now that Peter's piecing it all together, it seems even more bizarre that this woman wouldn't have told him. Unless she wasn't sure who the father was, a point that Peter keeps harping on. Which was possible. But still. Couldn't she have found that out?

"So, Dad. Who is she?" Carson asks.

Peter tells them that her name is Jeanine Randall and that he met her at work. Apparently, she'd met the children a few times at the company's annual picnics, and Lydia seemed to remember her, which would make sense. If she wanted Peter for herself, she'd likely try to get in good with his kids any chance she had. He tells them she changed her name when she moved away, and he doesn't know what it is. And he doesn't know her daughter's name or where she is. He doesn't tell them about Shackler, and I wonder why that is.

Lydia snaps out of her adolescent regression. The mature businesswoman is back, and she starts to discuss various scenarios and their options. Is it better to let sleeping dogs lie or go on the offensive and try to find her? Get ahead of any potential claims she might make? This daughter hasn't tried to find her father, as far as we know. Then Peter and Lydia start in on the legal implications.

His daughter is so well-versed in all of this that I'm speechless. She must have learned it from her grandmother. She's going on about retroactive community property claims, apparently concerned that this young woman might somehow find them and make a claim to the family fortune via legal or extralegal means, like a blackmail scheme. Most of the money is on Cynthia's side, so this seems ludicrous to me. But of course, she could ask for money from us. Back child support, maybe? Is that possible? She hasn't even surfaced yet, so this all seems a bit premature to me. I guess that's how it is when you have millions and millions of dollars. Someone's always lurking around the corner, trying to wrest some of it from you.

In the end, Peter informs them he will hire a private investigator, try to find out who she is, and we will all run the financial implications by our respective estate lawyers.

We're about to get up to leave when Carson stops us.

"Wait," he says.

We settle back down, and a chilly silence fills the room. Then Carson drops a bomb as he turns to his dad, finally putting it all together.

"Did Mom kill herself that day? Because of this woman? Because she found out about your affair?"

Peter cradles his head in his hands, his elbows resting on the table. He takes a few deep breaths. Then his eyes lift up to look at Carson.

"I can't say for sure. But I think so. And I'll have to live with that for the rest of my life."

TWENTY-ONE

It's Monday morning, and Peter's at work, happy for the respite from his personal troubles. They've gotten good news from the FDA. Well, it's sort of good news. Not an approval yet, but they can tell by the questions the feds are asking that it's close. There's nothing major in the FDA's response to their application. Nothing questioning the data or the methods. Only some picky stuff about format and a few requests for more detail in certain areas. That's usually a positive sign.

He hasn't wanted to get his hopes up, and he's not told Laura the full extent of what this might mean for them personally. Not because he's trying to keep it from her but because he doesn't want to get her hopes up only to have them crushed. Over the years, working at startups, he's found things can go south at any moment. A new study can come in revealing a side effect for the drug that hadn't surfaced before. A competitor could launch a drug with a better safety profile or price point. And even if it's a go, he's seen cases where the stock doesn't pop on approval—and sometimes even goes down—because it's already shot up as a result of all the hype, which might be the case in this instance. But, if the stars align, it will mean millions for some and tens of millions for others in the company.

You'd think that would make people giddy and excited. But it doesn't. It makes them tense and irritable because everyone's sitting on a pile of stock options they can't sell because the trading window is closed. That's standard procedure with incentive stock options; companies have to prohibit trading much of the time to protect against any SEC violations. So, they are all millionaires on paper, but it will evaporate into thin air if they don't get the approval.

The tension has been exacerbated by the merger and the fact that they've released a preprint—a preliminary research article—which shows that the drug also holds promise for lung cancer, a much bigger and more lucrative market than ovarian cancer, and that made the stock soar. But the company they're merging with wasn't able to reproduce the results, and if someone on his team screwed up, it's going to come down on him.

Daniel Chen, the senior scientist who made the discovery, pushed him to release the preprint against Peter's better judgment, and he's regretting now that he gave in. It would be better for everyone if this issue stays buried until after they secure the FDA approval, so Peter's been stalling on checking the data, and there seems to be an unspoken agreement that he doesn't need to rush it. Any wrong move, any negative press could send the stock tumbling.

Peter should be holding his breath like everyone else, trying not to blow down the house of cards. But it's bugging him, so he rechecks Daniel's data. Not in the spreadsheet they presented to senior management for the article but in the physical logs in the notebooks, which are kept in a safe in the lab. He finds some entries that look like they were changed, which can happen. Maybe someone wrote something down and then quickly realized the data was wrong. But in this instance, these entries happen to align with some of the issues the other team found when they couldn't repeat his team's results.

Peter puts the lab logs back in the safe and closes it.

Then something crosses his mind. The second email he got.

I won't tell if you don't.

He opens the safe again, takes out the logs, and snaps a few photos. Then he puts the logs back in, changes the pin pad code, and closes the door to the safe.

———

Shep steps into the coffee shop, not quite knowing what he hopes to accomplish. His shoulders sag a bit as he heads over to the table, and there's a tightness in his gut, a mixture of excitement and apprehension. It's been years since he left the force, and the life of a PI has not measured up to his expectations. He got into police work because he wanted to catch criminals, and he stayed for over a decade because he enjoyed the thrill of the hunt.

Although PI work has its upsides—not getting shot at, not getting bogged down in petty politics or municipal bureaucracy—it's not the same. There's not much at stake in most of his cases, and he feels like a bit of a sellout as he walks over to meet Dave Barker, a recently retired detective who led the investigation of Cynthia Foster's death nearly twenty years ago.

They engage in the requisite small talk about Barker's retirement, but it feels a bit perfunctory—they weren't close friends—and Shep's pleased when his former colleague soon cuts to the chase.

"So, what's on your mind, Shep? I'm assuming you didn't call me here to talk about my fly fishing hobby."

The former detective is a large, powerful man with smiling eyes and a perfectly bald head that gives his otherwise kind-looking face a menacing undertone. He's a legend of sorts around Silicon Valley, having cracked a number of high-profile cases over the years, and not the kind of guy you want to mess with.

"The Cynthia Foster case. From 2004." Shep knows that he's walking a fine line. He's representing Peter Foster, so he has to be careful to protect his client's interests. He doesn't want to give up too much.

Barker nods his head. "What about it?"

"The husband. Peter Foster. He's retained me."

"For what?"

"To look into some attempts on his wife's life. His new wife, that is."

Barker's eyebrows lift.

Shep holds up his hand. "No. It's not what you're thinking. I don't suspect he's got anything to do with what's happening now. But I'm curious about something. Why was it ruled an accident so quickly? Why wasn't there more of an investigation?"

"Personally, I thought it looked more like a suicide, given the woman's erratic history. Her mother didn't want to go there—and she had a lot of pull in town—and neither did the husband. I didn't see the point of pushing it; we'd ruled out homicide."

"Right." Shep took a sip of his coffee.

He'd given Barker an opening to share his views, and if the detective had any misgivings about the case, Shep is sure he would have voiced them just now. It seems that Barker's convinced it wasn't a homicide. But Shep's still not sure. And confirmation bias is a powerful psychological force; nobody wants to be wrong. There's a prolonged silence as Shep ponders his next move, still playing his cards close to the vest.

"I suppose I'm looking for connections that aren't there," he says at last. "If you thought the first Mrs. Foster was killed, maybe the same person is after Laura Foster. But probably not."

"Over a twenty-year period? That sounds a little far-fetched, Shackler. Maybe you've been watching too many cop shows." Barker smirks and his condescending snipe reminds Shep of what he doesn't miss about being on the force.

He's never been good at office politics, and he's not really a team player; he's definitely not a suck-up. He's a lone wolf type, an iconoclast, and he realizes that the institutional lifestyle never suited him, however much he misses the work. He wants to get up and leave, but that would be awkward, so he takes another sip of his coffee, sits back, and tries to feign interest as Barker regales him with war stories from his glory days on the force.

Shep can barely get a word in, which is fine with him. He's thinking about his lady friend—a shapely brunette with a sexy laugh—and their upcoming rendezvous, which promises to be a bit more entertaining than the present one.

TWENTY-TWO

I t's Monday and I'm back at the office, and it's so far going well. Yesterday was terribly upsetting for all of us over at Lydia's, and I'm trying to shake it off now and focus on work. Bethany and the CEO liked my idea of offering our program free to nonprofit organizations, so now I'm helping to vet some Bay Area organizations to beta test it. Mina's helping me, and we all feel pretty good about where things are heading.

Mina comes in with a Starbucks, which is absolutely perfect timing. I was just thinking I needed more caffeine, but I don't care for the office coffee.

"What's the occasion?"

"Emily brought it. As a thank-you. It's her last day." Mina places it on my desk.

I guess this means summer's over, but it doesn't feel like it. It's still pretty hot. Emily, our intern, filled in a bit on our team while I was gone. She picked up the slack like a pro, and we're all thankful for her efforts. I told her to contact me for a recommendation anytime. *I should be buying her a Starbucks. We're not even paying her.* Still, the coffee hits the spot, and I'm grateful. I take a sip and put it back down.

"Tell her thanks. Where is she?"

"Not sure."

"Did she get one for everyone?"

"No. Only the three of us."

Mina sees my brow furrow.

"Me, you, and Bethany," she adds. "Emily texted me this morning to find out what we all drink."

"That was thoughtful of her."

I take another sip and start to tell Mina about another organization we might want to approach as we get to work on my save-the-day plan. We're about ten minutes into it when we hear someone screaming.

"Someone help! Something's wrong with Bethany." I think it's her assistant.

I notice that my coffee is marked *decaf*. I don't drink decaf, but Bethany does because she's got some kind of heart palpitation issue. I was with her once when she drank caffeinated coffee by mistake. Her heart started racing, and her pulse shot up dangerously high. I bet the coffees got switched, and I explain this to Mina, who is now beating herself up for mixing up the coffees.

Mina and I race to Bethany's office while I dial 9-1-1. I have no idea how bad her condition is, and while paramedics might be overkill, I don't want to chance it.

When we get there, Bethany is pale and clammy. Her breathing is labored, like her heart is beating slow, not fast. She didn't look like this when it happened last time.

Mina takes one look at her and bolts back to her desk as she shouts back to us, "She's having an opioid overdose!"

In a flash, Mina returns with something in her hand. She rips off the packaging, tearing it with her teeth. "Narcan," she says as if everyone comes to work with a supply stashed in their purse.

By this time, Bethany is nearly unconscious on the floor, and we're trying to keep her awake. I hear faint sirens in the background, and they're getting closer.

"Are you sure?" I ask.

How could Bethany be having an opioid overdose? It seems unlikely, and I wonder if squirting Narcan up the wrong person's nose could make things worse.

There's a crowd around us now.

"Do something! She's fading," someone shouts.

Mina tilts Bethany's head back. She puts the Narcan applicator in her nose and presses the release button. Then she does it again, and soon my boss starts to come back to life.

The EMTs arrive, and Mina briefs them. They take over, and one of them tells Mina that she probably saved Bethany's life.

Then it dawns on me. The coffee. That coffee was meant for me. I was supposed to get the fatal coffee.

"Where's Emily?" I ask.

But I already know the answer. Nobody's seen her since she dropped off the coffees. She's long gone. Her cell is probably disconnected already. But why? What could Emily possibly have against me?

I dial 9-1-1 for the second time today.

"Police, fire, or ambulance?"

"Police," I say.

———

They took Bethany to the hospital, and the police are here. The two officers, a man and a woman, are both in their midthirties. We're trying to piece it all together. I tell the officers and our CEO, Chad, about the brake hose incident, and I explain my suspicions about the coffee, which they've taken to the lab for testing. Bethany was coherent enough to tell them she had no other way of coming into contact with opioids, and nobody here thinks she's a drug addict.

I tell them about the camera footage of Emily dropping her purse by my car the day before I came out to the driveway and noticed the fluid. The police want to see it, so I pull it up and show it to them. I can tell this is the first time Chad's seen it, and he doesn't look happy. Apparently, Bethany didn't share her concerns with him. The sling I'm still wearing is a constant reminder of the second attempt on my life, which I also tell them about. It's pretty obvious to me that I was the target, and Mina mixed up the coffees. But the police aren't jumping to any conclusions.

The male officer says he wants to talk to HR, so he goes on his way. We're pretty certain now that Emily Swanson is not her real name, and we're all wondering how in the hell she pulled it off. We weren't paying her, so she didn't need a bank account or any other formal documentation. But still. I'm sure we asked for some kind of identification.

And why would she be after me? Did Brent plant her here? Or did he win her over while she was on the job? He's good-looking and chatty with the younger women, but this seems extreme. He's not stupid, and would Emily do something like this simply because she had a crush on him? She seemed so competent and ambitious. I must be missing something.

Chad tells everyone to go back to work. All except Mina and me. We're supposed to go with the other officer, a woman with short, dark hair and a large frame. She dwarfs me, and I find her very intimidating. It's almost as if we are suspects. Do I need a lawyer? They tell us a detective is being assigned to the case, and I'm not sure what to make of that.

"Can I go get my purse and use the restroom?"

"Go ahead, but be quick," the officer says.

I run and grab my purse and head to the ladies' room. I call Peter and fill him in. He tries to hide it, but I can sense he's frantic. I tell him that I feel more like a suspect than a victim, the way they're looking at me. He says that's how they always act when they're investigating a potential crime. Everyone's a suspect—until they're not. He would know, I suppose. He says he'll call his attorney find out if I need one, but he can't imagine why they would suspect me. I'm the one being targeted.

When I get back, the police officer starts to bombard us with questions. What time did Emily arrive? How did Mina mix up the coffees? Why does Mina carry Narcan in her purse?

Mina discloses that growing up, she had a sister with a drug problem, and they'd lost her a few years back. I knew she had a sister who died, but I had no idea about the drug problem. If she'd had Narcan, she said, she could have saved her. So now she carries it all the time. Just in case.

The officer seems satisfied with her explanation but notes that she'll check out Mina's story. I suppose that's what they always say. She's simply doing her job.

Then she starts to ask me questions, and it feels a bit more like an interrogation. I remind her that I reported the brake line incident to the police, but she seems to think it's strange that Bethany didn't tell Chad that we came to look over security footage of the parking lot.

"Did you suspect anyone in particular here?" The officer is eyeing me, her head tilted to the side.

My heart is pounding in my chest. *I'm the victim here. Why is she looking at me like that?* Maybe that's how she looks at everyone. She's got a pretty severe face. On the other hand, she is asking me about potential suspects, so I suppose that's a good sign.

I explain that Bethany told me my promotion had ruffled some feathers, and I wonder if I should mention Brent. No, I decide; that could backfire. He and Chad are old buddies. Chad's pissed enough at Bethany and me as it is. Then an assistant whose name escapes me sticks his head in the door.

"Laura? Your husband said to check your phone. He's got some important information. For the case."

I look over at the officer. "Is that okay?"

"Sure," she says. "Go ahead."

I pull out my phone and see a few text messages from Peter. There are photos, so I swipe through them. Photos of a young blonde woman. A young blonde woman who was posing as Emily Swanson, who seems to have dyed her hair dark brown for the internship.

I know now who's behind all this before I even read his text message, and I feel my head start to spin. I'm afraid I'm going to faint, even though I'm sitting down. Nobody at work is targeting me. It's Peter's daughter. Ella Simpson's her real name, he says in his text. She's apparently "unhinged," and she's out to get me.

The fact that it's all going to come out to everyone—the whole sordid story of my husband's past—is the least of my concerns right now. This child of his isn't out to scare me; she's playing for keeps. For some bizarre reason, she wants me dead.

I reveal all of this to the officer and the mood changes. Suddenly, I feel radioactive, and I realize that my world is crumbling. The officer tells me they'll need to question Peter. I wonder if I should get an attorney before I start to divulge what I know, but if I refuse to answer questions, how will that look? I have nothing to hide. I'm not sure that's true for Peter, though.

—

A few hours later, I'm packing up my desk and getting ready to head home. It's hard to believe this is actually happening. I've been placed on unpaid leave pending further investigation, although they told me I could use my paid time off, a chunk of which has been used up by my biking accident. The CEO is borderline furious he wasn't told about the Sunday morning sleuthing and the concerns about my brake line; he claims he would have launched an investigation and perhaps prevented this "unfortunate incident." But I'm sure he's happy this is back on me and not on the company, and I can see the relief underneath the indignation.

It's clear that Bethany's job is also on the line, and the HR director has already been terminated for letting Ella Simpson pull a fast one. And the coup de grâce? Chad has named Brent interim Vice President of Monetization— probably the person he wanted in the position all along.

Thankfully, I've gotten pretty good at one-handed packing. I'm almost done gathering my belongings, but I haven't summoned the courage to leave my office and do my walk of shame. I guess it could be worse. They could have sent security to escort me out, which happened to an IT person a few weeks ago.

I look over at my doorway and see Mina hovering outside. Then she pops her head in. "How're you doing? Need any help?"

"Come in. I'm fine, thanks."

At least I still have one ally around here.

"I'm so sorry, Laura. This is totally unfair. You're the victim here."

"Thanks, Mina."

I'll miss working with her, and now she'll be stuck working for Brent.

"You should get a lawyer!" she proclaims. "Don't let them get away with this. They were the ones who failed to do a proper background check on the intern."

Peter has actually called an attorney already, but I don't want to disclose this to Mina, mostly to protect her but also because I'm afraid the walls have ears around here. I'll play the shrinking violet for now, then I'll go in for the kill.

"I understand their position. Right now, I want to focus on helping the police find Emily. Or Ella, or whoever the hell she is. You know, before she actually kills me."

We both smile. Then I widen my eyes and mouth, "Be careful" as my eyes dart up towards the camera.

"They don't scare me, Laura. Don't worry. I'm underpaid and being courted by many." She looks up at the camera. "It's an employee's market. Did you hear that, Chad? I want a raise!"

I shake my head and smile. "I'm sure going to miss you, Mina."

We hug, and she offers to carry out my box of stuff. I accept, and I'm happy for the support. The walk isn't as bad as I thought it would be. Lots of somber looks and well wishes. The fact that this might backfire on Chad makes me grin for a moment, but then I remember that someone is trying to kill me, I've derailed my career, and everyone knows my husband's an adulterer. My eyes well up, but I bat back the tears, hold my head high, and keep walking.

———

Peter's at the Santa Clara County police station. Although it's been nearly twenty years, it feels like yesterday. The detective who handled Cynthia's case has retired, and a new detective, an attractive woman in her midthirties with dark hair and a tawny complexion, sits across from him armed with the old case file. Detective Davis is her name. But Peter came armed this time too. He knows the drill. He's got his attorney friend, Tom Wilson, by his side, and he's not about to mess this up by saying anything stupid.

"I see you've retained a private investigator." She states this as a neutral fact, but there's an undercurrent of scorn in her voice, as one would expect; it's always perceived as de facto criticism of the police force.

Peter looks to his attorney, and Tom gives him a nod.

"I did, yes. When my wife's car was tampered with."

"I suggested it," Tom says, "and gave Peter the referral for Shep Shackler. He was concerned about his wife's safety, and rightly so."

"So, at the time of your late wife's death, you were having an affair? With this young woman's mother?"

"Don't answer that, Peter."

"If this daughter is a result of this affair, then it's relevant to the case."

"Then ask it in a different way."

"When did you find out that this child existed?"

"A few days ago."

"How?" Detective Davis is leaning back, arms crossed and head tilted to the side, looking eager for him to make a wrong move.

"From Shackler, the private investigator," Peter says. "And also from my daughter, Lydia. She did a DNA analysis and matched with a half sister. This all came out last weekend."

"And until then, you had no knowledge of Ella Simpson's existence?"

"He's already stated that," Tom says.

"I had no prior knowledge," Peter confirms.

"I imagine this might have come as a shock."

"This isn't a counseling session, Detective Davis," Tom barks. "Do you have a question?"

"Any idea why she would be after your wife?"

"Her mother's accident, maybe. She has nobody," Peter replies.

"That explains why she would want to find you, not why she would want to kill your wife."

"How would he know what's in this young woman's head? He's never even met her. Move on, Detective, or we're leaving."

Peter proffers a response. "Shackler said he called and gave you all the information we have. Along with his theories. You already know everything that I know about her. About her history of instability."

"Right."

Peter decides to go on the offensive and try to flip the script. "So what are you going to do about it? We need to find her. Soon. Before she harms my wife. Or herself."

Are they going to open up the whole case again and look further into Cynthia's death? That would be a disaster. But it wouldn't surprise him. He needs to keep their focus on finding Ella and call attention to the fact that his wife is the victim here.

"We'll do everything we can, Mr. Foster, and so will the Nevada police."

"If there's nothing more, my client and I will be going." Peter and Tom start to stand.

"Wait. I have one more question."

"Okay."

"Why did your PI request the old case file? From your wife's accident."

"Don't answer that, Peter," Tom says. "You'd have to ask him, Detective."

"I'll do that." Detective Davis leans back with her arms crossed, a faint smile on her face.

Tom turns to Peter. "Let's go."

They exit the station, then have a brief chat by their vehicles. The attorney tells Peter that if he didn't murder his wife, he has nothing to worry about. He says it so matter-of-factly that Peter's knees go weak. Does his friend actually think he's capable of murder?

"Of course I didn't murder my wife, Tom. And they know it."

"I know, Peter. That's exactly what I mean. You have nothing to worry about, so focus on finding Ella and keeping your family safe. I'll handle the police; don't talk to them without me there. Have Shackler keep me in the loop on everything, and make sure he keeps in touch with the police. I've got your back."

They start to part company, but then Tom turns back to Peter. "By the way, why *did* Shackler look up the case file?"

"I don't know, but I'll find out. And thanks for everything, Tom."

His friend goes on his way. Peter doesn't share Tom's optimism. He's worried, very worried, as he gets into the car to drive home and meet with Laura and Shackler to figure out what the hell to do next. He's so worried that he didn't even tell Tom the truth. That Shackler retrieved the case file because he thought Peter might have been a serial spouse killer. If his own PI thought it, others probably do too. At least Ella gets him off the hook for the attempts on Laura's life. But he feels the weight of it all on him. The daughter. The emails. The bad memories. The danger to his family. It's all his fault, and he has to figure out a way to make things right.

TWENTY-THREE

Shep Shackler is sitting in one of the stylish yet uncomfortable wingback chairs in the living room of the Fosters' new home. Peter and Laura are seated close together on their sofa. They've recently moved in, and the house is sparsely furnished, conspicuously lacking a dining set. What they do have is tasteful—light with clean lines—and he senses that Laura has done most of the decorating.

He knows this is a delicate situation. Peter Foster, he's sure, was keeping some information from his wife, and he's not sure how much she knows or how much Peter Foster has told her already, so he's planning to be as circumspect as possible. They all reached the house around the same time, so he didn't have a chance to check in with his client on how to approach things. He decides to start by recapping the events for them and giving them his take on everything.

Ella Simpson—known as Emily Swanson at the wife's office—is the daughter of Jean Simpson—formerly known as Jeanine Randall—the husband's ex-lover. Jeanine has been in a long-term care facility for the last three months with a traumatic brain injury, the result of a terrible car accident. Her memory is supposedly gone. She's bedridden and in and out of consciousness. The pair reside near Las Vegas, Nevada, where Ella's a rising sophomore at UNLV, the same school as Emily the intern, so that much of her story was actually true. Shep informs them that he's already given all of this information to the police.

Next, Foster gives them a rundown of the questioning he endured at the station.

"So. That was a pretty fast turnaround, Shep," Laura says. "You were able to find all this out about Jeanine and Ella? Today?" Laura's eyes are trained on Shep.

"Laura," his client says. "I, um—"

Shep holds up his hand. "Wait. Let me explain." He decides to give Peter Foster an out. "I have to confess, I've known about both of them for a few weeks. I figured it out on my own, and then I confronted your husband about the two of them more recently. Just a few days ago."

"Why?" she asks.

"Because I was suspicious. And worried about you, Laura."

"Suspicious of…?"

"It struck me as odd. The circumstances. Your husband's first wife dies in a freak accident. Then you have a freak accident. I had to make sure."

"Make sure of what? That it wasn't Peter's doing?"

"Yes."

She turns to her husband. "Is that what the two of you were talking about? The day you started without me at his office?"

"Yes," Foster says to his wife. "He asked me to come early. And he disclosed to me that he knew about both of our affairs. Cynthia's and mine. He asked what happened to Jeanine after Cynthia's death, and I told him I didn't know, which is the truth. I told him she left the company. Moved away. And then he told me what he told you today. He'd located her under a different name, and she's been incapacitated for the last three months. Since that ruled her out as someone who was targeting you, I didn't think there was any point in telling you about her."

"Ruled her out? Was she ever...ruled in?"

"Let's just say I was glad to hear that it couldn't have been her targeting you."

"So, she didn't go gently into the night?" she asks.

"Not quite." Foster lets out a sigh.

"And she never told you about this child?"

Foster looks away and then back to his wife. "No. I only found out a few days ago. Like Shep said. And I wasn't even sure she was mine. Jeanine was seeing someone else at the time of our affair. I figured it was more likely to be his child until you told me about the DNA hit, so there was no need to bring it up. And supposedly, Ella was out of the country. On a service trip to Mexico. I guess that was a cover."

Laura cradles her head in her hand. "Good grief. Why didn't you tell me, Peter? This is all such a mess."

Shep starts in again. "Laura, there's more. I dug into the daughter a bit more over the last few days. She's had some issues in the past. Psychiatric issues. My working theory is that she snapped when her mother had the accident, then she started looking for her biological father. She probably wants to eliminate anyone she perceives as standing in the way of her relationship with him."

"That's why she's after me."

"It's a working theory, but that would be my guess."

"How did she find out Peter was her father? I thought Lydia's app doesn't give any names or identifying information."

"No way to know for sure on that. And it doesn't even matter. Right now, we need to focus on figuring out where she is. What she'll do next."

Shep assures them that he's already working on that. He has a state-of-the-art system at his office with facial recognition software, and he's monitoring the vicinity for Ella. The police will be on the lookout too, in California and Nevada, where her mother is, but their resources are thin. He'll collaborate with them, as well as with Tom Wilson, Peter's attorney.

"I hate to bring this up now, but it's going to get quite a bit more costly. If you want my surveillance twenty-four seven, that is."

"Whatever it takes," Foster says.

Laura's hand goes to her forehead as she shakes her head, and Shep can tell it's going to be a hell of a night in the Foster household. The last thing he wants is to be in the middle of it, so he wraps things up and gets on his way, leaving them to sort out the marital issues, but not before giving them some suggestions on how to tighten up security at the house.

———

We see Shackler out the door, and finally, it all makes sense to me. Earlier today, I was wondering how this seemingly clueless investigator had managed to uncover all of this information in such record time. *I guess he's not so clueless after all.*

But I can't even look at Peter. I would ask him to leave, but I'm afraid to be home alone. So I head upstairs and warn him to stay away from me. My life is a total mess right now, and it's all his fault. My career has imploded, and I'm not safe in my own home. Or anywhere, for that matter.

I decide to stay at my parents' house in the city for a while, and I start packing up my toiletries. Then I notice something. The vial of oxy that was on my bathroom countertop. It's gone. *How can this be?*

Bethany's coffee was spiked with something, but they haven't said yet what it was. They were able to rule out fentanyl on the scene, but aside from that, it could be anything. Shep said that Jeanine had a bad car accident. So maybe Emily or Ella or whatever her name is could have gotten opioids from her. But still. My stomach is in knots now. Because facts are facts. The oxy was here, and now it's not.

Was she in my house?

Come to think of it, there have been a few times lately when I've temporarily misplaced things. Like they'd been moved or rearranged, but I thought it was Peter. Or my imagination. I have to tell Peter about this, but I don't want to talk to him. And I have to get out of this house, fast. Before I lose my mind—or my life.

———

Peter knows it's bad. How bad, he can't tell yet. Laura is upstairs. She asked for space, so the least he can do is give it to her. She's an understanding woman, but she's not a fool. He knows that he's dug himself a hole. He needs to protect Laura. He knows that. She's in mortal danger. But he has to admit the fact that Ella is his daughter complicates the situation. Even though he's never been into guns, if the situation were different, he'd run out and get one. But could he actually use it? On his own flesh and blood?

He's already called a security company to come and install an upgraded system. They were planning to do it anyway, but this ups the timeline. He's secretly hoping Shackler will locate Ella rather than the police. That he can go to Ella himself and try to talk her down. Navigate some kind of ending to all of this that's better than the nightmare scenarios running through his head. But all he can do now is wait. And pace around the house, wondering what will happen next. What his next steps should be.

Laura's been upstairs for about an hour when he hears her walking down the stairs.

"Hey," he says, bracing himself for what's to come. His stomach sinks when he sees she's carrying an overnight bag.

"The oxy that was on the bathroom counter. Did you move it?" Laura asks.

That wasn't at all what he was expecting. "What? No. Why?"

"It's missing, Peter."

"What?" Then he remembers her work incident. "Wait. You don't think...?"

"That she was in our home? What other explanation could there be?"

Peter thinks about it for a few minutes while Laura glares at him.

"The movers. One of them could have taken it. Or one of the delivery people."

Laura's looking off into the distance, her lips pressed together. Then she turns back to him. "That's actually a good point. I shouldn't have left it out on the counter. I forgot how hot a commodity it is. But I'll let the police know anyway. And I'll call and see if they have the results back yet on the coffee. I'm not taking any chances."

"I've got a security team coming today. To tighten things up."

"That's probably a good idea. But I'm going to my parents' for a while."

Peter doesn't like uncertainty, so he tries to nail her down.

"I understand, Laura. But how long is a while?"

"I don't know, Peter!"

Laura rarely raises her voice. He knows he should give her space, but he doesn't want to let her walk out that door. He fears she might never come back.

"Can we talk? Please?"

"Not now. I need some time."

Her left arm is still in a sling, so he offers to help her to the car. She accepts his assistance, and he tries to take that as a positive sign. He walks outside with his wife, helps her with the car door, tries to leans in and kiss her good-bye, but she grabs the handle and slams the car door shut before he can make his move.

Then Peter takes a step back and watches as his wife backs her silver Audi out of their driveway, stops to let some passing cars go by, and slowly goes on her way.

TWENTY-FOUR

I should be feeling something, but I'm not. I don't feel fear or anger or anything at all. I'm numb, and I know that I'm in for it once this all hits me. For now, I've started my drive north on 280. I watch the parched hills rolling past me as I search for a song on the radio that won't make me cry; I need to stay numb for now. How can my life turn on a dime like this? It's hard to believe. My job. My marriage. I'm almost forty and headed back home to stay with my parents. My life is in tatters, and none of it is my fault.

I have to do something to stop feeling like a victim, so I get off the highway after a few exits, pull into the parking lot of Stanford Shopping Center, call Sophie, and ask her to meet me for coffee before I head into the city. What's the rush anyway? I have nowhere to be. I'll see if she knows an attorney. Peter already consulted with one, but at this point, I'd rather find my own. She agrees to meet me, and I wander around the mall for a bit, waiting for her.

When she arrives, we get settled at an outdoor table at Starbucks. I haven't told her the details yet, only that there was trouble at work and it was an emergency.

I start in on it, and her jaw drops when I start to re-veal all the drama—Bethany almost dying of an over-dose, Mina bringing her back to life, and the fact that it was Peter's daughter Ella all along trying to kill me; she'd planted herself at my workplace. My life, my normally dull and predictable life, it's like a soap opera.

"Holy shit, Laura."

"You can say that again."

"I mean, where do you want to start? Your career? Your marriage? Your life?"

She throws up her hands, and we both start to laugh. I mean, it's so ridiculous you either have to laugh or cry. Then the tears start to roll down my face, and I'm laughing and crying at the same time. Sophie comes around and hugs me, and we stay like that for a bit. Then she takes me by the arms and gives me a firm shake.

"We're going to fix this, Laura. I promise."

I nod and wipe away my tears, and she heads back to her seat.

"Let's start with work," I say. "I need to talk to an attor-ney. See what my rights are."

"I can get you someone really good. Off the top of my head, I would say it's more on Bethany than you. She's the one who chose not to report it to the CEO if that's the transgression."

"She's been so good to me. I can't throw her under the bus."

"Laura, it's kill or be killed around here."

"I know."

She's right. I know this. It's taken me years to learn to assert myself, but it doesn't come easily. Maybe that's my nature or the result of spending my early years immersed in a culture that's less comfortable with conflict, but it doesn't matter. My inability to go for the jugular is holding me back in my profession. Either I force myself out of my comfort zone, or I need to change careers. As Sophie said, it's kill or be killed.

"They're the ones who hired an impostor and didn't fully vet her. You could start there. She did try to kill you, after all."

"That's exactly what Mina said."

I get a few names from her, and we go over the pros and cons of each of them. Should I go with someone like Chad? Or his complete opposite? A woman? A man? We decide to go with Veronica Garner, an African American woman in her early forties with a killer track record on both sides of employee-employer suits. I call her office and set up an appointment for later in the week. Then we turn to my marriage.

"What are you feeling? About Peter?"

"I have no idea how I feel. I'm numb."

Then I hear my phone buzz. It's the police department. I pick up, hoping against all odds that they've found Peter's daughter and that part of this nightmare is over. I feel a surge of hope for a short moment—but it's not why they're calling, and my stomach sinks again. There's some good news, though. Bethany's coffee was spiked with hydrocodone, not oxy. At least Ella wasn't in my house, that we know of.

But other than that, there's no new information at all on her whereabouts. Not at her home in Nevada or the long term care facility where her mother is. She could be anywhere, they say, and that doesn't make me feel any better. I relay this to Sophie, and she agrees it's better I stay with my parents for a while. I text Peter the update about the hydrocodone and turn off my phone.

"What do you think of the private investigator?" Sophie asks.

"He's good. Better than I thought."

I relay the fact that he figured all of this out before the police because he was looking into Peter's past, concerned that my husband might have been behind Cynthia's death and the attempts on my life, and we agree it's a good sign that he's looking out for me. I could hire my own PI, she points out, but it would take a while to get someone up to speed. It's probably better to stick with Shackler, but Sophie suggests that I meet with him on my own. After a bit, we say our goodbyes, and I head into the city.

—

Peter's at home waiting for Lydia, who should be arriving any minute. After he processed the shocking realization that this surprise daughter of his seems out to eliminate her competition, he thought of his children. Carson is living with two of his guy friends, so he's not too worried about his son but warned him about Ella just the same. But Lydia, all alone in that isolated house in the woods? This concerns him. He plans to ask her to stay with him until this all gets wrapped up.

He's trying to think logically. Why now? After all this time? What Shackler posited makes sense. After her mother's accident, something in Ella snapped, and she went searching for her father. But why wouldn't she simply try to reconnect with him? He would have done right by her. Why go to these lengths to eliminate Laura from his life? If only he could talk to her. Reason with her.

Lydia arrives while he's looking at photos of Ella, the ones from Shackler and some from Laura's company. With her dark hair, he notices again the slight resemblance to Lydia. It's in the jaw and the shape of the eyes, although Ella's eyes are dark like his, while Lydia's are bright blue like her mother's. A strange feeling of familiarity grips him, staring at a face that holds his DNA. Would he have the same reaction if he didn't know she was his child?

"Any news?" Lydia asks as she rushes through the front door.

"Nothing yet." Peter didn't send her the photos. He wasn't sure how she'd react, especially given the resemblance. With Lydia's history, he thought it best to show her in person rather than send them in a text.

"This is a nightmare, Dad. Where's Laura? How's she doing?"

Peter's a bit surprised that she's even asking about her stepmother, and he wonders for the first time if it might be difficult for his children if anything happened to their marriage. Even though it hasn't all been rosy over the years, their marriage has formed the bedrock of his children's stability for over a decade.

"She, uh…she went to her parents' house. For a visit." He's already told her about Laura being on leave from work.

"For how long?"

"I'm not sure."

"Did she get a lawyer? Those bastards. They can't do this to her. Can they?"

"I guess we'll see. Right now, I'm focused on finding Ella. And trying to keep everyone safe. Given the circumstances, Laura's probably safer at her parents' house. For now."

Lydia nods, but Peter's sure she's wondering if there is more to it. But they've got more important issues to discuss, so he changes the subject.

"Lydia, I have some photos of Ella to show you. Is that okay?"

"Is that okay? Of course, it's okay, Dad! I'm not a child." She shakes her head. "How else will I be able to track her down?" She flashes him a sly smile, and Peter has a sinking feeling that she's not entirely joking. She's been pretty possessive of him over the years, and she's got the instincts of a protector.

"She died her hair dark brown for the internship. But take a look at these." He hands her the phone, and she flips back and forth through the photos.

Her eyes widen, and Peter wonders if she notices the resemblance.

"Oh my God, Dad. I've seen her."

"What?"

"Yes. The girl from the coffee shop." She's tapping her finger on the phone screen. "The dark-haired one. It's her."

"What girl from the coffee shop?"

"This girl. I've seen her a few times when I ran in to get coffee. She sits at a table there; I grab and go. I noticed her looking at me a few times. Like she was checking me out or something. I didn't think much of it. Figured if I ignored her, she'd get the message I wasn't interested in her."

"When's the last time you saw her?"

"About two weeks ago. I stopped going there when I moved."

"We need to call the police. Now." Peter grabs his phone back and dials 9-1-1."And you're staying here with me until this all gets sorted out."

Then he and Lydia sit down and go over the logistics of getting a security team in place at the new house, and he tries to figure out a way to convince his wife to come back home. The thought of her out there where he can't protect her puts his stomach in knots, and he's regretting the decision not to level with her sooner.

TWENTY-FIVE

I'm getting settled in the guest room at my parents' house. Their place was built in the twenties, part of the economic boom back then, as were many others in the neighborhood. These days, a mix of historic and newer multicolored single-family homes and condos tucked a bit too close together follow the contours of the rolling hills as far as the eye can see. Theirs is modest compared to some but nicer than others. It's a narrow two-story home with two bedrooms and two baths, plus a spare room on the top floor that's quite small. It's a detached home, but barely, as it almost butts up against the home next to it.

There are two windows in my room, one on the side that's too close to the house next door to open the blinds, and one out the back with a nice view of the garden below. I'm feeling a bit claustrophobic, and I realize now that this is a very temporary solution. I probably should have left them out of it. Dad is still at work, Mom is beside herself with worry, and I'm regretting getting them involved. They don't need this kind of stress. And what if I'm putting them in danger too? What if Ella's following me? I decide I'm not going to stay for very long.

Where will I go? I have no clue. Maybe I should go to Honolulu for a few weeks. I've kept in touch with a close friend who still lives there. I can stay with her. Or I can get a hotel, which is probably safer—I'm a target now, after all, although it would be hard for Ella to follow me there. Perhaps the authorities are on the lookout for her at airports and that sort of thing.

But then I wonder how seriously the police are taking this. So far, there hasn't been any media attention, but, as Sophie pointed out, I could change that anytime I want. I've been reluctant to do so, and I plan on giving the police a few days to see what they can do. Chad and the board want to keep this under wraps, so they'd be upset if I went to the press, but why should I care about them? They're screwing me, and if this goes on much longer, the press will likely pick up on it anyway.

My phone buzzes. It's Lydia, so I pick up.

"Hi, Lydia. What's up?"

She's over at our house, and she informs me that, after seeing the photos on Peter's phone, she realizes that Ella's been stalking her. My stomach lurches, and I feel oddly protective of her as she tells me she's seen Ella a few times over the last few weeks at a local coffee shop she used to frequent before she moved. She and Peter alerted the police about this, and my stepdaughter will be staying at our house for the time being. Lydia's hired overnight private security to guard the premises. She and Peter discussed the pros and cons of each property and decided that our new home is easier to secure.

Then she tugs at my heartstrings.

"Laura, I know you're upset with my dad. And I don't blame you. But you need to come home. I know you two can get past this. And the safest place for you is here. For now."

She's making a good point, I know. But I need a day or two, because I'm not ready to talk to Peter yet. But I give her my assurance that I'll be back soon. A few days at most.

"Okay. Be careful, Laura. Please. I lost one mom; I can't lose another."

She thinks of me as her mom?

"I'll be home soon, Lydia. You be careful too."

"I will," she says.

———

I'm sitting on the comfy, compact sofa at my parents' house, staring into space. Bonkers is at my side, and I'm mindlessly petting his stubbly fur while he catches a nap. The downstairs is light and tasteful, with hardwood floors and large bay windows that let in a good deal of natural light, even on a foggy day. Normally, that's a plus, but today I realize that I'm pretty exposed here. Is this my life now? Sizing up window openings and assessing their threat levels?

My computer's open on my lap, but I'm not looking at it. I planned to start thinking about next steps, but I realize that until we figure out where Ella is, I'm stuck. I move to the kitchen table, in a nook off the living room, where I feel a bit more protected, and I vow to do something to try to move myself forward. The dog follows me and settles in at my feet. Soon his head lifts up as Dad comes through the door. He offers a halfhearted bark, looking for some attention, and Dad gives him a pat on the head.

"Hi Dad. Mom went out to do some errands."

I'm grateful for the rare opportunity to be alone with him. When I was young—elementary- school age—we were pretty inseparable on the weekends. We both loved the ocean, and he's the one who taught me to swim and boogie board. We also share a love of fitness and competitive racing, although he's predominately a distance runner, not a triathlete like me.

"Laura Loo," he says as he gives my shoulders a rub.

He sits next to me at their rectangular farm table, resting his forearms on the polished wood surface. "How're you holding up?"

"I don't know."

"Any news?"

I fill him in on the fact that Ella's been targeting Lydia too and that we've sort of bonded over it.

"Well, that's something, right?"

Typical Dad, always looking for the silver lining. He's the most positive person I know. I inform him that Lydia's staying at our house and hiring private security, and I tell him I'm going back there tomorrow. I expect him to protest, but he doesn't.

"How are things with Peter?"

I shrug. "I don't know, Dad. There have been so many secrets. I'm not sure if I can trust him anymore."

"It's a complicated situation, but I know he loves you. Do you still love him?"

"Yes. Very much. That's what makes it so hard."

Dad nods and looks away. He's pursing his lips, hesitating. Then he looks me in the eye. "Laura. Do you know how much is at stake here?" His eyebrows raise, and he puts his hand on mine, holding my gaze.

"Well, yes. It's my family. My marriage."

He shakes his head. "Sure, yes, but that's not what I meant. I've been reading up on Peter's company."

"His company?" I was expecting a lecture about the importance of commitment; this catches me off guard.

"Has he told you about the potential windfall? With the stock?"

"I, um, yes. Sort of. The stock. Yeah. He said if they get the FDA approval, it'll be good news for us. Financially. But he's been on pins and needles about it."

"Well, I would imagine."

This is blowing my mind. My father's been keeping tabs on the stock price of Peter's company? But then, he's an economics professor. I suppose it makes sense. Sort of.

"What are you getting at, Dad?"

"I know you're upset with him. But don't do anything rash, Laura. That money is half yours. Legally. And ethically. You've sacrificed everything for that family. And you need to get what's yours."

I'm flabbergasted. Is my father suggesting I should go back and patch things up with Peter for some stock gains?

I'd be fine without it. But then, I have to admit, I haven't been paying too much attention, and from the way my father's talking, it sounds like there's a lot more money at stake than I imagined.

"How much are we talking?"

"You don't know? Peter didn't tell you?"

"He didn't *not* tell me. I mean, he said the stock's gone up a lot, and I've never bothered to look into it. But he also said it could still go back down, so I've been taking it all with a grain of salt."

Dad nods. "Well, I think you *should* look into it, Laura."

What's wrong with me? Why didn't I check further into it? Most people probably would. I find myself thankful that Dad has my back. I remember that Peter gave me the log-in information for the account, but I never bothered to check it. This is on me, not my husband. And now I'm very curious.

"How much are we talking, Dad?"

"From what I've read, an amount that could change your life. And possibly the lives of others too, depending on what you choose to do with it."

TWENTY-SIX

It's early afternoon, three days after Ella Simpson tried to poison Laura Foster at her workplace. Shep is paging through the Cynthia Foster case file he obtained through an old friend of his on the force. Facial recognition software has turned up nothing on Ella, but then, he hasn't cast a very wide net. He's mostly staying local, his goal being to protect the family, leaving the wider search in Nevada and beyond to the police, so the fact that he hasn't spotted Ella might be good news for the Fosters.

Jeanine Randall, he's convinced, had more to do with the first wife's death than his client is letting on, regardless of Barker's opinions. It never made sense to him that Jeanine would cash out and vanish, especially given the fact that she was pregnant. Maybe she wasn't sure who the father was. But still. Eighteen years of child support is worth more than what she got from Foster. And it seems like she was crazy about the guy. Why throw in the towel? Unless you were running for some other reason.

From the case file, it looks like the police questioned Peter Foster, the victim's mother, and five witnesses who were on or near the trail at the time. It seems that nobody saw or heard anything out of the ordinary on the trail that day, yet an anonymous caller from a pay phone tipped them off that a hiker might have fallen down in the valley somewhere, but they weren't sure where.

The cause of death was clear; she died from the fall, and likely pretty instantly. Her head hit a ledge that jutted out as she tumbled down. From what they could tell, she fell feet first but slightly off-center. The manner of death was officially classified as "accidental," which makes sense in light of what Barker told him. They could have ruled it "undetermined," meaning it could have been a murder, a suicide, or an accident, and then the case would have officially stayed open all this time, fueling speculation and gossip. It had all the trappings of a sensational, media-frenzy case, so when the police ruled out foul play, it made sense that they'd want to close the lid on it. He can't help but wonder if things would have been different if they'd known about Jeanine Randall back then. A hard shove wasn't supported by the evidence. But what about a scuffle?

Surveillance cameras were far less ubiquitous then, so the authorities relied mostly on people's recollections, which are generally highly unreliable. Memory is fragile and imperfect, and Shep's seen his share of faulty convictions based on eyewitness testimony. Peter Foster was a person of interest initially, but he had an alibi. He was at his daughter's soccer game in Menlo Park, about twenty minutes from the trailhead. It seems nobody knew of Foster's affair with Jeanine Randall back then, so no one

questioned her. It was decades ago, so he's not very hopeful of finding anything to connect her to the scene, but he
feels he has to try.

A firm rap-tap-tap on his office door startles him, and
he stands up to open it. He's surprised to see Laura Foster
standing in front of him, his client's wife—without his
client. *This could get awkward.*

"Laura. How are you?"

"I'm sorry to barge in on you like this."

"It's fine. I was actually working on the case."

"Do you have a minute? I know I don't have an
appointment."

"Sure. Come in." Shep notices the dark shadows under her eyes; at least her arm is out of the sling. *She's been
through a lot lately,* he reminds himself.

"Any luck finding Ella?" she says.

"Not yet, but then maybe that's a good thing. I'm sur-
veilling the area, and she hasn't turned up."

Laura nods. "I suppose you've heard about Ella stalking
Lydia?"

"Yes, your husband told me."

Laura's phone buzzes, and she glances at the screen.

"Do you need to get that?"

"No, it's fine." She turns the phone over and lets it go
to voice mail.

Shep fills her in on what he's uncovered so far, which
isn't much.

"What do you know about Jeanine Randall? Are you
looking into her?" Laura's sitting on the edge of her chair,
biting her lower lip.

"In what way?"

"Do you think she could have put her daughter up to it?"

"That hadn't occurred to me. Why would she do that?"

"To get me out of the way. So she could have Peter to herself."

"Why now? After all this time."

"I have no idea. And...well, yes, I see that it doesn't make much sense in terms of the timeline." She shakes her head. "But I don't see why Ella would take it upon herself to do this. To come after me. So I was thinking, maybe it was her mother's doing."

"Anything is possible. But I'm focused on finding Ella. Her mother's no threat to you in her present condition."

"I suppose that's true." She looks down at the carpet. Then she turns to him and continues.

"Shep. What you said about looking into Peter? That you were worried about me?"

"Yes?"

"Thanks. For checking it all out. And for trying to protect me." She smiles a bit, but it seems an effort to lift the corners of her mouth to do it.

"You're welcome."

"So. You don't think Peter had anything to do with his wife's death, it seems."

"Not that I can tell. Why? Is there something I should know?"

"No. That's not what I was getting at. Peter seems to think Cynthia killed herself. Because she found out about the affair. Has he said anything to you about that?"

"That appears to be his working theory, although the manner of death was classified as 'accidental.' There was no suicide note, so they're only going on your husband's recollections of her state of mind when she left. But then, we haven't been focused on what happened to Cynthia. Why are you asking?"

"No reason in particular."

Shep nods, and there's an uncomfortable pause. He feels like she's dancing around the real issue. "So. Is there anything else I can help you with?"

"I'm not sure. I know what the police concluded, but I still can't shake the feeling that there's more to this than we know. Do you think Jeanine Randall might have had something to do with Cynthia's death? It seems odd to me that she suddenly disappeared so soon after it happened. Do you think she's dangerous? Like her daughter?"

"As I said, anything's possible, Laura. But I wasn't hired to look into that. I'm concentrating on finding Ella and keeping you safe. If you have concerns about the circumstances of Cynthia Foster's death and Jeanine Randall's role in it, you should go to the police."

"You're right. It's not important right now. But I can't shake the feeling that Peter's keeping something from me. I know my husband, and I'm sure there's something he's not telling me." She's looking him in the eye now, but Shep's not about to go there.

"Marriage counseling is not in my wheelhouse, Laura. You'd have to talk to your husband about that."

"Right. Of course."

Then she flips over her phone and punches in her code. Her eyes scan the screen.

"Will you excuse me for a moment?"

"Sure."

She heads into the foyer. He can see she has the phone pressed to her ear. Then she walks back in and stands in the doorway, stopping short of entering.

"Peter left me a message. The police called. They just caught footage of Ella in Nevada. They're getting close, he hopes."

"That's great news." Shep thinks he sees some color come back into her face.

"At least for the moment, maybe I can relax a bit."

They wrap up their brief, awkward interlude, and she goes on her way. It's a delicate situation and, he has to admit, a pretty intriguing case. Laura Foster's smart, and he's convinced she's right that there's more to the story than meets the eye. If her husband has any sense at all, he'll level with her before he loses everything. But as Shep said, he's not a marriage counselor, and their relationship is of little consequence to him.

He opens up the case file and continues reading where he left off.

———

It's late afternoon on Thursday, and I've just left Shackler's office, having learned little of any value. I'm planning to go back home tonight because I don't know where else to go. I feel rudderless, adrift in a sea of confusion, and I need to get grounded. I'm trying not to think about what my father told me, partially because I don't want money clouding my judgment about my feelings for Peter—and also because I don't want to jinx it. I'm pretty superstitious, and I feel like it's bad luck to count my chickens. Right now, we're in an uncomfortable financial situation, and that's the reality. Our expenses are a bit high on income, all of our cash went into the new house, and we can't sell the company stock.

I met with Veronica Garner, the attorney Sophie recommended. She informed me that it's almost impossible to win a case against an employer unless it involves a protected class violation, like race or gender discrimination. California is an "at will" state, so they don't need a reason to fire me, which I already knew. She suggested that we make an overture to the company and try to get them to settle. They won't want the negative publicity of a high-profile suit, she says, even if they would probably win. I told her I'd think about it, and she floated me a figure for her retainer. Needless to say, I don't have that kind of cash on hand.

Meanwhile, my brief meeting with Shep Shackler didn't make me feel any better. I can tell he's conflicted; he was reluctant to say much of anything. Peter's the one who retained him, and aside from making sure my husband's not a murderer, he's not likely to give up too much inside information. It's a measure of comfort to know that Ella's in Nevada, so I'm not looking over my shoulder every minute, at least for today. But then I'm pretty sure it's easier to obtain a gun there, so my imagination is still in overdrive, envisioning all kinds of crazy scenarios. I find myself grateful for the fact that my stepdaughter has the resources to hire private security to protect our family, but it is a bit humiliating, having to rely on her.

I need to kill some time. I don't want to be home alone, even if Ella's not a threat at the moment, and Peter and Lydia are probably still at work. I find a place to park and stroll around downtown Los Altos. It's early September, so it's still a bit hot in the daytime, but you can feel a slight chill in the air when the sun tucks behind a cloud this late in the day. I take in Main Street, lined with restaurants and salons, coffee shops, and trendy boutiques. The inviting outdoor tables sit mostly empty, waiting for the dinner crowd. I glance down at my nails, which are bare and boring. I haven't had them done since my accident. I decide to pop into my favorite nail shop and see if my nail tech is available. Kimi's the best, and I need to do something to make myself feel better.

"Laura!" She comes rushing up to me. "It's been a long time!"

"I know. Too long. Do you have time for a mani-pedi?"

"Sure! Sure! Pick your color. About five minutes? Okay?"

"Yes, that's great."

It's not very busy. Two nail techs sit and wait for clients. One's on her phone, and the other's thumbing through a magazine. A client is at the far pedicure station, texting on her phone. The meditative background music combined with the water feature at the door creates an aura of serenity, which is exactly what I need right now. The people here all look so calm, so normal, and I long to be like them—a regular person with everyday problems and concerns. I wonder if they can tell how screwed up my life is.

She calls me over, and I plop in the chair, engage in some chitchat about her boys, where she's been on vacation, the routine minutiae of daily life. I let my feet soak in the tub as she talks, and it feels great. I tell her about my accident and point out all the tender spots. She's careful to work around the areas that still smart a bit.

Forty minutes later, my toes are painted a rich plum color, shiny and perfect. She moves on to my hands, and she's even more mindful. I appreciate how careful she is with my injuries, and it's nice pretending for a time that a fall off my bike is my biggest problem. I select a more muted, neutral tone for my fingernails; sandstorm, it's called. After they dry, I leave, feeling a bit more refreshed and ready to finally face my family.

TWENTY-SEVEN

There are no cars at the house when I pull up, but the light is on in the living room. I press the garage door opener. It rises up, and I see Peter's car parked on his side of the garage. An inviting, open space sits next to it. I remember a time not so long ago when being relegated to the driveway was my biggest problem in life. Funny how things change. And why didn't I speak up for myself back then? I shake my head and vow to be more assertive going forward. Then I pull my car in next to his.

Before I can open my door, Peter's there, helping me with it.

"Hi," he says with a hesitant smile, his eyes wide and wary. I can tell he has no idea what to say—and neither do I.

"Hi." I look up at him, a little surprised by the fact that seeing his face comforts me a bit.

"Let me get your suitcase."

I pop open the trunk and allow him to retrieve it as I reach for my purse and exit the car. We're walking through the side door when I see him looking down at my toes.

"Purple." He gives his head a nod. "Pretty hot."

I can't help but smile a little.

But then it all comes back to me, and I take a deep breath and walk into the house ahead of him, at a total loss for how to handle this. We walk slowly through the kitchen, and it's painfully awkward. There's so much to say, but neither of us knows how to start. Then I turn around to face him. He reaches over and strokes my hair with his free hand, tucking it behind my ear.

"Laura," he says. It comes from a place deep inside him, uttered with a primal longing that makes me go all tingly in spite of myself.

I hear a thud as my suitcase drops to the floor, and our mouths meet in a frenzy of abandon. I can't even say who started it, but soon we're grasping for each other like the world is ending. My hands reach under my husband's shirt. I run them over the strong, smooth muscles of his back as we kiss. His hands caress me, and suddenly I long to be with him, skin to skin, just the two of us against the world. We fumble into the living room as I kick off my shoes, then it's up the stairs to our bedroom. At a loss for words, we decide to let our bodies do the talking, and they seem to have a lot to say.

—

A loud bang startles my head off the pillow. It's our front door closing. We must have dozed off, but I'm wide awake now—and frantic. Did we leave it unlocked? No, it locks automatically.

"It's probably Lydia. Don't worry," Peter says.

Our bedroom faces the backyard, so I throw on a robe and race to the guest bedroom. Lydia's Tesla is out front, so I take a deep breath to calm myself.

"Dad?" Lydia calls up the stairs. She must have heard the commotion. "Is that you?"

I call back, "It's me, Lydia. We'll be down in a bit."

"Hi, Laura. You two kids take your time up there." There's a playful tone to her voice: the abandoned suitcase, the flung shoes. I guess it's pretty obvious that we've mended some fences.

But have we? Not all of them. Not as far as I'm concerned. Sure, we still have chemistry. But so what? We still haven't actually talked about our problems. And we need to, so I go marching back towards our bedroom to confront him. Then I hear another car drive up, and I turn back to look out the guest room window. There's a black SUV outside driven by a guy in a uniform. *Must be the security guard.* Peter confirms this, and with the issue of our safety taken care of for the time being, I'm ready to lay my cards on the table.

"Peter. We need to talk."

"Nothing good ever follows those four words." I can see the dark circles under his eyes as they search mine for clues as to where my head is at.

"Not usually, no." I force a slight smile to get him to lighten up a bit.

"How bad is it, Laura? Like, on a scale of one to ten?"

"One being…?"

"I need to take the garbage out more."

"And ten?"

"You want a divorce."

"About a five," I say.

"So I still have a fighting chance." He shrugs and offers me a sheepish smile.

"Fifty-fifty. It's the best I can do."

"So. What is it you want to talk about?"

"I want you to tell me the truth—about everything." I keep my eyes trained on him. He looks away, and I know then that I'm right. He's hiding something.

"The truth?"

"Yes, Peter. All of it."

"About?"

"Don't do this, Peter. You know exactly what I mean."

"There are reasons, Laura. Why I haven't told you everything."

"I don't want reasons. Reasons are only more excuses. Why can't you trust me?"

"I haven't told you some of it because I've been trying to protect you." He's sitting on the side of the bed like he's planning to get up and leave. I'm standing towards the foot of the bed with my arms crossed.

"I don't need protecting, Peter. What happened that day? To Cynthia? And why did Jeanine just up and leave? It makes no sense. I know you're not telling me something. Now spill it."

"But I—"

"If you want to save this marriage, then tell me. All of it. I'm your wife, Peter. Your problems are my problems, whether I know about them or not, so at least let me in on what I'm dealing with, so I can try to get ahead of it."

My husband leans back on the headboard and takes a deep breath. I join him on my side of the bed. We're both facing straight ahead. I read once that men tend to open up more when they're not making direct eye contact. It supposedly makes them more comfortable. Hopefully, there's something to that theory. We're quiet for a bit, staring forward into space.

And then he starts.

"Cynthia left that day. Like I said. The day she confronted me about Jeanine and we had that argument. Lydia heard all of it, so I didn't go running after Cynthia. I figured she'd come back after she cooled off."

"Right."

"Lydia didn't want to talk about any of it. When I went up to her room, she was already in her soccer uniform, and I didn't press it. Figured I'd talk to a professional first. See what they suggested."

"Where was Carson?" So far, he hasn't told me anything I don't already know, but I let him continue at his own pace.

"Sleeping over at a friend's house. I was due to pick him up later that morning, after Lydia's game."

I nod my head.

"So, I'm getting ready to take Lydia to her soccer game, and I get a call from Cynthia. 'Tell your psycho girlfriend to stop following me,' she says. She tells me she saw Jeanine in her car, following her, on her way to Windy Hill, where she was going to hike."

A chill goes up my spine as I think back on that day, out on my run, when I heard Carl coming up behind me. Some days it's crowded there, but sometimes not, and there are stretches that can be pretty deserted. There's a steep drop-off at the top of the trail where it meets Skyline— steep enough for a paraglide launch. That's apparently where she fell, but there were hardly any people that day and no witnesses. The launch site was closed that day due to high winds, which happens often.

"I told her it was probably her imagination and pleaded with her to come back and talk things out. But that was the wrong move. She accused me of calling her crazy and hung up on me."

He turns to me, and I can see the trepidation in his eyes—and now I finally understand. Although I've had a hunch about this all along, that something more sordid than an accident happened that day, I suddenly realize that I've wanted to be wrong. The implications of what I think he's about to tell me start to bounce around in my head.

Peter goes on to explain that he called Jeanine, but she didn't pick up, so he took Lydia to her soccer game, made an appearance, and then snuck off. He drove past Jeanine's house, but her car wasn't there. Then he drove to the parking lot of the trailhead and saw Jeanine's car parked near Cynthia's. But he had to get back to the game. He didn't have time to try to find them.

"I was about to drive away when Jeanine came rushing out of the trailhead. She looked rattled and confused, looking over her shoulder like she was worried she was being followed. I half expected Cynthia to come out after her, but she didn't. And then Jeanine got in her car. I didn't want to be seen with her there. The lot had gotten more crowded, so I moved my car out of her view. Then I followed her. She pulled over a mile or so down the road on Alpine, and I could see her sitting with her head in her hands. I pulled over behind her. I figured she'd had some kind of confrontation with Cynthia. She seemed upset, so I went over to talk to her."

At this point, I want to stop him. To press rewind. What if Jeanine killed her and Peter helped cover it up? Will I be an accomplice? But I can't unhear what I've already heard. So, I sit still, my eyes wide with anticipation while Peter collects his thoughts, and I brace myself for what's to come.

"She was surprised to see me, but then she told me everything was fine. That we could be together. That she told Cynthia about us: how I was in love with her, not Cynthia, how I was only staying out of guilt. Which wasn't true, by the way. Then she told me Cynthia had seen the light and was willing to let me go. At that point, I had no idea about Cynthia's accident. I figured my marriage was over, but I never wanted to see Jeanine again. And I told her that. Then it all went south from there."

"Cynthia's…accident?" I ask.

"Huh?"

"You still think what happened to Cynthia was an accident?"

"Well, I guess we've taken to calling it that. It's a euphemism."

"For suicide?"

"Well, yes. What else?"

"You don't think Jeanine might have had something to do with it?"

"What are you getting at?"

"How do you know Jeanine didn't push her off that cliff? That they didn't have some kind of altercation?"

"We're pretty sure she jumped, Laura, based on the position of the body when it landed. Although Jeanine's words might have pushed her in that direction. The police ruled the manner of death accidental, but only because her mother didn't want the scandal of a suicide. Her mother wanted it kept quiet, and she has a lot of pull in this town. That's why there wasn't much of an investigation. Coupled with her erratic history, it added up. We both tried to keep all that under wraps. The children were too young to process all of it."

I nod. It's starting to make sense. "Then what happened?"

"I left Jeanine on the side of the road and raced back to the soccer game to get Lydia."

"And you didn't know until later that day that something happened to Cynthia?"

Peter hesitates for a moment, and I start to feel bad for him, having to relive it all. Then he looks me in the eye. "I found out she was dead when the police came to the door."

"And Jeanine, she decided to just leave town?"

"Can we leave that part of the story for another time? Please? I really need a break from this."

"Sure."

I'm not done with this conversation, but we can take a break. I should probably give him some space now. I have

"Any idea who it might be?"

"Yes. A guy named Daniel Chen. He's a senior scientist on my team. He hounded me until I released the preprint, against my better judgment."

Shackler nodded.

"And I worked with him years ago. At another firm."

"Would this, perhaps, be the same firm you were at when Jeanine Randall left town?"

"It would."

"So maybe this Chen guy is onto you."

"Maybe."

"And this all might be connected."

"I think so. The first email: *I know what you did. I won't tell anyone.* It came right about the time we all realized that the data in the preprint might be off. The second one: *I won't tell if you don't.* That one came right after I started digging into the computer files, which Daniel would have known I was doing. The documents are all shared. After that, I went back to the lab logs—the notebooks we keep in the safe—and I saw that some entries were crossed out and corrected, ones that match the issue we're having. Only I have the code, but I changed it anyway just to make sure."

Shackler agrees that it sounds much more likely that the lab guy sent the emails and not Peter's daughter. If Daniel knows that Peter was behind the press leak that got the stock to rise at the other company years ago, he's probably going to hit him with some kind of demand any day now. Peter and Shackler discuss the options and come up with a plan. A plan to finally end this, once and for all.

Peter heads out, eager to get home. But as he's getting into his car, his phone buzzes with a text alert, one that sends him rushing to his office.

We got the approval.

When he arrives at the office, the place is buzzing with excitement, peppered with an undercurrent of desperation. The company has opened the trading window, and people are racing to file the appropriate paperwork and place their trades before loads of stock gets dumped on the market and possibly lowers the value. But Peter's got one piece of business to attend to first. He pulls out his cell phone, opens an app, and presses record. Then he calls in Daniel Chen.

"I guess this is good news, right?" Chen looks sheepish, and Peter's even more convinced he's right about him.

"Except for one thing," Peter says. "I checked the lab logs, Daniel. I noticed that some of the data entries were changed. Is there anything you'd like to tell me?"

The color drains from Chen's face. "I know how it looks. It was a mistake. My mistake, Peter. But I fixed it. It works now."

"What are you talking about?"

"Okay, when I pushed you to release the preprint? I was close, very close, and I knew I could get the drug to work for lung cancer. But I needed to get out that publication before my review so they'd keep me on. I was only temporary, remember?"

"Yes, I remember." Peter didn't actually remember, but he was mulling over the implications. Daniel would be desperate to become permanent so he could stay on until they got the approval and reap the rewards. Although the preprint wasn't a dealbreaker, he could see how Chen might perceive it that way.

"So, yeah, the data in the preprint. I exaggerated it to make it look better than it was. That's why the other team couldn't reproduce the results. But I figured out later how to make it work, so I went back and changed the tables and the logs. Then I told the other team I'd made a mistake in my instructions to them for the experiments, and I told them how to fix it. We got the news today that they were able to reproduce the results."

"So it actually works now?"

"Yes. It works."

This is very good news for Peter, and he thinks for a moment that maybe he shouldn't rock the boat, at least until he cashes out some stock. But he needs to find out the truth about Chen.

"Daniel. The emails. It was you, wasn't it?"

Chen shuffles his feet, stalling for time, obviously mulling over how to play this.

"Tell me the truth, Daniel, and this'll go a whole lot better for you. Lie to me again, and you're toast."

"I'm sorry, Peter. Yes, it was me. I had a hunch back then. When we found out someone leaked that fake story to the press, the one that got the stock to rise, I figured you might have been in on it, but I kept it to myself."

"What made you think it was me?"

"I overheard you and that woman. From IT. I could tell something was wrong. You two were arguing. Then she cashed out and disappeared a week later. I figured maybe you were in on it together."

"Well, we weren't. And I have no idea what you're talking about."

Chen's hand goes to his forehead. "I'm so sorry, Peter. I have family who's counting on me. Back home. I didn't make much off my stock at the last few jobs. Bad timing. I need this job. And money to bring them all here. It was nothing personal. But when I found out you were onto me—"

"So your plan was to blackmail me? So I'd keep what you did quiet?" Peter's not in the mood for a sob story. He needs to get the man on his phone, clearly admitting what he did.

"Yes."

"So what is it you want from me, Daniel? Money?"

"No. Nothing at all. I want nothing from you. I only want you to stay quiet like I stayed quiet for you. I don't want any trouble, Peter."

"You should have come to me, Daniel. Leveled with me. I went to bat for you to get you this job."

"I know."

"What you did is a crime. Fabricating the data to get the stock to rise."

"I know that too. I'm sorry."

Peter shuts off the recording and shows him the phone. "It's all recorded now, Daniel."

Chen looks down at his feet and then back up at Peter. "What are you going to do?"

"I'll tell you what. You take your gain. Cash out your stock. Now. Then give your two weeks' notice, and we go our separate ways. But I'll keep this recording, just in case. The statute of limitations has run out on the press leak, Daniel. Even if it was me, which I'm not saying it was, nobody can be prosecuted for that. What you did is an actionable federal crime. Do we have an understanding?"

"We have an understanding."

Chen exits the office with his head hanging low. With that out of the way, Peter hops on his computer to reap his rewards.

———

The house is quiet this afternoon, so I'm taking advantage of some rare alone time, although I know Lydia and Peter are due home any minute. It's been a strange week. I no longer feel like I'm on vacation. I feel like I'm unemployed—which I am, for the first time in my life. And although Lydia and I have been getting along pretty well, we can't do this forever. This property is smaller than our other house, and it feels like we're on top of each other. I think about leaving for awhile, and going to Honolulu, but we don't have much money.

I realize that nobody is to blame. Not really. Not even Peter. It's simply a series of difficult, if tragic, circumstances, so I try to power through. Bethany and I have been talking about starting a new company. She has some ideas and is looking for venture capital. It's a long shot, so I'm not counting on it. I'm surprised she's not more upset with me, but all of her ire is directed towards Chad and the other principals.

I go into the kitchen to fix some dinner. I like to cook, and I'm pretty good at it, so I've been experimenting with different dishes to give me something to do while I figure out what to do with the rest of my life. Today I'm making shrimp masala. I turn the burner on under the oil and garlic, and a savory smell fills the room. I add some ginger and a pinch of curry. The garlic sizzles, and I hear a pop as one of the spices combusts in the pan.

Then I hear the whir of the pin pad, and the front door creaks open. Delicate footfalls pad towards the kitchen. I dump the shrimp in the pan and stir frantically to get an even coating of spices on them. It smells great.

"Hey, Lydia. Hungry?" Nobody answers as I give the shrimp another stir, lower the heat, and turn around.

"Hello, Laura."

I've never had a gun pointed at me before. It's even more terrifying than I could have imagined. My feet sink into the floor like my body's giving up. It seems to know it's futile to protest. I know the door was locked. It locks automatically. She must have been watching the house and seen us punch in the pin pad code. Maybe she has been in here before, and it wasn't just my imagination playing tricks on me. That thought sends a chill up my spine.

"Hi, Emily." My hands lift in surrender. "I mean, Ella. How did you...?" Without really thinking, I reach down and turn off the stove.

"Don't move!"

My stomach lurches and I'm sensed with an over-whelming feeling of dread. Her hands are shaking. I wonder if she knows how to fire a gun or if she's even held one before. She's sweating, and somehow the fact that she's so nervous seems even worse to me than if she were comfortable with it. There's no telling what she might do.

"I have nothing against you, Laura. But you're standing in the way of fate."

"It doesn't have to be like this, Ella."

"Yes, it does. I read the letter. After I did the DNA test and saw I had a half sister. I found it. In my mother's closet."

What letter? What is she talking about?

But I don't dare challenge her.

"I see."

"My mother told me my dad died a hero in Iraq. She had photos of him. And her. She had this whole story. It was beautiful and tragic. But it was a lie. That was my uncle. And then she finally told me the truth about my father, after I found the letter and confronted her. And then I ran away, and she had that horrible accident—looking for me." Her eyes start to water, but she catches herself. "And it's all my fault."

"That must have been horrible, Ella. I'm so sorry."

"My mother and father. They still love each other, you see. And you're in the way."

"I'm in the way, you say?"

"Yeah."

"So, what do you want from me?"

"I want you out of the picture. I know my mom will re-member if I bring my dad to her. And then she'll get better. This is all my fault. I shouldn't have yelled at her that night. I told her I hated her for lying to me. She drove off to find me after I left. I have to make it up to her. Then they can finally be together. And she'll forgive me. I know it. She's done so much for me. I need to do this for her."

I decide my only chance is to play along.

"I understand, Ella. And none of this is your fault. But I'm planning to leave him anyway. I can't take all the lies. I know he was lying to me all along. And it's true, he's in love with another woman. So there's no need to harm me, okay? It will only make things worse."

"I don't believe you. Where's my dad?"

"He'll be home any minute now, and then we can talk this out. But you need to put the gun down."

Her jaw stiffens, and she hardens her stance. "No! You'll call the police. I'm not stupid, Laura. Let's go into the living room. And don't try to grab a knife, or I'll shoot you. I swear to God I will!"

She keeps the gun trained on me as she directs me with its movements. "Turn around," she commands. "Walk that way." Her wrists jerk the gun to the right, and I wonder if she might fire it by accident.

My mind is focused on survival as I walk, looking around for anything I can grab to try to disarm her, but we've not finished decorating yet. There are no large vases, no big lamps—those are still on back order—nothing I can use to defend myself.

We turn the corner into the living room, and my heart nearly stops beating as I take in the sight before me. It's Lydia with a gun pointed at Ella and, by default, aimed in my direction.

"Drop it, Ella."

Lydia has a gun? When did Lydia get a gun? And unlike Ella, she seems pretty comfortable with it.

We're in a standoff now, with Ella's gun on me and Lydia's on Ella. This is a disaster. I was pretty sure I could have talked Ella down, but now she'll be desperate. I hear faint sirens in the background, and I don't know if that's good or bad. Lydia's rational enough to drop the gun if the police come, but Ella's delusional. She might have a death wish.

But we don't have to wait for the police, because I hear a car drive up. It sounds like Peter's SUV. Someone's going to get shot before this is all over, I'm pretty sure of that, and it's anybody's guess who it will be. I want to call out to him, warn him, but I don't dare. Not with his two daughters waving their weapons around our living room.

Peter bursts through the door, and Ella spins around to face him. With her gun off me, I duck behind a chair, and then I try to calculate my chances of tackling her from behind before someone's gun goes off.

"Ella!" he says.

"Dad!" Ella replies.

Peter freezes when he sees she has a gun. For a moment, I'm hopeful that Peter will be able to talk her down. My husband's eyebrows raise as he takes it all in: Lydia to his right, Ella in front of him. Ella's gun is tilted down a bit like she might drop it, but she doesn't. Lydia's gun is still pointed at Ella, and the younger woman knows it. There's no good way out of this, save for Ella giving up. Peter's eyes dart back and forth between the two of them.

Then he hurls himself into the air, inserting his body between Ella and Lydia, trying to take Ella down. A gunshot rings out, and he falls to the ground. Ella screams and runs out the door as Lydia and I rush towards Peter.

"Dad!" Lydia cries out.

Has Peter been hit?

He's on the floor, struggling to push himself up. He's not dead, thank goodness. Was he shot? Or was it Ella? Or nobody?

Then we hear a car come skidding to a halt.

"Oh my God!" a voice cries out.

There's a moment of silence and then the thundering pop of another gunshot.

Peter pushes himself up and runs out the door as the insistent, deafening whine of police sirens fills the air.

TWENTY-NINE

Peter runs across the street on autopilot, barely noticing the woman in the driver's seat of the car, holding her head in her hands in despair and disbelief, obviously traumatized by what she witnessed. He runs over to Ella's body on the ground with a gun lying next to it, but he instinctively turns away as his stomach lurches. The blood. The smell of gunpowder. It's all too overwhelming. But then he notices a blood-stained piece of paper a few inches from her hand, and he quickly bends down and picks it up.

He's still trying to process everything that happened in the house: Lydia with a gun on Ella; Ella with a gun on Laura. He wonders why he has any sympathy at all for the young woman who caused it all. But when he looked into her eyes a few long moments ago, he felt a connection—a rather strong one.

If I didn't know she was my daughter, would I feel the same?

"Peter. Are you okay?"

It's Laura. She places her hand on his back. He looks over at his wife, feeling conflicted and confused, hoping she can at least try to understand on some level what he's going through. But she's not a mother. She's never had the visceral feeling of seeing yourself in the eyes of another human being, of knowing on a primal level that it's your job to protect them.

"I'm sorry, Laura, but it's not her fault. Not in the larger picture."

"I know. Don't worry about that now."

Two police cars come to a screeching halt. Two ambulances arrive next, joining the two police cars already blocking most of the street. Neighbors sneak hesitant peeks from their doorways and windows, unsure what to make of it all.

The driver is still in her car, sobbing, and Peter wonders why he's not having more of a reaction. It's then that he feels a burning sensation in his left arm. He looks over and sees blood seeping into the fabric of his beige polo shirt. Laura notices it too, and her eyes widen.

"Peter. Were you hit?"

He lifts up his sleeve a bit, and his arm stings even more when the air hits it. There's a cylindrical mark, a bit deeper than a scrape, on the outer edge of his shoulder. It's raw but not very deep. "It must have grazed me."

He suddenly feels a little light-headed, but he's not sure if it's due to the wound or simply the general stress of the situation. The burn is on his left side, so it must have been Ella who discharged her weapon. That's a bit of a comfort to him. Better than Lydia having to explain herself. *Is her weapon even legal?* Peter had no idea she owned a gun.

A pair of EMTs tend to Ella although it's obvious that she's gone, while two police officers, a man and a woman, invite Laura and him to go back into the house. Another male officer is with the driver, who is just now getting out of her car.

"She came out of nowhere. I almost hit her. And then she took the gun and turned it to herself and ..." but the driver didn't need to finish the sentence. It was obvious to everyone what happened next.

Peter starts to feel nauseous as he takes it all in, barely able to process all of it. Then the female officer notices his arm.

"Let's get that looked at." Then she turns to Laura. "Ma'am? You can go into the house with Officer Taylor. Sir, you go with the EMT."

Peter protests, insisting that he's fine, but the officer pushes back. They have procedures, she informs him in a tone that makes it clear this is a directive, not a suggestion.

Peter does as he's told, and watches Officer Taylor, a kind-looking young man who appears to be in his mid-twenties, escort his wife into the house.

"Thanks for your cooperation, Mrs. Foster." The young officer is polite and comforting, not like the ones who grilled me at work. I wonder if that's due to his age or simply the different circumstances.

I've just about finished telling him what happened, and it sounds even more bizarre the more I reflect on it. Peter's troubled love child tried to kill me four times, and then my husband risked his life to try to keep us all alive. I'm trying to focus on the fact that Peter was willing to sacrifice him-self to end it all and save us—and not dwell on the realiza-tion that he's got a soft spot for Ella. The fact that it bothers me at all makes me feel like a monster, which I'm not. But she did try to kill me, so I can't be too hard on myself.

They've called the detective assigned to our case and filled her in on the news; they can stop looking for Ella Simpson here, in Nevada, and everywhere except the morgue.

He questioned Lydia, too; she offered a matter-of-fact explanation for the weapon, and she's got all the requisite permits. Gran, she said, insisted on it when she moved out on her own. A woman of means needs to be able to protect herself, Gran said. *Rich people problems.*

But then again, what would have happened to me oth-erwise? Lydia may have saved my life. And now she and her handgun can move back to their own place. Me? Even after all this, I wouldn't be caught dead with a weapon in my home. I hate guns, and I'm even more adamant about it now that I've stared down the business end of a barrel.

Peter comes in, a bit pale. His face looks twisted like he's in pain. "She's gone," he says. Which we knew, so I'm assuming he's saying this more to himself than to us.

"I'm sorry," I reply.

Although this makes our future much less compli-cated, it's such a sad story, and I feel for him. This, on top of the tragedy that's already befallen this family. Even Lydia looks somber, and I wonder if she felt any kind of connec-tion to her half sister or noticed the resemblance at all.

I stand up and embrace my husband. Then he releases me and shares a moment with Lydia. Officer Taylor gives us space, and I'm grateful that he's so perceptive and compassionate. But our home is still a crime scene, he reminds us, and we need to get out of the way and let them do their thing.

"I'm going to see Christopher," Lydia says. "We haven't seen much of each other lately, with all that's been going on. But first, I'll pack up my stuff and head home. Give you two your privacy back."

"There's no rush," I say.

"Thanks, Laura. But it's fine. And I've already texted Carson. He's relieved that it's over."

Carson. Right. We've left him out of the loop on all of this, again. We need to reach out to him more. He's so low-maintenance I almost forget about him sometimes, but that's no excuse.

"And I'll call off the security too." Lydia seems pretty calm about all of this, and the fact that she's taking charge is fine with me.

The police have already questioned Peter, but they will be here for a while processing the crime scene. They reminded us that it's an ongoing investigation and we shouldn't venture too far or leave town. The last time I heard that, back at the office, my heart started to race. But I'm not too concerned about it today. I'm a pro now. That's what they always say.

THIRTY

Two days have passed since Ella tried to kill me. We haven't talked about it much to each other, although we've had our fill of talking to the police. We haven't really connected that much about anything; we've both been sort of going through the motions the last few days, but we're trying to find our way through this and back to each other. Now Peter and I are at our favorite Italian restaurant, tucked in the back, and it reminds me of our dinner years ago when Peter first professed his love to me. Something behind the sadness in his eyes is fighting to break through. Is it that same happy memory?

I haven't had a chance to ask him about the letter Ella mentioned. I want to but maybe not now. I told the police about it, but Peter was still outside. Chances are he knows as little as I do, and we can leave it for another time.

"I actually have some good news. I was planning to share it with you when I got home the other day. But then..." Peter shrugs.

"Right. So? What's the news?"

He smiles and looks me in the eye. "The FDA approval. We got it. Late that afternoon."

"That's great!" My eyes widen, but I try not to look too excited, being mindful of his emotions about Ella. I fight to suppress my grin.

"It's okay to be happy, Laura. You've been through so much. We all have. And I'm so relieved that you're out of danger now and this nightmare is over. I'm sorry it's all so… complicated."

"I know, Peter. It's okay. Really. Let's not focus on that tonight."

"Great idea."

"So, have they opened the trading window?"

"Um, yes. About that. I was planning to talk to you before I acted on it, but I stopped by the office that day, and the consensus was we should place a trade as soon as possible, at least take some of the gain, before everyone joins in. So I cashed out enough to tide us over. Less than half of it. Sorry I didn't talk to you first. It was all kind of frenetic."

"I trust your judgment."

Peter nods.

"And?" I say.

"And what?" He smirks.

"Stop it, you. How much do we have to 'tide us over'?"

He smiles and floats me a figure.

I widen my eyes, but only for show. My dad and I had already calculated it. "I guess we'll have to make do."

"I love you so much, Laura." He takes my hands in his, raises them to his lips, and kisses them softly.

"I love you too, babe."

"So, what do you want to do with the rest of your life?" Peter asks.

"What do you mean?"

"I mean, you can do anything you want now. We've got enough money. Start a company. Start a nonprofit. Train for the Kona Ironman."

"It's a bit too much to process right now. Nobody's trying to kill me anymore, so I'll sit with that for a bit. What about you?"

"I'm already doing what I want."

"Biotech?"

"Curing cancer."

"A worthy cause. I need to find one. I'll think it over and get back to you."

I can do anything I want now, and somehow that thought terrifies me a bit. But I'm sure I'll get used to it.

———

I'm in bed, wrapped in Peter's arms, and I can hear his heart beating in his chest. It's a sound I haven't heard in a while, and it soothes me. I think about all we've been through, and it amazes me that we've come out of this with our relationship intact. He's gently stroking my hair, and I don't want to break the comfortable, post-lovemaking silence. But then he speaks.

"I love you," he says. He's still stroking my hair.

"I love you too."

I roll over so I can look at him, and he props himself up on his elbow.

"I guess things are looking up," I say. He brushes back the hair from my face. There's something on my mind, and I've been weighing out whether or not to bring it up.

"Seems like you and Lydia are doing much better these days."

"I guess all of this craziness brought the two of us closer."

"Nice that something positive came out of it. She's a good one to have on your side."

"That's for sure."

I think about the fact that she may have saved my life. What would Ella have done if Lydia hadn't pulled a gun on her? And I'm glad that it's all behind us.

But is it really?

"Peter?"

"Yes?"

"When you said that you were relieved it couldn't have been Jeanine after you found out about her accident, do you think she's... dangerous?"

"Huh?"

"I mean, it crossed your mind, that she could be targeting me. Why?"

"She's bedridden, Laura. With no memory or functional capability."

"She could recover," I offer.

"I think she's pretty far gone."

"You didn't answer my question."

I actually had Shackler investigate this for me, and from what he found out, Jeanine isn't *that* far gone. It's not like she's brain-dead. They say she's in a "minimally conscious state," with no memory of her previous life but with some intermittent periods of rudimentary awareness. It's possible she could recover. Not probable, but possible. But I don't want Peter to know I've looked into this. How would that look? It seems so insensitive, but then he's not the one who had four attempts on his life.

Peter flips to his back and stares up at the ceiling in silence for a few moments. Then he turns his head to me.

"Jeanine was pretty vindictive in all of this. Said all kinds of nasty things to Cynthia. She knew what could happen, that Cynthia was unstable, and she did it anyway. I feel like she was trying to push her over the edge. Figuratively speaking. But then, she was angry, and for good reason."

"Right."

"But she didn't come after you when we first got together, so I don't see why she'd do it now, even if she could."

"Okay. But I still don't get why she left right after Cynthia died."

"We had words, Laura. She knew it was over, and she felt humiliated. I lashed out at her. Blamed her for the suicide. But I can't talk about this anymore right now, okay? We've been over and over this so many times. Can't we finally move on? Please?"

He sits up and swings his legs over the side of the bed like he's going to get up and leave. I put my hand on his shoulder to stop him.

"Don't leave. I want to move on. I really do. And I promise I'll never say another word about it again."

At least not to you.

My husband gets back in bed and leans against the headboard. I put my hand on his thigh and stroke it gently. He smiles at me and grabs his book off the nightstand. I decide I've had enough of this for tonight, but the truth is, despite what I just said, I'm not going to feel completely at ease until Jeanine Randall is dead and buried.

THIRTY-ONE

Peter's sitting in Shackler's office, which looks quite tidy and professional compared to a month or so ago: sleek new office furniture, a fresh coat of paint, more flattering lighting. A large filing cabinet has replaced the stacked-up boxes. *Nice to see the hefty fees he's charging me are being put to good use.* They've got some unfinished business to discuss, and then Peter's hoping to close out the case and put this all behind him.

"So, you got the approval?" Shackler asks, spinning his pen between his fingers as he leans back in his comfy new ergonomic chair.

"Yes. We did."

"Congratulations."

"Thanks."

"So, how did it go with your lab guy?"

Peter's about to brief the investigator on his little interlude with Daniel Chen when Shackler's cell buzzes.

"Will you excuse me for a bit? It's an emergency of sorts."

"Of course." Peter ducks into the foyer, which has retained its vintage look. Shackler closes the office door behind him.

Peter doesn't have a lot of close guy friends or anyone he can confide in, and he has to admit Shackler's grown on him. He's a stand-up guy, and Peter's impressed by the fact that he looked into Cynthia's case to protect Laura, even if it was because he suspected him. Shackler's also not stupid, and Peter senses that he might uncover something later, on his own, about what actually happened the day of Cynthia's death—and that wouldn't be good.

It was a cold fall morning by Northern California standards—in the low forties. He'd gotten the call from Cynthia around eight thirty claiming Jeanine was following her, and he'd been trying to reach Jeanine with no luck. When he arrived at the soccer field for Lydia's game, the team was still warming up. He delivered Lydia to her coach, made the parent rounds, and ducked out without anyone noticing. He had about ninety minutes at most.

He raced over to the parking lot at Windy Hill Preserve. When he spotted Jeanine's car near Cynthia's, he knew it was game over for his marriage if he didn't intercept her. Jeanine would go for the jugular, make it sound as horrible and sordid as possible, and he could hardly blame her. It's not like he tried to lead her on; he simply changed his mind once he got to know her. But she had voice mails from him. Text messages saying he loved her, and he knew she'd use them. She'd threatened it many times when she was in one of her angry moods. Then she'd do a one-eighty. Start crying. Pleading with him not to be mad at her. It was sad, and he felt bad about it. But until that day, he had no idea what she was actually capable of.

When he arrived, he saw Jeanine stumbling out of the trailhead, looking rattled. He didn't want to be seen there talking to her. He stayed in his car and followed her to the turnout, where she pulled over like he told Laura. And that's where the story diverges.

He walked up to her car, and she put down her window.

"Why were you following Cynthia? I told you. It's over between us, Jeanine. I'm sorry if I hurt you. I really am. But you have to accept it and move on."

"No, Peter. It's not. We can be together now."

Her eyes were red and swollen, and he gathered there had already been some kind of confrontation. *Damn it.* He was too late.

"What does that mean, Jeanine? What happened?"

"I'm sorry, but it's for the best. She didn't deserve you."

It hit Peter that Jeanine was speaking of his wife in the past tense, and he lost it. He opened the door, pulled her out of her car, and pushed her up against it.

"What the hell did you do, Jeanine?"

"Peter! Stop! You're hurting me!"

"Sorry." He was pressing too hard as he gripped her arms, the adrenaline surging inside him. He relaxed his grip but kept his hands where they were, forcing her to look him in the eye.

"Did something happen? Did you kill her?"

Then her look turned stone-cold, like something in her snapped. "No! I didn't kill her, Peter. Calm down! And get your hands off me. She got what she deserved."

He removed his hands and let a car pass by, but then he gripped her jacket and pulled her in close.

"What does that mean? Tell me what happened, Jeanine. *Now.*" He spoke through clenched teeth, his face a mere inch or so from hers, and his heart was pounding in his chest.

"I told her the truth! Since you were too much of a coward to do it yourself. How you were better off with me. How great the sex was with me. I showed her some of your steamy text messages. I told her you thought she was a terrible mother. That the kids would be better off with me. I was hoping she'd see that it was better for her to let go and let us be together. And I think she finally saw the light."

Peter's anger exploded. He started to shake her, and he could feel his face flush with rage. "What the hell have you done?" Her head wobbled back and forth like a rag doll's. He saw the fear in her eyes, came to his senses, and let go. But he'd already gone too far.

"You bastard! How dare you lay a hand on me?" She shoved him back towards the road. "I did it for you. For us. You've never been happy with her, Peter. Admit it."

He ran his hands through his hair as sweat dripped down from his temples, trying to figure out a way to salvage this. Peter had always tried so hard to control his temper, especially around women. How had he let this happen?

"I have to try, Jeanine. We have children. You knew that going in."

"This is all your fault, Peter. You think you can use me like this and then throw me away when you're done? I'm sure people at work know about us. I'll be forever branded. And you get to go on and live your life? With your rich heiress wife, who doesn't give a crap about you or her children? I don't think so!"

She reached for her car door and grabbed the handle. Peter walked towards her, holding up his hands in surrender. "Jeanine. Calm down. Nobody knows about us."

She got in her car and slammed the door. His stomach sank.

What have I done?

Peter's head was spinning, trying to figure out a way to undo the damage. "I'm sorry. Wait. Please. We need to talk."

"Get away from me!" She started up the car.

"Where are you going?"

"To ruin your life," she called out to him through the open window. "Like you ruined mine. I'm reporting you to the police, Peter. You assaulted me just now."

"Please, Jeanine. Be reasonable. I didn't assault you. I'm sorry. I just got carried away. We can work this out."

"And then I'm going to frame you for murder."

"Murder?" His stomach lurched. "So you did kill her? Jeanine!" Peter was yelling at her, but he'd lost his leverage. She was about to drive off.

"I didn't kill her, Peter. I already told you that."

"So she's okay?"

"I didn't say that either."

He crouched down and looked her in the eye, appealing to her sense of decency. "Quit messing with me, Jeanine.

Please. My marriage is over. You got what you wanted. I'm sure she'll divorce me. Isn't that enough for you?"

"No, Peter. It's not."

"What else do you want from me?" Peter was expecting her to say she wanted him, wanted to get back together. But she didn't.

"What do I want? I want to leave here and never come back. And to do that, I need a million dollars. And you're going to get it for me."

"Right. And why the hell would I do that?"

"Because if you don't, like I said, I'll frame you for murder. I'm sure you left bruises on my arm when you grabbed me. You don't know your own strength. I'll use them to prove how dangerous you are. It's always the husband, Peter. Who do you think they'll believe?"

"What murder, Jeanine? What are you even talking about? You just said Cynthia was alive."

"No, Peter. I said I didn't kill her, which is true. She jumped when she found out the truth about us. A million dollars, Peter. Or your life is over."

Jeanine sped away, leaving Peter and the remnants of his broken life on the side of the road. At the time, he wasn't sure what to believe. Mostly, he was hoping that Jeanine was simply messing with his head and that Cynthia was fine. But he called for help, just in case, from a pay phone up the road.

After his worst fears were confirmed, he still could not bring himself to believe that Jeanine was capable of cold-blooded murder. At the time, he figured it was more likely that Cynthia committed suicide, as Jeanine said. But now that he thinks about it, he could imagine them having some kind of altercation. Maybe Jeanine didn't kill her intentionally. Maybe there was a scuffle, and Cynthia fell. He'd never know for sure. But back then, he realized pretty quickly that his best shot was pushing the suicide theory, calming Jeanine down, and getting her out of town. And luckily for him, his mother-in-law wanted to shut down the investigation as quickly as possible.

Shep's door opens and snaps Peter back into the present.

"Sorry about that. You want to pick up where we left off?" The PI is standing in the doorway of his office now, poking his head into the foyer.

Peter came so close to unburdening himself to Laura about this that he could taste it. If he were a religious man, he'd go to confession. But he's not. So he's decided he'll divulge all of this to Shep Shackler. This also has the added benefit of invoking privilege, so Shackler can't use it against him, which would be the case if he found out on his own. A win-win.

"Sure." Peter stands up and strolls back into the office. "So where were we?"

"Actually, Shep, there's something else I want to tell you first." He sits back and crosses his legs. "About Jeanine and my late wife. And the day she was killed. Off the record, that is."

"Okay, then." Shackler puts down his pen, leans back, and crosses his arms.

Peter takes a deep breath and clears his throat.

"Whenever you're ready. Take your time."

And then Peter starts in, recounting the events of that fateful day. He's trying to read the investigator, but Shackler's got a pretty good poker face. The man seems unfazed like he'd already suspected something was up. *Good thing I decided to tell him the truth.* When he finishes, the investigator's nodding like it all makes sense to him now.

"I always suspected there was more to it. So it was you? Who called for help from the pay phone?"

"It was me. Yes. At that point, I still wasn't sure if anything had even happened. I thought, or maybe I hoped, that Jeanine was only messing with my head, trying to make me sweat, but I wanted to get help there as soon as possible, just in case."

"So you didn't know for sure until the police came to your house? That she was dead?"

"Right."

"Wow."

"Yeah."

"And you got Jeanine her money. Through the stock scheme."

"Yeah."

"And she left town."

"Yes. But I pointed out to her that since she was the one who'd followed Cynthia, I could just as easily implicate her. Plus, they concluded pretty quickly that the manner of death was accidental, so she lost most of her leverage. The position of the body. If she'd been pushed hard intentionally, it would have landed differently. Or that's what they concluded. Cynthia's mother didn't want it classified as a suicide, although that was the general consensus, and she didn't want much of an investigation either. I think she knew about Cynthia's affair, and she didn't want to bring the tabloids down on the family. But nobody knows about Jeanine being there that day, and I'd like to keep it that way."

"I see."

He doesn't feel the need to tell Shackler that he buttered up Jeanine by telling her what she wanted to hear. And by sleeping with her one last time, which, in hindsight, turned out to be a very bad move. He still cared deeply for her, he'd professed, but they couldn't be together after all that had happened; surely she could see that. But it wasn't as sordid or manipulative as it sounded. He cared about Jeanine, even if she wasn't "the one." They'd known each other for years and were friends prior to the affair. And he knew she was right; it was all his fault. He felt better about the fact that their last encounter was a tender one. He even left her a nice love note, hoping it would ease her pain and lessen the chances of her retaliating in the future—another bad move. He flashes back to the weathered piece of paper he found near Ella's body.

What we had together most people never experience in a lifetime. I'll always care about you, but you know we can't be together now, not after everything that's happened. You'll always have a place in my heart, and know that I'm with you always. All my love to you.

Still, the guilt ate away at him over the years, along with the fear that Jeanine would resurface and retaliate, which is why he abstained from relationships after Cynthia's death—until he met Laura. Peter had no idea where Jeanine had gone, and he hoped after all that time, she'd moved on too, but he was still holding his breath for the first few years he was with Laura. If he'd known about Ella, he'd have done right by her, but it was too late to dwell on that. Hopefully, the fact that he'd risked his life to try to save their daughter somehow evened the karmic score a bit.

"And how did it all go with your lab guy?"

"Let's just say I don't think he'll be bothering me anymore."

After filling him in on the Daniel Chen situation, Peter exits Shackler's office for what he hopes will be the last time.

Shep has to hand it to Peter Foster. For a time, he thought the guy was a tool. But he's pretty smooth; he underestimated the guy for sure. Telling him the whole story about Cynthia's death before he had a chance to dig it up himself? Brilliant. Now Shep's hands are pretty much tied, at least if he wants to stay in business as a PI.

Foster's not a murderer, but he did withhold information, and he did lie to the police. Now, nobody will ever be the wiser. He says he told most of the story to his wife, but who knows? She seems like a nice lady, better than the other two he got involved with. And for a moment, Shep can't help but wonder if it all didn't work out a little too well for the guy.

But it's not his problem, and Shep's curiosity's been satisfied—at least for now. The case is closed, and he's got a nice fat, juicy invoice to send off to the nouveau riche Fosters, which will fund a much-needed vacation. Somewhere nice. And maybe some new furniture for the lobby.

THIRTY-TWO

It's been two weeks since all the drama unfolded, and it seems like our family is getting back to normal. We've gotten our dining room set—a light midcentury made of solid maple about half the size of our former one, with comfortable upholstered chairs a shade lighter than their wooden legs. We're hosting the kids for dinner tonight, and it feels like a big moment to me. The past is gone, and we are all moving forward. Carson's here, and Peter's chatting with him in the living room. I place a tray of cheese and crackers on the coffee table and sit with them. They drink beer out of the bottle while I sip my Pinot Grigio.

"How's school going?" Peter asks. He's nearly halfway through the first semester of his senior year, and we're all wondering what his plans are for the future.

"It's fine, Dad." Carson's a quiet one, like his father. We never know for sure what's going on in that mind of his. He's always been a good student and an easy child, although I sense there's more to him than meets the eye. All of the recent revelations must have had an impact, but I can't get a read on him.

"We haven't seen much of you lately. What have you been up to?" Peter asks.

"The usual. Hanging out with friends. Studying."

I wonder if he's dating someone, but I don't want to put him on the spot. As if reading my mind, he finally discloses something.

"Oh, and, well, I'm seeing someone. A girl I met in my LSAT prep class." He smiles, and I see him blush a little. In that one sentence, we've gotten more breaking news than in the last year of conversations with him.

"Wait. LSAT prep class?" I say. "You're applying to law school?"

"Yeah, didn't I tell you?"

"Um, no," Peter says. "I think we would remember that, Carson."

"I think it's great! What made you decide on law school?" That's probably a stupid question, and I'm not expecting much of a response.

"Nothing in particular. Just something I've been think-ing about for a while."

"Okay," I say. "Now, tell us about the girl." I'm happy that they met in the LSAT class because that means he's not doing it simply to please some young woman.

Carson gives us the rundown. She's a senior at a nearby college, and they've been on a few dates, and that's about as far as we get when Lydia knocks on the front door and I let her in. She joins us in the living room. I get her a glass of wine as she settles into a chair across from Carson and her dad. When I come back, she's got a giant grin on her face, but she's uncharacteristically silent. It feels like she's playing some kind of game. When I come back with her wine, we're all looking at each other, waiting for someone to speak.

"So, did you know that Carson's decided to apply to law school?" I say.

"Yes! He told me. You didn't know?"

"I guess we were the last to find out," Peter replies.

I think about mentioning the fact that we've all had a lot on our minds lately, but then I think better of it. We all want to move on and forget the trauma of the last few months. Lydia still has this Cheshire cat grin on her face, and I'm wondering what the hell is up. Then she brings her left hand to her face, and I see it. A giant rock glistening on her ring finger.

"Lydia? Did you and Christopher—"

"Yes! We got engaged!"

She jumps up and runs over to me. We hug, and then she moves on to Peter and then to Carson. And then, of course, we get the entire rundown on the proposal. How he did it, where he did it, and how she felt when he did it. We've only met him in passing, and this seems a little rushed to me, but I don't say anything.

Then I look over at Carson, his thunder officially stolen, and I can't help but feel for him, always in Lydia's shadow. But he seems fine with it, if I had to guess from his body language, and maybe even a bit relieved that it's taken the pressure off him and our prying into his love life. I let them relax and talk and head into the kitchen to put the finishing touches on dinner, our first family dinner in our new home.

As I start to make dinner, I notice I'm not very hungry. I actually feel a bit nauseous, and I haven't been sleeping well. My hands are shaky and my pulse is racing again.

Everything seems perfect, so why am I still so anxious?

It could be the aftermath of all of the stressful events in our lives. I realize that my life, up until the last few months, has been delightfully dull, and I like it that way. Ella's out of our lives, and, although the truth coming out the way it did was hard on all of us, we've all grown closer from it. But there's an undercurrent of tension, and there's only one explanation I can think of.

Jeanine Randall. She's the elephant in the room. Maybe Peter isn't concerned about her, but I am, and I bet the children are, too. And I need to do something about it to make me and my family feel more secure. As I said, I won't be completely comfortable until she's gone for good.

———

Shep's final check from the Foster case came in. It was a big one, and he realizes he misses the case, but not because of the money. It's back to the same old boring ones as before. A cheating spouse. A missing dog. Yes, someone actually hired him to find a missing dog. Money is money, and they're paying him handsomely, but he feels like maybe he needs to do something more with his life.

It's too late to join the FBI or make any major career changes. He gave up his job on the force years ago, thinking it would help his marriage, but it failed anyway, and he still hasn't found anyone he wants to settle down with.

After Foster's nightmare stories, he's even more reluctant to get serious with anyone. He's still seeing the same lady, though. An attractive accountant who's happy to keep things interesting yet casual; she's perfect for him.

His cell phone buzzes and it's an unfamiliar number but it's from the local area code, so he picks up. To his complete surprise, it's Laura Foster—and she wants to retain his services to keep tabs on Jeanine Randall and her medical condition. *Laura Foster's a smart lady. I'd be wary of Jeanine, too.* Laura asks him for a meeting time, and he has to fight the urge to tell her to come right over. He asks her to hang on while he stalls a bit, not wanting to appear too eager.

"I can squeeze you in tomorrow. Around ten," he says.

"Tomorrow at ten sounds great."

Then he goes on line and books a trip to St. Lucia for himself and his lady friend, for a few weeks out. A vacation will do him good; he knows it's a little odd to be this excited about Laura Foster's phone call but there's something about this case that makes him feel alive. Maybe getting some distance from work will do him good.

———

I feel so much better now that I have that appointment lined up. We're seated at the new table, and I am closer to my family than ever. After living like an outsider for so long, it's great to finally feel a part of it. My stepdaughter almost saved my life, and I look over at her and marvel at how far we've come.

Peter and Carson are talking about his future in the field of law, and Peter offers to introduce Carson to his lawyer friend and maybe have him intern there.

I'm still not used to the fact that my life is my own now. That I can do whatever I want. I've lived around fabulously wealthy people for over a decade, and while we've never been destitute, I've always felt a bit out of place in terms of income level. I don't want money to change us, and I vow that I'll do something positive with it, and not just for myself.

"So Carson?" I say when there's a lull. "Are you planning to tell us any more about this new friend of yours?"

He blushes again, but I wanted to give him a chance to tell us, since he was interrupted by Lydia's news.

"She's nice," he says. "We're going away for a long weekend soon." Then he goes back to his dinner. I take that as a sign that it's at least somewhat serious, and that makes me smile. Then Lydia chimes in.

"Speaking of going away, I'm thinking about a destination wedding."

I catch Peter's eye and we smile at each other. It's comfortable and happy and warm, and I hope that it stays this way forever.

THIRTY-THREE

I t's been nearly a month since the final attempt on my life, and things are getting pretty much back to normal. My former company imploded. Wrong place, wrong time. They didn't want to pursue my idea of letting colleges advertise to students, and with the sudden proliferation of free AI apps on the market that can write essays, nobody's going to pay for ApplAI. They're liquidating. I really dodged a bullet, and I have to laugh at the fact that I mean that literally as well as figuratively. Never did I think I'd get fired and then stare down the barrel of a gun in the space of a week—and then have it all turn around. Life is good now, so I've decided not to pursue any action against them; there's nothing to take, and I want to move on.

I'm walking into The Reef, a small bistro on Route 1 across from Ocean Beach, to meet my parents for lunch. When I spot them in the lobby, Dad has his arm around Mom, and he's talking softly into her ear. Then he notices me as I walk up to greet them.

"Laura." Dad squeezes me tight. My mother tears up a bit but catches herself. She pats her eyes with her fingers and smiles at me. It's the first time I've seen them since the nightmare ended, and we're all experiencing a bit of let-down stress.

"I'm fine, Mom." I hug her as the hostess stands back and waits for us to have our moment.

"Right this way," she says after a bit, and we follow her.

It's late afternoon, and she seats us at a table near the window. We can see the ocean with its rolling whitecaps across the way, and it reminds me of happy times growing up on Kailua Beach. I want to get back home more often, and now I'll be able to do that. I'm even planning to try to qualify for the Kona Ironman this year, a lifelong goal of mine that's within reach now that I'll have time to train.

They fill me in on the latest happenings with my brother and his family, who are planning to come out for Christmas so we can all be together. They were visiting him when all of this drama with Ella came to a head. I know they're dying to ask me *What now?* and while it's my father's nature to exercise restraint, it's curious that my mother has contained herself for this long, so I'm not surprised when she starts in a moment later.

"So, Laura. We were wondering—" Mom says.

"Dotty!" Dad widens his eyes at her as if they'd decided beforehand that she wouldn't pry. He's smiling, though. My mom is my mom, and we both love her for it.

She offers a halfhearted apologetic shrug.

"What I'm going to do with the rest of my life?" I smile.

"Basically."

"I've got some ideas." I can predict what's going to come next.

"Laura, with that kind of money, you could make a real difference in the world."

"I know that."

"Well, what's Peter planning to do?" she asks.

"Peter?"

"Yes. Peter. Your husband?"

"He's not planning to do anything. He's staying at his job."

"Really?" Dad says.

"Yeah. He's a true believer. He wants to cure cancer. They've got a lot of ideas and ample funding. He's not planning to make any moves."

"And you?" Mom asks. "Have you thought about a nonprofit? Something in your wheelhouse? Women in STEM, maybe?"

Dad shakes his head. "Give her some time, Dot."

"It's fine, Dad. I actually have made a decision."

"Oh?" Mom's brow furrows.

"I'm starting an accelerator. For early-stage female entrepreneurs."

"That's an interesting way to go," she says.

"Only two percent of VC capital went to women in 2021." Dad spouts figures like my mom drops literary references. He's on top of all of it and immediately sees the bigger picture.

I can tell my mother's a bit disappointed that I'm not starting an educational foundation or tackling homelessness, or taking on another one of her pet causes. Then she and Dad get into a brief debate. Dad lectures her about the merits of capitalism over socialism. Mom points out its excesses: the widening wealth gap, worker exploitation. I lean back and take it all in.

"Anyway," I interrupt, "that's what I'm doing."

"That's great, honey," she says.

I've decided to hire Mina as my executive director, I tell them, and I've already contacted Bethany and asked her to pitch. She's drawing up a proposal, and I'd be thrilled to fund her idea—if it's a good one.

And then we move on to other topics because, beyond that, there's not much to tell. Not a lot is changing. Peter's staying at his job. We're staying in our house, although I'm going to rent something in Honolulu and go back and forth, partly because I want to reconnect with my past but also because it's easier for in-state residents to qualify for the Kona Ironman. Lydia and Christopher's engagement means we'll also be planning a wedding. They're thinking of having it in the islands, so I've offered to do some of the legwork. I'm thrilled that Carson's decided to apply to law school, even if it sort of came out of the blue. He wants to practice corporate law, which is good; I can't see him as a litigator.

We're trying to focus on our present and forget the past, and after getting the news that Jeanine Randall died, I'm feeling a whole lot better. If that makes me a horrible person, then so be it. I've never thought of myself as the type of person who could be happy about someone's death, but then I never thought anyone would try to kill me. And I'm still not convinced that she didn't push Cynthia off that cliff. But I've had my share of drama and mind-blowing revelations for one year, and I don't need to know any more. For now, we can simply move on and enjoy be a normal, happy family.

EPILOGUE

One month later

My hands are shaking and my stomach is in knots. I've played the video Shackler sent me over and over, and I'm still not sure if he's simply seeing things that aren't there or if he's possibly onto something. It was taken the day Jeanine Randall was pronounced dead. A young man with dark hair in an orderly's uniform walks out a side door of the care home she's in. He looks around quickly, rips off his mask, scratches his nose, and puts it back on. Then he disappears from the camera's view. He never looks directly at the camera, so it's hard to tell for sure, but he does bear a striking resemblance to Carson, my stepson, as Shackler pointed out.

What should I do?

My mind is racing and my palms are getting sweaty as my mind runs through all the possible explanations. Of course, there's a strong probability that it's not him. It's hard to tell from the video. It could be anyone.

Right?

But then I flash back to the dinner we had at the old house, when Carson asked about his mother's suicide. That look on his face. It was a look I'd never seen on him before, however understandable his anger was to all of us.

Could it be him in the video?

I remind myself that Shackler took it upon himself to look into my husband and Jeanine Randall, so I doubt he will let this go, even if I tell him to stop. But I have to try. I have to give Carson the benefit of the doubt until I have more information. Even if it's him in the video, it doesn't mean he killed her. Maybe he just went to see her, to get some kind of closure.

But what should I do right now?

I'll tell Shackler something to throw him off Carson's trail, make up some kind of alibi for Carson. He's not a police officer, so I don't think that could get me in any legal trouble. I can always backpedal and say I got my days mixed up if anything comes of it. He might not believe me, but at least I can buy myself some time and figure out how to find out the truth on my own; I'm starting to regret bringing him into this.

Because the timing is positively terrible. In all the confusion, moving from my home to my parents and back, I missed some of my birth control pills. When I realized yesterday that I was about a week late, I hoped it was caused by all the stress from our recent happenings. But today I decided I'd better find out for sure.

About an hour ago, I found myself shocked but a little excited by the two solid lines on the pregnancy test I held in my hand. I've never wanted children of my own, so I was surprised by the warm feeling that enveloped me as I took it all in. We don't have money problems, and most of our troubles are behind us. If there were ever a time in my life that I could handle this, it's now.

But what about this video?

I pick up the phone, call Shackler, inform him he's mistaken, that Carson could not have been in Nevada that day, and I tell him his services are no longer needed.

It's not Carson. It can't be.

And that's all I can handle for now.

———

Two months later

I'm sitting at an outdoor table at Peet's Coffee in Menlo Park, which sits across from a small, grassy town square with some benches and trees. Calling it a park is a stretch, but I guess that's what it is. Hip-hop music blares out from the exercise studio a few doors down. I'm looking over Bethany's proposal on my computer when I stop and glance across the park and notice him.

He's a small boy, around seven I'd guess, and he's bouncing his way diagonally across the square to the rhythm of the music towards his parents. One beat, he kicks up his leg. The next, he spins around. He circles back a few times, flashing his hands in the air. Then he crouches into a faux break dance position and spins around.

I smile as I watch, his total lack of inhibition stirring something deep inside me. The excitement of simply being alive, the wonderment that only a child can feel at every-day life—and before too long, I'll have one of my own. I'm not giving up on my dreams or on any of my goals though, including the Ironman or my accelerator. And I'm not going to take much time off from work either. I love what I'm doing, and I can handle doing it all.

It came out in casual conversation that Carson was away the weekend Jeanine Randall died, on a getaway with his girlfriend who we have yet to meet. I relayed that information to Shackler and washed my hands of it. I've never been the type to go looking for trouble, and I don't want to start now.

But I must confess, in the dark of night, I still think about that video now and then. I wake up and picture the look on Carson's face that night at dinner, and I start to feel a pounding in my chest. I breathe through it, hoping that the burst of adrenaline isn't having a negative effect on my baby. And then I tell myself it's not him. It can't be him. It will all turn out okay. Maybe there will come a time when I need to look into this further—but not right now. Now I bury it, down deep, and move on with my life.

Peter and I went to our check-up today. All is well, the baby's healthy, and I'm feeling so very fortunate. I cross my fingers in the hope that it stays this way. Before I get lost in my work again and forget, I shoot off a text to my stepchildren with the breaking news about the newest addition to our growing, blended family. I'm anxious to share it, to make it real. I type out a message and send it off with my phone cradled in my left hand. My right hand goes to my belly as I stare down at the screen for a few long moments, my sent message nestled safely in its comfy blue bubble.

It's a boy!

Acknowledgements

I am fortunate to have had two amazing stepmothers, both of whom I kept top of mind as my protagonist developed. Rosalind Storms, my late stepmother, provided steady guidance and encouragement when she joined our family during my confusing middle school years. Although we lost her to cancer far too early, before I even graduated high school, I continue to marvel at how well she managed our family at such a young age. Ginny Traymore, my stepmother, continues to provide support, wisdom, and laughs on a regular basis. She has remained a part of my life even as my father has passed on. Both of these amazing ladies were excellent role models when my husband and I blended our families over a decade ago, and I became a stepmom myself. I am grateful that I have so many amazing family members, both step and biological, including my daughter, stepson, brother, and three stepbrothers who all enhance my life in myriad ways. With family, the more, the merrier—most of the time.

Thanks to the many people who made this book possible, including my talented editor Julie MacKenzie who elevated and refined my prose, and my beta readers and friends who provided valuable reader feedback which helped shape and improve the plot and enhance the character development. A special thanks goes out to the Team Sheeper triathlon racers, my husband included, who walked me through the more technical aspects of bike racing, provided insight into the Santa Cruz race course, and brainstormed some truly terrifying cycling scenarios with me. I am now even more amazed by all of you and what you do. Thanks to my husband for his unwavering support for my books, his reading and rereading of my manuscript, and for all the years he's spent in biotech trying to cure cancer and fight infectious diseases. And don't worry, all of his exes are still alive and well.

Finally, thanks to my readers. You make all of this worthwhile. I appreciate the support more than you know. You are why I keep writing. If you have time to leave a review, it would be greatly appreciated. I read and consider all of them, and it helps me improve my craft. For updates on my next novel, a mystery/thriller set at a desolate boarding school in the dead of winter, sign up for my mailing list at www.bonnietraymore.com.

About The Author

Bonnie Traymore is an author, historian, and educator. As a world traveler, she loves to include vivid settings in her novels. Originally from the New York City area, she's lived in Honolulu with her family for the last few decades. When she's not writing, she enjoys being in the classroom with young minds, keeping her work fresh and current. She's also an accomplished non-fiction writer, historian, and veteran educator with a doctorate in United States History. She has taught at top independent schools in Honolulu, Silicon Valley, and New York City, and she's taught history courses at Columbia University and the University of Hawai'i.

Please enjoy a sample of *Killer Motives:*
A Hudson Valley Mystery
Book 1, Hudson Valley Series

ONE

As Angie made her way to the bedroom, resigned to a night alone in her empty, chilly new house, her imagination was playing tricks on her. The creaking floorboards reminded her of skeleton bones knocking together and the wind whistling through the windowsills called out to her like spirits in the night. She didn't mind a little fear, though, because it was the only thing keeping her from succumbing to the urge to kill herself. If she felt fear, didn't that mean she wasn't quite ready to die?

She looked down at her outfit, the red fabric clinging to her firm, sexy body that men loved to conquer. It wasn't easy being a woman who every man wanted to sleep with but few really cared to know. Then she heard a car pull up and her heart leapt. Maybe he'd had a change of heart! She dashed into the bathroom to clean the runny mascara off her face. She heard a knock at the door and started down the stairs, trying hard not to get her hopes up only to have them crushed again.

Although he knew what to expect as he drove the last curve of the dark road to his destination, he was uncharacteristically nervous. It was not very late--just about nine in the evening--but the crescent moon offered up little in the way of illumination. The thick fall foliage that lit up the sky by day now veiled the area in darkness and shadow. He dimmed his lights on approach and scanned the area looking for other cars or some sign that he'd been spotted, but only one car was in the driveway--hers--and the lights were all out. He slowed his car to a stop as he pulled it in behind hers, hovering between park and reverse, letting the engine punctuate the silence as he observed his surroundings. Nobody else was here. Nobody else knew. He was just being paranoid. He sat there weighing his options, unable to shake the unsettling feeling that someone was watching him.

"Is that you, Nick?" Victoria feigned concern as she heard her husband coming through the doorway from her perch atop the staircase, holding a laundry basket in front of her like a shield. The faint smell of oil and garlic from their uneaten dinner lingered in the air.

"Of course it's me. Who else would it be? I ran out to meet my client. The Shady Hill property."

"Why didn't you tell me you were leaving? I was worried." She made her way down the staircase, curious to see how this would play out.

"I didn't know where you were. I got a text from her. She couldn't get her key to work. She was locked out. I had to run over. It's all good now." Nick stopped to hang his keys on the holder. A grocery bag hung from his forearm.

"Getting a key to work? For over two hours?" She walked past him as she spoke, struggling to play it cool although her stomach was in knots.

"Come on! You know how she is. I stopped over there, gave her my spare, she had all kinds of issues, as usual. Then I stopped by the store. We needed coffee. Dutiful husband. See?" He held up his shopping bag and waved it back and forth.

"Well, you could have texted me. You missed dinner." She walked into the living room and placed the laundry basket on their accent chair, stopping to pick off a stray piece of lint that had landed on one of its navy stripes.

"I'm trying to be more focused on my work, bring in more money. This is a big sale. Don't I even get a 'congratulations'?" He ambled to the sofa, mumbling something under his breath, as the bag ripped a bit and dangled from his arm. He plopped down and stretched his arms across the back, giving the soft Italian leather a squeeze. "Speaking of which, did you go somewhere? Your car was in the driveway when I left."

"Me? No. I was doing laundry. Dutiful wife." She motioned to the basket. "I pulled it into the garage when I took out the recycling." She didn't really remember pulling the car into the garage, she'd been so rattled.

"You didn't leave me much space. I could barely get my door open." He reached into the shopping bag. "And I also happened to pick up a bottle of champagne." She looked at him, confused. "To celebrate?" The closing?" He lifted it out of the bag and showed it to her, as if she'd never seen a champagne bottle before. "I wanted to surprise you."

"I don't like surprises, Nick." Was she supposed to feel guilty now? Did she ruin his little celebration?

He smiled in that sly, sexy way that used to send tingles through her body as he stood up and walked over to her. His voice was warm now, inviting. "Come on. You used to like my little surprises, as I recall, at least at certain hours of the night..." He went in for an embrace. When she tensed up, he backed off, keeping a light hand on her shoulder. "Something wrong, Victoria?"

She had no choice but to look at him. In their ten years of marriage, the only signs of the decade on him were some gray flecks in his dark hair that added a measure of gravitas to his boyish affect and matching stubble that accented his square jaw and olive skin. If it was possible, he was even more attractive than when they'd first met. Too bad it was wasted on her. "It's late." She backed away.

"Right." He looked genuinely defeated. "But really Vic, we could try harder to get some of that back. I want to try harder. I really do."

She turned from him and made her way back up the curved wooden staircase, down the hall, and into their spacious master suite to shower and get ready for bed. She had liked it in the beginning, the casual way he called her "Vic," the freedom it gave her to break free of the dead weight of her heritage. "Nick and Vic," he'd laugh. Now it just annoyed her. But she didn't want to think about that now. She was drained. Ready for a hot shower and sleep.

She peeled off her clothes and jumped in the shower, trying to avoid any further interactions with her husband. As she stood under the pulsating jets, her tense neck and shoulder muscles started to relax. Then a sharp pain jolted her as some of the water dripped onto her scraped up fore-arm. Damn it! It had just stopped hurting too. She cut the shower short and toweled herself off, lightly dabbing the moisture from her throbbing arm. The gash had closed up pretty nicely but the scrapes, although not very deep, were still really raw.

She heard him come in their bedroom as she embarked on her nightly skin care routine. He walked up to his matching sink to brush his teeth, keeping his distance as he grabbed his toothbrush from its holder. They stood side by side, in a sort of stand-off, not looking at each other, not talking. She could see in the mirror that he was sneaking glances at her.

"So, how's that deal on the Cole painting going?" He reached over into her territory to grab the toothpaste. "Didn't you say there were some problems?"

"I think we got it figured out. Foreign buyer, cash, ran into some issues. Charles is working on it with the IRS or the KGB or whoever it is he has to placate. I'm out of it. He'll make it work." She continued to dab her eye cream into the crevices, dotting and pressing as directed.

"At least I hope he makes it work. This buyer doesn't like to be disappointed."

"Charles," Nick said in a garbled British accent, his words obscured by the electric toothbrush in his mouth. "Charlie boy needs to get over himself. He's not very street smart. He's gonna get himself in trouble one of these days with those foreign buyers. They don't screw around."

She ignored him, immune to his constant digs about her upper crust background. Funny how he didn't seem to mind the perks it afforded him.

He stopped brushing and rinsed. "What's with that scrape on your arm?"

"Oh, I was running at Rockefeller. My toe hit a rock. Sent me barreling into a tree branch." She continued her routine, moving on to her neck cream.

"It looks nasty." He put his toothbrush back in the holder, wiping the excess foam from his mouth with the back of his hand. He turned to her with a look somewhere between admiration and curiosity.

"Why are you looking at me like that?" she asked.

"You don't need all that stuff, you know. You're only thirty-five. And you're still the most stunning woman I've ever seen." Nick offered up his best lover-boy smile, and she failed to suppress an eye roll. "What? Don't roll your eyes! I'm serious. And you know it's true, too, I'm not just saying it."

She believed him, which somehow made it even worse. Sure, her complexion was flawless and it complemented her sensibly cut, medium-length honey-blonde hair with subtle highlights perfectly, but she thought for a moment that she looked very pale and bland next to her dark and handsome husband. Maybe that's how he saw her. Boring.

Vanilla. She quickly quashed those thoughts. This was his problem, not hers, and she was done with his head games. He should have stuck to talking about business.

"I don't look like I need all this stuff because I have all this stuff and I use it religiously. Ergo, I need all this stuff. But thanks." She really hoped he would just give it up and go to bed. Finally reading her signals, he turned and made his way out of the bathroom.

"And don't forget we have my function tomorrow," she called after him. "You can make it, right? It's the first one in a long time. We need to make an appearance together." She was looking forward to her charity event this year, even more than usual. It was the first one in a long while and she was hungry for some social interaction.

"Yeah, I can make it. I told you. I'm all yours now. Don't worry. The house closed. It's a new chapter. It was a nightmare, drilling a new well, all the crap we had to do to make this work. I'm surprised it wasn't on an Indian burial ground. All to live on that creepy hillside. I hate it up there. I should get a double commission." Was he expecting her to commiserate?

"Well, the customer's always right, as they say." She was running out of face creams. Would he just go to sleep already?

"I'm getting sick of real estate anyway. I might want to do something else. I need a change. You were right, it's a grind, even at the high end." His Catholic guilt was on steroids. Was he regretting the affair? Time to do some damage control?

"Let's talk about it another time, okay? I'm tired." After a few minutes of glorious silence, she felt the coast was clear enough to head to her side of the bed.

She listened to the familiar sound of Nick's rhythmic breathing and the steady pattering of the rain outside. An earthy smell wafted through the window which she had forgotten to close. The cool air felt nice on her face. When she was confident he was down for the count, she pulled the covers over her head and looked again at the images on her phone. She finally had the proof she needed to get rid of him with minimal damage to her bottom line. She should have felt jubilant, but she just felt empty. Maybe that was to be expected? Ten years of marriage, and it hadn't been all bad. She wanted desperately to sleep, but the throbbing from the scrape on her arm kept her awake as her restless mind replayed the events from earlier that evening--over and over and over.

She'd been cooking dinner when she heard Nick's car start. The next thing she knew, she was in her car, driving. She wasn't angry. It was like she was looking down on herself as this other person drove her car mindlessly into the night. She wasn't thinking about what she would do when she got there. As she turned to drive up the dark, winding road, reality started to seep in. She was more careful now as she drove around the bends on the way up the hill. She parked her car on the side of the access road on the way to the house. Her phone was on the passenger seat. She took it in her right hand with her keys in the left. She hadn't thought to grab her purse, but she remembered turning off the stove.

She started walking towards the house, down the short access road. It was pitch black. No streetlights. She used her phone's flashlight to guide her. She was wearing flats which were a little too big in the cooler weather and her feet lifted out near the heel. The shoulder was rocky and uneven so she slowed down. About half way down the road, she stumbled on a rock. She lost her balance and fell into the brush, grasping for the spiny tree branches with her right hand. They broke her fall but she dropped the phone and her keys. Why hadn't she left her keys in the car? The phone was easy to find in the dark, but not the keys.

As she searched for the keys, it dawned on her that she could have just hired a private detective. She could certainly afford one. But she had come this far, and she needed to know the truth. Now. Tonight. Soon she was at the house. Nick's car was in the driveway. She waited a bit, not sure if she could actually bring herself to go in and confront him. Then she looked up. It must have been fate. She could see them now in an upstairs window, locked in an embrace. They started kissing. She was snapping away on her phone--photo after photo after photo. She felt a rush of excitement as adrenaline coursed through her veins. Her heart was ticking like a metronome. She had him, dead to rights!

Then they moved out of her view and her mood shifted. She felt a rush of panic and her face flushed, realizing how desperate she would look if someone saw her or spotted her car. What would her mother think? It felt creepy here now, surrounded by the dark woods, like she could disappear into them and never be seen again. She retreated, heading back to her car, careful to watch her footing this time. When she was inside her car, she locked the doors and took a moment to compose herself before she started on her way back home. It wasn't until she was driving down Bedford that it was light enough for her to notice the nasty gash on her forearm, bleeding into the teal silk of her three-quarter sleeved blouse. She pulled over and started to sob.

TWO

A body was found at the bottom of the stairs at a home in Pocantico Hills, off Bedford near the border of Sleepy Hollow. It looked suspicious so they'd called in Major Crimes. That's about all he knew. He and Lexi had gotten the call about fifteen minutes ago and it was now just past eight in the morning. Already all hands were on deck. Jack had expected this to blow up fast, but not this fast.

"Watch out, Jack!" A media van almost backed into them while Jack was trying to park the car. He swerved a bit to avoid it and blasted his horn. Lexi could be a bit of a backseat driver but it didn't bother him too much. Besides, he hadn't actually seen the van. Parking was already tight. There were two police cars, the media van, and the forensics team vying for turf, in addition to what was probably the victim's car in the driveway. It was almost impossible to turn around, so he just parked the car where it was, blocking in the van. He had little tolerance for the press.

The property, although a short drive from town up the hillside, felt more isolated than it was, which was fine for some people but not likely for everyone. It was the kind of place about which urban legends would circulate, like sightings of Washington Irving's ghost at nearby Sunnyside or the famed spirits of Estherwood Mansion

288

in Dobbs Ferry. Even in a region rife with spectral spec-ulation, this property stood out--not great for a murder investigation.

"The media's here? Already? We don't even know for sure if there was a murder!" Lexi's voice went up an oc-tave as she spoke. A reporter and her team were setting up. This was their first homicide call in a while, and it was squarely in the high rent district.

"It's a dead body two weeks before Halloween on the Sleepy Hollow border. What do you expect?" Jack knew it would be harder if the press got involved this early, but there was not much they could do about it now.

Lexi shook her head, registering her disapproval. She didn't seem to like it too much in Westchester. She had been here just over a year--a promotion. Maybe it would grow on her like it had on him. They were both veteran New York City cops and had endured much more unfortu-nate beats--gang and drug infested--where murders were so common place, they didn't even make the news. It was a luxury to have so few that they became spectacle, but people around here wouldn't get that, and neither would the press. The uniformed officers had already taped off the crime scene and the press knew better than to think that they would comment this early in the investigation, but that didn't stop them from trying as they got out of the car and headed for the house.

"Was this a homicide?" "Do you have any leads?" They weren't taking photos or video just yet. Jack held up his hand as if to shield the two of them as they headed for the front door.

It was a larger house by most people's standards but undersized for the area. It seemed pristine at first glance--recently fixed up--but he could tell it would be a money pit, an older home solidly built but set on a sloping hillside surrounded by tall hemlocks and mature black oaks that blocked the sun. It looked to be about three thousand square feet, with the lot about twenty thousand. There was a realtor's sign in the yard. Had it just been sold, or was it still in the process? He recalled that there had been a string of real estate agents murdered years back, before his time, a serial killer who had never been caught.

They made their way up the entry stairs to the front door landing. There was no screen door, just a large dark wooden door--high end--with a dead bolt and handle lock combination. Jack thought that it seemed inadequate protection for the caliber of the home, but then this wasn't a particularly high crime area. Still. As they entered the foyer, he noticed a side table with some real estate flyers, business cards of various agents, and some booties under the table. To his left, a body was lying at the bottom of the stairs, appearing to be a woman, with an officer looking down on her. He whipped his head around toward them when he heard them approach, protecting his turf.

"Jack Stark and Lexi Sanchez. Major Crimes." Jack waved to him and smiled as they logged in and donned their gloves and shoe coverings. Officers here weren't normally very territorial, but he made an effort to be gracious just the same. The officer motioned to them to come over.

"Gary Johnson." He offered them a quick raise and lowering of his hand. "Thanks for getting here so quickly."

"So what do we know?" Jack was taking inventory of the surroundings while trying to keep his distance from the body until the Medical Examiner arrived. It was a pretty gritty crime scene. Lots of blood, typical of a head wound, and some twisted limbs from what was apparently a nasty fall. He turned to look at Lexi. She looked a little peaked. It never really got any easier.

Officer Johnson filled them in. "Female, forty-two years old, Angela Hansen. Found at the bottom of the stairs. Looks like she was hit with a blunt object and she tumbled down the stairs. I guess there's a chance the injury could have come from the fall, but I don't think so. And see that bruising on the neck? That's certainly not from the fall. It looks like she was hit from behind and then fell down the stairs. My best guess it happened last night sometime. The temperature was pretty consistent in here, so it shouldn't take too long to get time of death. We wanted to call you in right away." Jack had already noticed a thermostat on the wall set to 68 degrees.

"Thanks for looping us in so quickly." Jack studied the back of the victim's head from his vantage point, trying not to contaminate the body. She had landed face down with her head to one side, dressed in a tightly fitting red dress, not the kind of outfit a woman wore for a night home alone. Long, flowing dark hair fanned out all over the stairs and the landing. He moved in closer. He could see there were some marks around her neck, but they weren't consistent with strangulation as a cause of death, at least not ligature strangulation.

Then his eyes focused out from the body to its immediate surroundings as he got his bearings. He took a look around the first level. The front door led into the foyer. To the right was a den and laundry area, a full bathroom, and an attached garage filled with boxes. There was another door to the backyard in the mud room by the laundry. Built to accommodate the slope, the main living area was on the second floor. He made his way up the stairs and took a spin around the second level which consisted of the kitchen, living room, the master suite, and two other bedrooms with another full bath. Only the master suite had furniture in it. He went back to the kitchen and saw that a few necessities had been unpacked. There was an open bottle of wine, about two-thirds full, with one wine glass in the sink.

He went up and down the stairs a few times, observing the blood spatter and the angle of her body trying to imagine the crime. From the spatter, it was clear she was hit at the top of the stairs with something hard before she fell. Maybe a fight at the top of the stairs? A crime of passion? It didn't look premeditated. Not likely a serial killer. He was getting ahead of himself, but then that was to be expected. It had been a slow few months in homicide.

"Does it look like anything was stolen?" Lexi looked around at all the boxes and general disarray. It was sort of a mess, but an organized mess.

"Hard to tell. It looks like she was moving in. There's stuff everywhere. Lots of boxes, all over the house. Some half empty, but it doesn't look ransacked. Looks more like she was in the middle of unpacking, but hard to say for sure. It'll be hard to see if anything was stolen with the state it's in. Records show the sale recorded two days ago. Nice housewarming, huh?" Johnson's voice was a little shaky, even a bit emotional, which seemed odd to Jack. He looked too old to be a rookie. Maybe she looked like someone he knew.

"New owner then. I wonder if she even changed the locks. We need to talk to the agents, see who might have had access." Jack made a mental note.

"One thing is, we found her purse but no cell phone so far. Johnson motioned to the purse on a table in the den, the contents of which were being cataloged by the crime scene unit. "There's about fifty dollars in the purse, credit cards, license, all that stuff. But we can't find the cell. We'll keep looking. I guess it could be anywhere."

"Good to know, that's significant." Jack scribbled something barely legible on his notepad which was about the size of a deck of cards. "Any signs of a break-in? How did you even get the call?" He was asking too many of the questions, as usual. He reminded himself that he needed to back off a bit and let Lexi break in, build her confidence.

"No signs of a break-in. The plumber called it in. She had someone scheduled for early this morning. When she didn't answer the door or her cell, he got concerned. He tried the door and it was unlocked, so he came in and found her, called nine-one-one and here we are."

"What woman doesn't lock her door?" Jack pulled on his chin with his thumb and index finger, deep in concentration. Johnson nodded in agreement. Lexi was listening while sketching the scene, a specialty of hers. "And how did those vultures find out so fast? Smelled it in the air?" Jack pointed his thumb back towards the door and the reporters outside.

"No idea. Police radio? Tip from the plumber? You know how this place is. News like this travels fast. You better think of something to tell them. It'll help if we can control the narrative a bit." Johnson was absolutely right about that. He certainly knew this area pretty well.

"Does she have any family?" Lexi finally chimed in.

"She's the sole owner of record. We found an ex-husband in Orlando and her parents live in Brooklyn, but that's about it so far. She seems new to the area, used to live in the city. Looks like she worked in finance. I'm gonna go check with the teams in the other rooms, see if they found anything useful."

"We'll wait here with the victim. Thanks for the update, Officer Johnson."

"Gary."

"Thanks Gary."

While he and Gary were bonding, Lexi had been taking copious notes in her notebook along with her detailed drawings and sketches. She was a total type A which worked to his benefit. He could see she already had almost two full pages.

"How's your thesis coming?" Jack liked to needle her. Their banter may have seemed callous to people who didn't understand their world. It was a way to blow off steam, a way of keeping a part of their humanity in the face of all the horror they saw on a regular basis. It probably kept them from going insane.

"Let's compare notes." Lexi snatched his notepad from his hand without missing a beat. She was younger. Quicker.

"'Cell?' 'Locks?' Wow, very observant, Jack. Bravo. You've practically solved it."

"I don't like to get bogged down in the details."

She shot him one of her looks. "If she just moved in, she probably has a moving inventory or an insurance policy we could check to see if anything of value was taken."

"Great thinking, Lex. Why don't you get started on that and I'll try to track down her real estate agent while we wait for the ME's report to come out." The Medical Examiner's report was a just formality to Jack. He already knew it was homicide. A beautiful single woman murdered in her home in a safe, upscale neighborhood. They needed to get some answers--fast!

THREE

Nick was driving to his office in Tarrytown when his cell buzzed, an unknown caller. He was still reeling from the night before. He hesitated for a moment and almost didn't answer it, but that was considered bad practice in his business. It might be a potential client. All he wanted was for things to go back to normal. He picked up. "Hi, this is Nick." A click and a pause.

"Nick Mancusio?"

"Yes, Nick Mancusio." Another longer pause. What the hell. Say something. "Hello? *Hello?*" He was about to hang up. Probably a scam call. Then he heard the phone cutting in and out and someone talking. For such a swanky neighborhood, they sure had crappy cell phone reception. The caller spoke up again, louder this time.

"This is Detective Jack Stark with the Tarrytown Police Department. Are you there?"

"What? Yes, I'm here. What is it?" He felt his heart race as his hands gripped the steering wheel a little tighter.

"Do you know an Angela Hansen? I think she was your client in a recent real estate transaction?" The detective's tone was neutral, not threatening, but there was something about the way he disclosed the fact that he already knew something about him and their relationship that made Nick more nervous.

"Yes, yes I know her. We just closed on a property, up on Shady Hill Lane. Why?" What could he say? He couldn't lie about that.

"She was found dead in her home this morning. I'm a homicide detective. We'd like to talk to you as soon as possible. See if you can shed some light on this." He slammed on the brakes to avoid running a stop sign, although his was the only vehicle at the intersection. Coffee spilled on the console and his folders on the passenger seat went flying. His mind was blank. It's not like he couldn't think of anything to say. It was more that he couldn't find his words. This was a detective trained to pick up on cues. He didn't have time to mull over how to play it. He was taking way too long. Finally, he spoke.

"Dead? What? Oh my God. What happened?" The car behind him honked. He turned right and pulled over.

"I can't get into that right now. I can explain more when I see you. We could come to you or you could come down to the station." Down to the station? That sounded ominous.

"Can you give me half an hour? I have to rearrange my schedule. I can call you in thirty minutes with a time and place."

"I'll call you. Be sure to pick up." The detective hung up.

Nick dialed another number. It went to voicemail. "Jeff, it's Nick. Call me. It's an emergency."

"What are you doing here?" Jeff was visibly annoyed, standing tall behind his desk, his arms folded like a sentry. Nick had driven straight to his office unannounced, and had interrupted him while he was on a call.

"It's my client. Angie Hansen. The police called me. Jeff, she's *dead!* They found her body this morning. In the new house." Nick started to pace, trying in vain to dispel some of the nervous energy that was clouding his judgement.

Jeff's jaw dropped. He came around his desk, walked a few paces over to the door, and shut it. He turned back to Nick. "You mean *my* client, the client *I* gave to *you*, is dead? What the hell happened?" Right. In all the chaos, Nick had almost forgotten. She was his client too, a big law suit.

"I have no idea. The police want to meet with me. Some homicide detective called. I didn't know what to do, so I came here. They're calling back soon. I'm supposed to tell them where and when I can meet. What should I do?!" Nick rubbed his neck as he continued to pace, thankful that it was spacious enough in the office to distance himself from Jeff.

"Homicide?" Jeff walked across the room and stood by the window, gazing beyond the town a few floors below them out towards the Hudson River. He turned to Nick. "So she was murdered?"

"I guess? I don't know! They wouldn't tell me much. They said they'd explain later. I'm freaking out."

"Why? Did you kill her?"

"Of course not! What kind of a question is that?" Nick knew that Jeff had a sick sense of humor, but this was pushing it.

"Then what are you so worried about? Seems like this is a much bigger problem for me than for you." Typical Jeff.

"I was there last night. Maybe they know I was there. Do you think they know?" Nick's palms were sweaty and his heart was still racing, not just because of the detective, but also because he was anticipating Jeff's reaction to what he was shortly going to disclose.

"So? You're her agent. You can explain that pretty easily. I still don't see the problem. And will you stop pacing and sit down? You're freaking me out." Nick stopped his pacing and sat in an armchair, as requested, his head in his hands. His leg was bobbing up and down, shaking the seat. He let the information sit with Jeff for a moment.

"Wait. Please. Tell me you weren't sleeping with her. For Christ's sake, Nick. Tell me!" His voice was getting louder and Nick motioned to him to keep it down. "Even you can't be that stupid, right? *Right?*"

Nick looked down at the carpet, trying to avert Jeff's signature death stare. He could hear that Jeff was now the one pacing around. He wished he could make himself invisible. Nick looked up and continued.

"I'm sorry Jeff. I don't know how it happened, it just did. It was a big mistake! I've been trying to break it off for weeks. She was still calling me, texting me. There were some issues about her key not working last night. I went over. We talked more. She wasn't happy, but she was calmer. She seemed to be getting it. She was alive when I left, I swear. Upset, but alive."

"Are you *insane?* This was a big case for me! A clear-cut harassment suit, worth millions. High profile. I could have made a fortune, not to mention the publicity. I told you it was a delicate situation. That she was vulnerable. Unstable. And you *slept* with her? You're supposed to be my friend! I went out on a limb for you and you screwed me."

It was all true. Jeff had warned him, and Nick could see just how screwed Jeff was. He had already put a ton of hours into the case, all on contingency, and now he would get nothing. Nick would still get his commission. It was totally unfair. And there was nothing he could do to change it.

"I'm so sorry. It was a major screw up. I'll make it up to you. But Jeff, I slept with her. I didn't kill her! It's not my fault your client's dead. Can we table this until later? Please? Just tell me. What should I do?"

"You should get yourself castrated." Jeff had a right to be upset, Nick knew, but he was hoping that decades of friendship would count for something. They had been friends since college, both disappointing each over the years, and up until now, he figured they were about even. Nick waited, knowing that anything he offered in the way of an excuse would just piss him off more.

"I'm a civil litigator, not a criminal attorney. I don't give that kind of advice." His voice was calmer but his look was still menacing.

"I need something. Now. Please. Anything. They're calling, any minute now. Should I meet with them? Or should I get a lawyer first? What should I do?" He hated feeling this desperate, being at people's mercy. How had it come to this?

Jeff looked at him and shook his head. Nick waited. Finally, he spoke. "Meet them at your house. You'll be more relaxed. The station is too intimidating. Come clean about the affair. To everyone. If you didn't kill her, there's no evidence, so you should have nothing to worry about. Prints in the house, DNA, whatever, it can all be explained. But if they catch you in a lie, you're toast."

"If I tell them about the affair, it'll destroy my marriage."

"That's the least of your worries. If they ask you and you don't tell them, it'll look worse. Way worse. That in and of itself could be a crime." Jeff's advice was solid. Still, Nick found himself trying to recall if there was any evidence of the affair now that Angie wasn't alive to disclose it.

"You wanted my advice, that's my advice. Take it or leave it. Now I have to get back to work. You can see yourself out." Jeff shooed him out the door. As Nick made his way down the hallway to the elevators, his phone rang, right on schedule.

―――

Victoria was home working off some nervous energy as she put the dishes away and wiped yesterday's smudges off the white Shaker cabinet doors. Out the kitchen window, the sun sparkled magically on the Hudson River reflecting the scarlet and gold of the fall foliage clinging to its steep banks. Her melancholy mood from the evening before had turned to excitement, bolstered by a bit too much caffeine on an empty stomach and her Alanis jams playing in the background. She had already called her attorney and had an appointment for next week. She would put all that out of mind until then. Today, she had a meeting scheduled at her office at eleven this morning, an important one, and her benefit dinner tonight. It was now half past nine and she needed to get going. She was almost finished emptying the dishwasher in her methodical manner--only a few cups were left--when her cell phone vibrated against the granite island countertop, its dark surface blending in with the stone. She reached over to grab it. There was a text from her husband: *It's an emergency. Call me.*

There were also three missed calls from him and a voicemail. Nick was not given to hyperbole. Quite the opposite. He was actually a bit too laid back, never worrying much about anything. He had never sent a text like that before. She called immediately, not bothering to check her voicemail, putting it on speaker as she finished her chores.

"Vic?" His voice was soft, almost apologetic. He didn't seem hurt or in danger.

"Nick. What is it?" She felt mildly annoyed, already.

"I have something to tell you, and I'm warning you it's pretty shocking." Was he actually going to confess about the affair now? Over a cell call? That was totally unlike him.

"I have to get to work, Nick. What's so urgent?" She was starting to wish she'd ignored his text.

"My client. From the Shady Hill property. The one I went to see last night? The police called me. She was found dead. At her house. This morning."

Victoria placed the last clean mug on the counter. Dead? A heart attack or something? No. The police wouldn't call Nick for something like that. There had to be more to it. She picked up the phone and took it off speaker.

"What happened?" She wasn't sure she wanted to know the answer.

"I don't know, but a homicide detective is meeting me at the house any minute now. They called and wanted to meet with me in person. 'See if I could shed some light on it,' was how he put it. Jeff told me to meet them at our house, not at the station."

"Homicide? She was murdered?" Victoria had to hand it to Nick. This certainly reached the bar of 'emergency.'

"They didn't say that, exactly. He said he'd tell me more in person. I don't know much more than you do at this point. What if I was the last person to see her alive, Vic?" Nick's voice was shakier now, almost panicky.

"So? You're certainly not responsible for her death?"

"That's what Jeff said."

"What does Jeff have to do with this? You called Jeff before you called me?" She thought that sounded like the actions of a guilty person, reaching out to your attorney friend. But guilty of what?

"He's an attorney! And he knows her! I told you, remember? They had that law suit going. Let's not do this now. *Please!*" His tone was harsher now, devoid of sentimentality. "I just wanted to give you a heads-up. The detective might get there before I do. They'll probably want to question you too. Tell them I'm on my way. I'd appreciate some support. I'm your husband, Victoria, please try to remember that." He hung up.

She picked up the mug she'd left on the counter, looking out to the sun's rays sparkling on the Hudson, her thoughts suspended in the timeless currents of the flowing river. It was all starting to hit her now, just what a disaster this was. The photos that were supposed to liberate her from the marriage were now a liability, potentially placing her at a crime scene. What do detectives look for? Means, motive, and opportunity? She had two out of three for now. Should she be worried? And what about Nick? He was acting strangely last night, and she'd attributed it to a guilty conscience. The affair, she assumed. But could it have been more? She knew Nick wasn't overtly violent, but anyone could commit murder given the right circumstances. What if the woman had gotten pushy? Demanding? Threatening? How far would Nick go to protect what was his? She needed time to think, consult with an attorney. But she didn't have the luxury of time.

The gate buzzer sounded, jolting her out of her stupor, and the mug slipped from her hand, shattering into pieces on the travertine tile floor. She quickly picked up the big chunks, but the shards of porcelain would have to wait.

If you enjoyed this sample, check my website for current retail availability: www.bonnietraymore.com